INFINITE RETRIBUTION

EXODUS UNIVERSE

ROBERT STADNIK

ISBN: 978-1-953865-05-2 (Paperback)
ISBN: 978-1-953865-06-9 (eBook)

Library of Congress Control Number: 2021903188

Any references to historical events, real people, or real places are used fictitiously. Names, characters, and places are products of the author's imagination.

Books Fluent
3014 Dauphine Street
New Orleans, LA
70117

PROLOGUE

DATE: SEPTEMBER 2146

LOCATION: HUMAN SOLAR SYSTEM, NEAR MARS

"The Onixin, Senfo, and Quix ships will comprise the defense fleet. Our capital ships will remain in the rear of the formation, supporting planetary defense of Mars."

Commander Annette Nikols and her captain, Rich Melicoast, were not happy about Admiral Vespia's orders. Their ship, the AURORA, was part of a large armada waiting for the Screen invasion force to appear in the solar system. Instead of being included in the battle plans, the capital ships were being relegated to the sidelines, deemed too inferior to go toe-to-toe against any Screen vessel.

Captain Melicoast wasn't taking the orders lying down. "We've been training for this for years. This is our home and we should be dictating the battle strategy, not taking orders from traitors and their alien allies."

"I'm not interested in coddling your ego!" Vespia shouted back over the communications line. "In case you forgot, one of those alien ships disabled the SOLARA in a single shot. You will follow my orders, or I'll have you removed from command of the AURORA. Is that clear?"

Captain Melicoast had no choice but to concede. He knew

that the AURORA and the other capital ships were not equipped to fight against any alien vessel, friend or foe. What bothered him was that the admiral was supporting the battle plans of a traitorous cadet that had stolen TERRA's experimental starship. "Acknowledged, Admiral. But I will be filing an official protest with the council when this is over."

"I am the council," Vespia replied before cutting the communication line.

The captain returned to his command chair and sat down, rubbing his forehead. He had not made a friend in her, but didn't care. He was certain other members of the council would listen to him when this was all over. The traitors needed to be held accountable for what they had done. They'd stolen the EXODUS. They'd angered the Screen enough that the aliens were coming here to wipe out the human race. It didn't matter to him that the traitors had cobbled together an alliance of alien races to help defend the human solar system. They'd gone against a long-standing policy that had kept the peace for nearly a century. Even if the defense fleet and capital ships were victorious, he was certain lives would be lost.

Annette Nikols, the captain's executive officer, approached him. "We could still engage the Screen during the battle. With all the ships out there, there'll be so much going on that no one will notice us moving to the front lines."

Rich chuckled at her suggestion. "A tempting offer."

"We may be at a tactical disadvantage, but that shouldn't stop us from joining the fight," she said. "We have the right to defend our star system. We know our defensive capabilities better than our alien 'friends.' And the EXODUS has been gone for three years. They don't know what enhancements we've made to our defense network."

Rich nodded in agreement. If they could participate in the battle in a more offensive manner, it could garner the captain some fame. He could see it now: the hero of the AURORA bravely taking his ship into battle. "Have tactical and operations analyze the Screen data provided to us to develop an offensive strategy."

Annette smiled. "With pleasure," she said as she headed

over to operations.

Years before, when the EXODUS had escaped the solar system, the AURORA had tried to stop her, but the capital ship's weapons had been ineffective against the experimental starship. It had been an embarrassment for the seasoned AURORA crew. Now they had an opportunity to redeem themselves and show both the returning EXODUS and alien allies what they could do.

After a few minutes of consulting with tactical and operations, Annette returned to Captain Melicoast. "We're all set. Just give the word and we'll head into the fight when it starts."

As the captain nodded, his tactical officer alerted him. "Sir, sensors show the EXODUS has just entered the solar system. They're on a direct course towards Mars."

"The traitors have come home," Rich muttered in disgust, trying to contain the anger welling up inside of him. He had over thirty years of military experience. Being forced to take orders from a cadet was incomprehensible. He still had a hard time believing Admiral Vespia had agreed to let this John Roberts call the shots.

Annette felt the same as her captain did. There was no justification for these rebels stealing the EXODUS. The human race was now in danger. The presence of these alien 'allies' did little to ease her mind. The Screen armada easily outnumbered the ships defending the solar system.

The communications officer made an announcement. "A wide-band transmission is coming from the EXODUS to the entire fleet."

"Let's hear it," Rich ordered.

"This is John Roberts of the PHOENIX. I'm taking command of the fleet. We're transmitting our battle formation. Review it and reposition your ships."

Rich's blood boiled at hearing the cadet's voice. He had caused so much upheaval by taking the EXODUS: pitting TERRA against the government, inciting fear among the population, almost inciting a civil war. What's more, this traitor had had the audacity to change EXODUS's name to PHOENIX. He wanted to personally take Roberts to some vacant building and execute him with a shot in the head.

"Acknowledge John Roberts's orders under protest," Rich instructed the communications officer. He looked over at Commander Nikols. "Be prepared to execute the tactical plan. We will not sit by."

"Yes, sir."

Little did the captain know that Annette had another plan. She had served under him for many years and knew of his ego. If they engaged in the battle and survived, Captain Melicoast would take advantage and garner all the attention. She could see him bragging that it was his tactical genius that allowed the AURORA to engage the Screen and survive.

Annette couldn't allow that to happen. She was long overdue for a promotion and could see it delayed if the captain carried out his plan. When this was all over, Annette would ensure the removal of Captain Melicoast and her ascendancy to ship commander of the AURORA.

CHAPTER ONE

DATE: MAY 21, 2151

"Today is a momentous day not only for TERRA, but for the entire human race," Admiral Karla Vespia proclaimed to the audience in front of her. "For almost five years, our engineers have worked diligently to build the newest generation of starships. We have relied on our capital ships to defend the solar system for many years and they have served in that capacity with distinction. These ships you see behind me"—she referred to the three blue-and-gray starships hovering in space outside the viewing windows—"will carry humanity forward as we join our allies in space exploration."

The crowd gathered at Luna Station broke out in applause. The attendees consisted of TERRA officers, government officials, members of the media, and visiting delegations from the Aldarian, Onixin, Quix, and Senfo homeworlds. With all the high-level officials gathered in one place, security had a heavy presence to ensure the ceremony occurred without incident. This was the first official gathering of delegates from the alliance and the government had made it clear that TERRA was to use as much security as needed. Hosting such a prestigious event was important in elevating humanity's reputation in the alliance.

When the applause died down, Admiral Vespia continued. "These new starships will launch humanity's mission of exploration and will defend the solar system." She motioned to the ships behind her. "The SOLARIS, INFINITY, and DISCOVERY represent the culmination of efforts begun by our flagship, the PHOENIX, and the alliance it cemented." She glanced at the officers standing to her right. "We've handpicked these officers to command these ships and carry us forward into a new era as we continue to build upon the foundation of friendship with our new allies."

After another round of applause, the admiral concluded her speech. "It is with pride that I officially commission the TCS SOLARIS, INFINITY, and DISCOVERY into service."

With her speech done, the dockmaster launched three wine bottles towards the newly-minted starships. The bottles struck the hulls of each ship and shattered, officially commissioning TERRA's first generation of starships. The crowd erupted into applause one last time before Admiral Vespia stepped down from the podium to mingle with the delegation.

The previous day, Karla had attended a debriefing of the alien delegates that explained what would occur during the ceremony. One of the items discussed was that, as a symbolic gesture, humans hurled bottles of wine at ships going into service. The admiral had seen the look of confusion from the delegates, as none of them understood why humans would choose such an unusual method of launching ships.

As Admiral Vespia stepped down from the podium to mingle with the delegation, Captain Annette Nikols turned to her fellow captains and shook hands with them. After congratulating the DISCOVERY's captain, she turned to the captain of the SOLARIS.

"Congratulations, Captain Diego," she said as she extended her hand.

Jacob Diego shook it. "You too, Captain."

"I want to thank you for all the help you provided during INFINITY's build."

"My team and I were happy to help," Jacob assured her, making it a point to give credit to the officers who were part of the construction project. "I have to say I was impressed by your eagerness during construction. Very few people have the appetite to learn one alien technology, let alone several of them."

TERRA's new starships were based upon the schematics that the PHOENIX had provided, which included technologies from all the alliance worlds. There had been a lot of turnover in the engineering bureau, as officers had been unable or unwilling to learn how the technologies worked. What should have taken only about two years to build had been delayed until TERRA officers with the aptitude to learn and willingness to take on the challenge could be found.

TERRA could have solicited the alliance to provide more engineers to help build these ships, but along with the government, they'd limited the number of aliens working on the project. It was important that humans carry the mantle of responsibility and enjoy the achievement as their own.

Annette nodded to Jacob. She'd taken pride in learning about all the technologies incorporated into these new ships. "How do you feel about our first assignments?"

Jacob didn't waver in his response. "Makes total sense."

The SOLARIS was to patrol space around the solar system while the DISCOVERY was to patrol the space nearest the Cresorian homeworld. Given the hostilities the Creosorians had exhibited during the past four years, TERRA felt a show of strength was necessary to prove that humanity wasn't weak and could defend itself if necessary.

As for the INFINITY, it would patrol the space once claimed by the Screen as their own. Even though the race had been eradicated and their homeworld now occupied by the alliance, TERRA felt it important to investigate those star systems previously controlled by their former enemy.

The systems should have been investigated by the alliance, but the Onixin, Senfo, and Quix were unwilling to remove any of their ships from defensive patrols of their own home systems. In addition, they had lent some of their vessels to TERRA to patrol the solar system until TERRA got its first batch of ships into service.

Annette noticed Jacob's response had been brief. He wasn't

one to elaborate or volunteer any more information than what was requested of him. She had tried asking him about the ship he had served on previously as executive officer, the SOLARA. TERRA had decommissioned the ship a few years ago, when they'd started construction of the new ships.

Annette found it odd that they would scuttle the SOLARA before a replacement was ready. She'd heard rumors that it had been involved in some classified operation that resulted in the ship being severely damaged. But she'd never gotten confirmation if that was true. When she'd asked Jacob about it when they started working together, he'd given her the same line that TERRA put out: the SOLARA was old and no longer needed to be in service. Annette found that to be an odd statement, as the SOLARA was the youngest capital ship in the fleet and the other vessels were still in service.

Annette switched subjects. "I've read the long-range sensor reports from the alliance. None of them picked up any evidence of life on any of the life-supporting planets discovered in former Screen space. I expect INFINITY's mission will be uneventful. The DISCOVERY may see some action with the Cresorians."

Jacob looked disappointed. "I hope not. Even though they've declared war on the alliance, I don't want us to get into a fight with a former ally. I'm hoping they'd think twice before trying to engage one of our new ships."

The Cresorians had descended into chaos since the Screen's defeat. Leadership on their homeworld had changed so many times, the alliance had lost count. Despite the formal declaration of war, there was no outright fighting going on. Two years ago, a batch of eleven Cresorian raiders had tried attacking a Quix military cruiser. All the raiders had been destroyed, while the Quix ship barely suffered a scratch. Since then, the Cresorians had limited their attacks to civilian ships.

Annette wasn't a fan of the Cresorians. She understood that Jacob had worked with them during his tenure on the PHOENIX, the ship whose crew was responsible for bringing the alliance together. She could respect a fellow officer not wanting to go to war given his personal history with them. The Cresorians had also helped the alliance defeat the Screen. It was unfortunate that their internal issues had degenerated them into a lawless race, but Annette was a military officer who looked at the facts. The Cresorians had chosen to make humans an enemy, and thus Annette would treat them as such.

As for the alliance, Annette had not initially been a proponent of being a member. She felt that humanity had been forced into banding together with the Onixins, Senfo, Aldarians, and Quix out of necessity to eliminate the Screen threat. But over the years, she'd seen the usefulness of collaborating with their allies. The alliance was providing security to the solar system until TERRA could get its fleet up and running, and had provided numerous advanced technologies that would have taken humans many years to develop.

Annette nabbed a glass of sparkling water from a passing waiter and held it up. "I hope none of us are forced to engage them. Here's to a successful first mission for both of us."

Jacob grabbed a glass of champagne and raised it as well. "And to the success of these new SOLARA-class starships."

Despite today's celebrations, none of these new ships would be leaving the solar system for another few months. They were still ironing out some of the kinks in the propulsion and operating systems. But the command council felt that today's ceremony would give the construction crews the jolt needed to finalize testing of the ships.

Admiral Vespia approached the pair. "I'm glad to see two of my officers enjoying themselves before their maiden missions."

"I was thanking Captain Diego for his help with INFINITY's construction," Annette said.

"Captain Diego helped accelerate construction on all the ships," Vespia clarified as she looked at him. "Your help has been critical in getting them completed. You'll also be happy to know that I just received confirmation that Earth's orbital shipyards will be coming online next week."

"And seven more SOLARA-class starships will be launched by next week as well," Jacob added. "Now we just have to get them staffed."

One of the biggest challenges for TERRA was finding officers to serve on these new ships. SOLARIS's crew were mostly transplanted from the capital ship SOLARA, while Captain Nikols and the captain of the DISCOVERY were left to pick their crews. But it was proving difficult for TERRA to determine who would serve on the seven new ships coming into service. Except for the SOLARIS crew, no officer had any experience in space exploration. TERRA had decided to select officers to command these new ships and let the ship commanders choose their crews.

"You've done a great service to TERRA," Karla said to Jacob. "Despite the delays in construction, you managed to produce a class of starship that will serve our needs."

To get a compliment from the head of TERRA was a rare occurrence. Admiral Vespia was tough. She demanded a lot from her officers.

"I'm just as anxious to get our new fleet established." Jacob's personal experience made him realize the importance of having a strong military. Although it had occurred four years ago, his adventure on the SOLARA through a jumpgate was still fresh in his mind. The SOLARA had been completely ill-equipped for the mission. It was only with luck and help from the alliance that the ship had returned home.

So far, the only starship in TERRA's fleet conducting deep space exploration was the PHOENIX. Since its departure, TERRA had received only a smattering of transmissions from their flagship. Although PHOENIX reported encountering some friendly races, they also came across hostile species who wanted nothing to do with peace. Those transmissions only made TERRA focused on building new starships as quickly as possible so it could defend the solar system in the event a hostile race appeared. They could not depend on the alliance for defense indefinitely.

A junior officer approached the trio. "Excuse me, Admiral. Yearden Thresha would like to speak with you."

Karla acknowledged her aide before turning to Jacob and Annette. "Best of luck on your missions, Captains."

Both captains nodded to her. "Thank you, Admiral," they said in unison.

As the admiral left, Jacob turned to Captain Nikols. "Have you had a chance to meet with your Onixin navigation officer, Kordif?"

"Not yet. I'm still having a hard time accepting the idea of an alien serving on my ship." She saw Jacob was about to say something, but held her hand up. "I know you've had positive experiences working with aliens on PHOENIX and SOLARA. I accept we need the alliance, but I'm old-school. It's going to take time getting used to working with aliens on our ships."

Jacob smiled. "As long as you're open to the idea. Just remember they're here to help us."

"I know things can't go back to how they used to be. We're in a new world now. The Screen are gone, TERRA's working with alien militaries, and PHOENIX's out there exploring the galaxy." Annette was careful with her words. She still considered the crew who stole PHOENIX to be traitors, but she reminded herself the outcome had been positive.

It helped that she worked closely with one of those 'traitors'—Jacob, who'd been part of the crew who'd stolen that ship. He was a dedicated man who did what he felt was right. How could she stand in judgment of him? If his actions had freed the human race from the Screen threat, then she was willing to give the other traitors the benefit of the doubt. She just didn't agree with how they'd gone about it.

"If you need any insights about the Onixins, let me know," Jacob offered, referring to the reptilian race. "I've worked with several of them in the military exchange."

To foster better cooperation with the other alliance members, TERRA had started a military exchange program so that officers from each alliance's military served in one another's organizations. Captain Diego had Fotell, a Senfo, who served as his operations officer on the SOLARA. After a brief stint back home after the jumpgate mission, Fotell had returned and would be serving in her same capacity on the SOLARIS.

Annette appreciated his offer. She had met a couple of Onixins during INFINITY's construction and had had some brief interactions with them. "Thank you, Captain. I've read Kordif's biography and think his qualifications will serve us well."

Jacob was glad that one of the more tenured officers was keeping an open mind about things. In the last few years, many long-serving officers had been forced out of TERRA. A big part of this had been due to the government's decision to have Earth Security (ES) take over TERRA. During PHOENIX's Screen mission, TERRA had gone rogue from the government. When the Screen threat had been eliminated, the government had quickly reasserted control by putting ES personnel in key TERRA positions. Last year, ES had been officially dissolved and merged with TERRA.

Annette's former ship commander, Rich Melicoast, who she'd served under on the AURORA, had been a casualty. He'd been the first ship commander removed from his post after the Screen's defeat, court-martialed right after the alliance's victory in the solar system. Details of the charges were deemed classified, and the specifics of his court-martial were never made public. Many speculated that TERRA's low regard in the public's eyes had forced them to take decisive action against their own officers, and Captain Melicoast had been one of those casualties.

Once he'd been removed from command, Annette had been promoted as the AURORA's captain. She'd never discussed publicly what happened. In fact, she never discussed Captain Melicoast at all. Jacob had spent a lot of time with her and had never heard her mention his name or his removal as captain of the AURORA. It was as if she had erased him from existence.

"Hey, Dad." Jacob turned to see a young man in a red TERRA cadet uniform approach the two captains.

"Chad," Jacob smiled, patting his son on the shoulder. "I'd like you to meet Captain Annette Nikols. She and I worked together building these new ships."

"It's good to meet you, Captain," Chad said politely.

"Likewise," Annette replied as they shook hands. "Your father's told me a bit about you. First year at the Academy, correct?"

"Yes, sir," Chad confirmed.

"Chad's going to be interning at the engineering bureau this summer," Jacob said proudly.

"That's quite an accomplishment," Annette remarked. "Congratulations."

"Thank you. Dad gave me a tour of the SOLARIS. It convinced me I want a career designing starships."

"Chad's shown an aptitude in catching on to how some of these alien technologies work," Jacob added.

"I think that's an admirable ambition," Annette said. "We need a lot of engineers to build these ships. If you like, I'd be happy to give you a tour of the INFINITY."

Chad's eyes lit. "I'd like that very much."

"Contact me tomorrow and we'll set something up."

The young man's DAT beeped, and he quickly checked it. "It's Mom. I better get this. It was nice meeting you, Captain Nikols. I'll see you later, Dad."

Jacob smiled as he watched his son head off.

Annette could see how much his son meant to Captain Diego. "He seems like a nice young man. I'll bet he's going to be a fine officer."

"Yeah," Jacob muttered. He still struggled with not having had a hand in his son's upbringing. He'd sacrificed being a parent so he could be part of the EXODUS Project. His idealism had outweighed his parental obligation, and it was something he had to live with. Luckily, Chad was happy to have his father back in his life, and Jacob had been able to establish a cordial relationship with his ex-wife.

"What about you, Captain?" Jacob asked. "Any kids?"

"No, I never felt I had the time to have a family and pursue a career. I give a lot of credit to officers who manage to balance the two. I don't regret my choice."

At the other end of the viewing gallery, Admiral Vespia was talking to delegates from the Senfo and Quix homeworlds. They intercepted her as she headed to meet Yearden Thresha. Instead of declining to talk so she could meet the Yearden, she elected to remain and chat with them.

It was almost comical interacting with members of both these races at once. The Senfo were barely three feet tall, while the slug-like Quix were over seven feet in height. Two bots maintained a position a few feet behind the Quix. When they walked, or slithered, along they left behind a gelatinous substance they secreted from their lower bodies. The bots cleaned up the residue as the Quix moved around.

Admiral Vespia's discussion with the delegates was interrupted by a soothing voice behind her. "Excuse me, Admiral."

She turned to face an Aldarian garbed in flowing robes. "Yearden Thresha."

They had met once, shortly after PHOENIX's return to the solar system. Thresha was the spiritual leader of her people, the Aldarians. Although part of the alliance, they only participated in a consultative role. The Aldarian race totaled all of 300 people, so they remained on their homeworld in order to reconstitute their population. Thresha's presence here was deemed necessary given the momentous occasion of the launch of humanity's first batch of starships.

"I was hoping I could have a word with you," Thresha requested.

Karla nodded to the Quix and Senfo delegates. "Excuse me." She motioned Thresha over to a window where they could speak in private. "I hope our amenities have suited your needs. I know this is the first time you've left your world in four years."

As the Aldarians looked similar to humans, except for the ridges running horizontally and vertically on their foreheads, Karla had to remind herself that Thresha was an alien. Unlike the other Aldarians, Thresha's eyes were completely white. From what Karla knew, Thresha's original eye color had turned white when she was selected as Yearden, a title given to the Aldarian's spiritual leader. The Aldarians had never provided a scientific explanation for the phenomenon and Thresha's eyesight was not impacted by the color change. Other Aldarians had eyes similar to humans.

Thresha smiled. "Your people have been most gracious to me. I do not wish to subdue your celebration; however, I feel I must impart some advice to you."

The admiral was intrigued. "And that is?"

"Your people are entering a new age. They are preparing to venture out into the stars, and I am concerned whether they are ready for the challenges that lie ahead."

"Well, I'm touched you're concerned for us." Karla could barely hide the sarcasm in her voice. "I wasn't aware you've become an expert on human history to make such a judgment."

"I learned much about your history during my time on PHOENIX. As the Screen lost their way when they came to this galaxy many cycles ago, your people must not lose their way as they take these first steps into the unknown."

Karla was in no mood to listen to the ramblings of some alien spiritual leader. "I'm sure we'll be fine. I would think you'd have more confidence in us, given your time on the PHOENIX. You've personally witnessed what we humans are capable of. My officers reviewed PHOENIX's logs of its first missions and are prepared for what's out there. We'll be fine. Now if you'll excuse me."

Admiral Vespia didn't wait for Thresha to say another word as she walked away from the Aldarian.

Thresha turned and joined her friend, who had been watching from a distance. It wasn't hard to spot him, as he was wearing an elaborate white gown adorned with diamonds. It was accentuated by his orange-red beehive hairstyle.

"How'd it go, sweetie?" Chris Anne asked.

The two had been friends for years, having met on PHOENIX. The famous singer from Earth had come to this event as part of the Senfo delegation. He had been living on the Senfo's home-world, Flutori, teaching them the art of music. This art form did not exist in Senfo culture. They'd invited him to live with them and teach them how to create music. Chris Anne was so revered by the Senfo that they'd created a special position for him in the Commonality, the governing body that led the race.

"She is not concerned about the officers assigned to these new starships being able to handle the challenges of space exploration."

"I don't know Admiral Vespia, but from what I'm told, she's a tough cookie," Chris Anne said as he fiddled with his sparkling white dress. Even though he wasn't performing, he always wore one of his dresses while out in public. He had to keep his image up, whether on Flutori or back here in the solar system. "She's not going to accept the word of an alien who has a hunch. You gave her some advice and it's up to her to take it or leave it."

Her friend's words did little to ease her worries. Although she had remained on Aldaria since leaving PHOENIX, Thresha made it a point to keep tabs on the humans' progress in building up their starship fleet. It was humans who'd protected the Aldarians and she held a special place for them in her heart. She knew that out of all the alliance races, the humans were the most vulnerable, given the current state of their military. She worried that they were too eager to build up their fleet without taking the time to consider what expansion into deep space meant. The crew of the PHOENIX knew the perils, but that ship was gone, out exploring the far reaches of the galaxy. Only a few of those crewmembers, like Captain Jacob Diego, remained behind to impart what they'd learned to others.

Chris Anne could see that she was still worried. He tapped her chin with his finger. "It'll be okay, sweetie. Let's think positive that the crews of these new ships will be successful."

Thresha appreciated his upbeat words. It was why he'd been a good morale officer on the PHOENIX. "Of course. Your people have proven themselves capable despite their differences. I am sure their endeavors will yield fruitful results." Despite those words, a part of her still worried for them.

Karla headed over to the buffet table, not to get food but to approach her nemesis. "The shrimp is really good. You should load up before the Onixins eat it all."

Admiral Michael Forsent turned to Karla. "Admiral Vespia, I'm allergic to shellfish."

Karla smiled. "I know. Eat up."

Admiral Forsent was a member of the TERRA command council. He was originally from ES, and had been placed on the council when TERRA was reorganized. He and Karla frequently clashed with each other. It was routine for them to engage in an argument during council sessions. Karla was always thinking of some way to get him off the council but so far, her efforts had been futile. But she was a patient woman. It might take years, but she would succeed.

"Isn't there a pine box you can crawl into and expire?"

Michael asked.

"And miss your wonderful demeanor? I wouldn't think of it."

Michael chuckled and looked around. "I must say this looks to be a success."

"I'm surprised you're saying that, considering you voted against holding this ceremony."

"Two other council members voted against it as well," Michael reminded her.

"Who I'm sure you convinced to vote no."

"You got your way. That's all that matters."

"Why, Admiral Forsent. I do believe you're starting to get it."

Michael chuckled again, as if he were enjoying their banter. "Well, I'd love to stay and chat, but I better meet some of these delegates and dispel any misinformation you may have given them about me."

"I only talk about important people," Karla said as she watched him walk away. Even though he was a thorn in her side and constantly interfering with her agenda, at least he made their interactions entertaining. In a way, she enjoyed having him as her nemesis.

CHAPTER TWO

DATE: JULY 2, 2150

Annette waited patiently in the hangar bay control room, browsing through her holographic DAT of the litany of items that needed to be done before INFINITY's official launch. INFINITY would be the first SOLARA-class starship to leave the solar system and the captain wanted to be sure they were ready. She refused to allow any hiccups to occur as it would not reflect well on her. Since coming on board, she'd had all departments provide her regular updates on their preparedness for launch.

"Shuttle Luna-6 is inbound," the hangar officer announced.

Annette closed her DAT and looked through the observation glass onto the hangar deck. "Clear them to land."

The officer opened a communications line to the shuttle. "INFINITY hangar bay to Luna-6, you're clear to land. We have pad A-5 cleared for you."

"Acknowledged, INFINITY."

Annette watched as the shuttle appeared at the hangar bay entrance and made its entry. Having the hangar bay located on top of the ship made it much easier for auxiliary craft to come and go. When PHOENIX had returned home after the Screen mission, its schematics had been downloaded and used as a template to design the SOLARA class. One of the design elements SOLARIS had incorporated was having the hangar located at the top of the ship.

"Shuttle has landed," the officer announced as it touched down.

"Thank you." The captain exited the control room and headed down to the hangar floor to greet the shuttle's passenger. By the time she reached the hangar, the side door of the shuttle had opened and the person she was expecting emerged. "Welcome aboard the INFINITY, Commander Rola."

The tall young man stepped off the shuttle and saluted the captain. "Commander Frank Rola, reporting for duty." His dark hair and olive complexion, along with his height, made for an imposing figure. Annette could see the leadership qualities emanating from his physical demeanor alone. She was impressed.

"At ease, Commander." Annette stepped forward and extended her hand. It was out of protocol, but she'd learned that it was okay to do some things her own way. Offering her hand in friendship was one way to break the ice with her new executive officer.

Frank didn't hesitate and shook the captain's hand. "Thank you, sir."

"We don't have anything pressing to address. I can show you to your quarters and give you the rest of the day to get settled."

"Thank you, but I'd like to get up to the command deck and start familiarizing myself with the ship." He paused, as if realizing he might have implied he hadn't prepared himself for this assignment. "I'm sorry. I didn't mean to say I'm unprepared. I've read up on all of INFINITY's specifications and her sister ships. I . . ."

Annette smiled as she held up her hand. "No worries, Commander. I was the same way when I started my stint on the JORDAN. You don't need to worry about impressing me. Your service record speaks for itself. You have my full confidence; otherwise, I would not have selected you for this post." She motioned for him to walk with her. As they left the shuttle bay, she continued. "I want to congratulate you for what you've achieved. No one's ever become an executive officer as young as you."

"It's you I should be thanking. You're the one who selected me for this post."

Annette knew he was being modest. "You've excelled at everything you've undertaken. I'm sure you felt you needed to prove yourself because you're a mute." She purposely used that negative term to gauge his reaction. He might have achieved XO status, but if he was to be a successful executive officer, she needed to make sure he had thick skin.

Frank was blunt in his response. "It was exactly that reason I worked so hard. I knew people were watching me, hoping I would fail. I had to prove my abilities to everyone."

Mute was a term given to people who were descendants of Nuclear Holocaust survivors. It was a popular belief that they had genetic defects that required more specialized care. To ensure they received such care, they were banned from living on Luna and Mars, and were not permitted to serve in either Earth Security or TERRA.

Many officers, including Frank, hid their genetic profile using concealment devices in order to serve in TERRA. When the ban was lifted, Frank stepped out into the public arena and revealed he was a mute. His gamble paid off and he was allowed to remain in TERRA. Even though his position was safe, he'd known he needed to demonstrate to his peers and superior officers he was capable of serving in the military. Just because TERRA struck down their policy didn't mean that would change people's minds.

At the age of thirty-one, he'd become the youngest officer to be promoted to executive officer (some would argue that Julie Olson was the youngest XO at age twenty-four, but others pointed out she'd attained her position without TERRA's official approval).

"I appreciate your honesty," Annette replied. "Your record and actions speak for themselves, which is why you're here. Your genetic lineage is irrelevant to me."

Frank was relieved to hear those words from his new captain. He had encountered bigotry in some of his previous assignments from those who felt he was incapable of performing his duties, despite his accomplishments. "It means to me a lot to hear that," he said as they stepped onto a lift.

"Command deck," Annette announced to the computer. "Have you reviewed the biographies of the senior staff?"

"Only a few of them. I'm a little nervous about working with an Onixin. I've never worked with an alien before."

The alliance had established an interspecies program where officers of the alliance militaries could serve on different ships. Very few TERRA officers had participated in the program, unwilling or too intimidated by serving on an Onixin, Quix, or Senfo vessel. However, many individuals from the alliance races clamored to serve in TERRA so they could work with humans. Since it was the consensus that it had been humans who rallied the local races to defy and defeat the Screen, many aliens wanted the opportunity to work with humans, to learn how they operated.

Despite the large number of aliens serving in TERRA through the program, Frank had never worked with one. Now here he was on a ship that would have an alien as part of the senior staff.

Annette spoke to abate his worries. "I've worked with some aliens during INFINITY's construction, but not the Onixins. From what I've read, their culture appears to be similar to ours. Just be yourself and you'll be fine. Keep in mind that the microns don't always translate every word in an alien's language." Microns were nano devices that allowed aliens to converse with one another without knowing each respective language. But the devices were not perfect and sometimes an alien word would come through that sounded truly alien.

"Good to know, sir."

The lift beeped and the door opened. Annette motioned for Frank to step off first. "After you, Commander."

Frank exited the lift and was amazed by what was in front of him. This was not like any command deck he had ever seen on any of the capital ships he served on. INFINITY's command deck was huge. Stations and terminals were laid out spaciously, unlike the cramped area of a capital ship. Compared to the bronze or dull silver colors of a capital ship's hull, the INFINITY's command deck was bright and vibrant, with a combination of white and blue colors.

The terminals were missing the mechanical buttons and levers found on capital ship terminals. Instead, they were flat, with virtual button displays, made to be rearranged at a whim by the officer manning the station. INFINITY had been constructed based on a combination of various alien technologies. The biggest challenge was getting these very different technologies to interface and work with each other.

"Most of the senior staff are either finishing up last-minute duties on INFINITY or at Luna Station," Annette explained as Frank walked around the command deck. "You'll meet all of them at the senior staff meeting tomorrow morning."

Frank only nodded, barely paying attention. He was enamored by this new ship, whose technology was far more advanced than anything on a capital ship. When he'd accepted this assignment and began reading up on SOLARA-class starships, he'd realized there were a lot of new things that he would have to learn. The weapons were more destructive, the n'quardin power grid more efficient than plasma energy. Fighter bots were used as fighters instead of Interceptors manned by pilots. Even the shield system was foreign to him.

Once Annette felt she had given her new XO sufficient time to look around, she invited him to follow her. "Join me in my office, Commander."

Frank complied and followed the captain to her office, located near the lift they had stepped off earlier. When they went inside, he was impressed. Captain Nikols's office was far bigger than an office on any of the capital ships. Not only did the captain have her desk, but silver couches were situated on the walls on either side of it. There was also a small table against the wall, holding several glasses and two water decanters. The captain even had her own washroom in the back corner. This was luxurious indeed.

On one wall was a large portrait of the TCS AURORA. Frank knew that the captain had served on only two ships before this one: the JORDAN and the AURORA. She'd served over twenty years on the AURORA, building her career and rising to the rank of executive officer. When Captain Melicoast was expelled from TERRA, she'd been promoted and assumed command of the ship. Barely a year after commanding AURORA, she'd transferred to the Luna shipyards and assisted with the construction of TERRA's new starships.

It was common knowledge that TERRA was decommissioning their capital ships. Frank concluded that Annette had been made aware of those plans and transferred from the AURORA to ensure she would command one of the new starships.

Annette took a seat behind her desk, motioning for Frank to take one of the chairs on the other side. "I'm sure you'll have a lot of questions about how this ship operates," she said.

"I'm still a little surprised this ship has a smaller crew complement than the SOLARA did," Frank remarked, referring to one of TERRA's old capital ships. "INFINITY is easily twice her size." The SOLARA had a crew complement of about 532 people, whereas INFINITY's crew numbered 518.

Annette understood his confusion. "Everything on this ship is bigger. The decks are longer, wider, and taller. The crew quarters are like apartments and have living areas, bedrooms, and kitchens. It was decided that larger spaces are good for the officers' mental well-being, especially for long-term missions. With all the new technologies installed, we simply don't need as many officers to operate this ship."

That made sense to Frank. "Regarding the ship's tech, it's going to take me time to get familiar . . ."

Annette raised her hand to interrupt him. "I'm not worried about your ability to learn how this ship operates. Your service record demonstrates a commitment to tackle new challenges. I have no doubt you'll be up to speed in no time."

The commander appreciated the captain's faith in him. "Thank you, sir."

Annette waved her right hand over her left wrist to activate her holographic DAT. She sent the display to the monitor situated on the wall opposite the AURORA's portrait. Pictures of several individuals appeared.

"Even though you've read their biographies, I want to go over the senior staff with you." She started at the top of the list. "Lieutenant Martin Singer will be our senior communications officer. I served with him briefly on the AURORA. He's spent the last couple of months training on SOLARA-class communications systems."

Annette moved to the picture of the person displayed below Martin. "Next, we have Lieutenant Ingrid Erikson, who'll be our senior operations officer. She spent two years on the GENESIS and six years on the AURORA. She has comprehensive knowledge of ship operations. I don't anticipate any problems for her acclimating to how things are run on the INFINITY."

The captain moved onto the picture of the Onixin. "Viv'r Kordif will be arriving on the ship late this afternoon. I met him a few weeks ago on Luna and am impressed how well he seems to work with humans. All reports say he's been an exemplary participant in the exchange program."

"I thought Onixins only had one name?" Frank said.

"They do. Viv'r is Kordif's military title. It's equivalent to a second-class lieutenant. Since it's a proper name, the micron doesn't translate it into English."

Frank nodded as he reviewed the Onixin's bio. "He participated in the Battle of The Solar System?"

Annette nodded. "From what I read, his ship was in the thick of the battle. It'll be good to have someone with actual navigational combat experience. I plan to use his expertise to come up with battle exercises for the crew."

This made sense to Frank. Even though the captain had been present during the Screen's attack on the solar system, the AURORA and the other capital ships had been relegated to the back of the fleet under the protection of the Ni ships. Given TERRA ships' inferior offensive and lack of defensive capabilities, they'd seen very little action during the battle.

Frank recognized the next name on the list. "Is that the same Dr. Myers who served on the PHOENIX?"

Annette nodded. "One and the same. He's the only medical officer we have with actual interspecies medical experience. The others are still on the PHOENIX. Dr. Myers has agreed to train the medical teams on all three ships. He'll start with INFINITY and stay with us for two missions before moving onto the DISCOVERY and SOLARIS. Once he's trained our staff, he'll recommend which doctor should be promoted to chief medical officer." Annette was not overly enthused about having a former member of PHOENIX serving on INFINITY. But he had valuable experience that would serve her ship's medical team well, so she was willing to offer him every courtesy.

Frank was anxious to spend some one-on-one time with the doctor. He'd heard all sorts of stories about PHOENIX's adventures during its Screen mission, but had never had an opportunity to speak with an actual crew member. Plus, Dr. Myers's actions had helped solidify Frank's position in TERRA after revealing his mute status.

They reached the bottom of the list. "Finally," Annette said, "we have our chief engineer, Commander Ronan Anvil."

Frank smiled. "I know Commander Anvil. I served with him on the JORDAN while we were both operations officers there. He'll be an excellent addition to the crew."

Annette was pleased to hear that her new XO had a previous working relationship with one of the senior staff. "He's proven his worth to this ship. He's been here a week ironing out some last-minute problems that have cropped up with our systems."

Frank took one last look at the senior staff's biographies. "We've got a good mix of experienced officers. I look forward to working with them."

Annette stood up. "Good. I'll let you go and handle any tasks that need to be completed before we leave. I'll send the to-do list to your DAT. Kordif will be arriving at 1630 hours. I'd like you to meet him in the hangar when he arrives."

"I look forward to it, Captain." Although Frank was nervous about meeting an alien one-on-one, he reminded himself that the captain had put her trust in him. He would not disappoint her.

Annette stood. "Dismissed, Commander."

Once Frank left her office, she sat back down, relieved. The initial meeting with her executive officer had gone better than expected. She had scrutinized the service records of hundreds of officers vying for INFINITY's XO post. She'd been tempted to place someone she knew from her days on the AURORA, but had decided against it. She'd already staffed half the ship's crew with officers from that ship, and several admirals had warned her that awarding an AURORA officer in the XO position would appear as if she was showing favoritism.

The TERRA admirals even implied that Earth Security might elect to increase their presence from the forty-eight officers already assigned to INFINITY to a much higher number. The last thing she wanted was a crew of mostly ES officers. This was a TERRA starship and only TERRA officers should be allowed to serve here. But internal policies dictated that ES be involved in most of TERRA's operations, including the operation of the new starships.

Annette reluctantly accepted she would have to deal with ES going forward. Luckily, she'd been able to arrange that ES personnel worked strictly in security. She didn't want them working in multiple departments on INFINITY.

Annette looked over at the portrait of the AURORA and smiled. She missed that ship. INFINITY was far superior to her old capital ship in every way, but the captain had spent over twenty-two years serving there and had a lot of fond memories. AURORA would always have a special place in her heart. She hoped that maybe INFINITY and AURORA could conduct a joint mission together before AURORA's decommissioning. It would be nice to work with her old colleagues again.

——— ——— ———

Commander Rola took his time heading down to engineering, paying attention to his new surroundings. He had the computer verbally guide him to his destination so he wouldn't get lost. The captain was right; they had made this ship bigger in every conceivable manner. On any of the capital ships, two officers could barely walk down a corridor side by side. Here, the corridors were wide enough to easily accommodate four people at a time.

The silver metallic hull seemed to have a shimmer to it, as if the ship itself was pulsating with life. Frank felt fortunate to be here.

Even with the aggressive construction schedule building these new ships, it would be a challenge staffing them. TERRA had a long list of officers who had applied for a post on a starship.

The problem was finding qualified candidates to serve on them. The most qualified officers were the ones who had served or were currently serving on one of the four remaining capital ships. Going from a fleet of four to a planned fleet of several hundred starships meant TERRA would face a staffing shortage. To resolve the problem, many of these vessels would be manned by people coming right out of the Academy. There had already been discussions to increase enrollment numbers so that the Academy could train a larger numbers of officers.

Although the ship was large, it didn't take much time for the commander to reach engineering. When he arrived, Frank was amazed at the size of the area. The old capital ships had never been designed for faster-than-light travel and therefore were not originally equipped with hyperdrive engines. As a result, their engineering compartments were small. When space exploration became possible, engineers had to figure out how to cram hyperdrive engines into the capital ships so they could perform patrol duty outside the solar system. Frank recalled how difficult it had been to work in the JORDAN's engineering section after it got its engine. Officers were constantly bumping into each other. A couple of engineers even had to transfer out of the department because the area became too claustrophobic for them.

INFINITY's engineering section was a large rectangular area comprising three decks. The entire area was open, with two levels of catwalks hovering above, accessible by a variety of small lifts and ladders. Up against the far wall pulsated the hyperdrive engine. It was housed in a copper-colored casing, with bits of light shimmering through the needle-sized openings that dotted that portion of the hull. Frank found it odd that the engine was embedded in the wall rather than situated in the middle of engineering. According to the specs, its placement provided better efficiency.

"Well, I'll be. Look who finally shows up." Frank turned around to see Commander Ronan Anvil. The chief engineer had a warm smile on his face. "Took long enough for you to get down here," Ronan said as he approached the commander. The two shook hands and patted each other on the shoulder.

"It's good to see you, Ronan." A feeling of relief and gratitude came over Frank at seeing his friend again.

The engineer nodded in agreement. "You don't know how happy I was when I learned you got assigned here."

Hearing those words put Frank at ease. He'd heard through the grapevine that Ronan had applied for the XO position, and hadn't been sure how his friend would react to Frank once he arrived. It seemed the chief engineer harbored no hard feelings.

Frank elected not to address the issue. "Captain Nikols says you've done a remarkable job getting things in order."

"I've learned so much in my short time here compared to my entire career in the fleet," Ronan admitted as he ran his hand through his short blond hair. "What do you think of the ship so far?"

Frank looked around. "I'm overwhelmed. I can hardly believe what she's capable of. We never had such advanced systems on the JORDAN."

"I heard Captain Diego tried to get Senfo computer systems installed on these new ships, but TERRA wouldn't allow it," Ronan said. "They weren't willing to trust having semi-sentient alien computer systems run our ships, so we're stuck with dumbed-down human-made ones. Don't get me wrong, what we have is still way more advanced than the ones on the old bucket of bolts we used to serve on."

Frank chuckled at Ronan's description. "How's your sister doing, by the way?"

"She's good. She still asks about you."

Frank had dated Ronan's sister, but his ambition to excel and the amount of time he spent away from Earth had put a strain on their relationship. She'd even moved to Luna, hoping to convince Frank to transfer to a post at TERRA headquarters, but it never happened. Frank wanted a career on a ship and wouldn't consider working at a ground-based facility. The breakup had been difficult and, although Ronan had taken time off to be with his sister to help her through it, he'd never blamed Frank. Ronan knew that TERRA officers had to make sacrifices to move up the ranks, and understood why Frank had put his duty ahead of his personal life.

"Next time you talk to her, give her my regards." Frank considered reaching out to her, but didn't want to exacerbate any bad feelings by contacting her. It was nice to hear that she had gotten past their breakup and was doing well. He changed the subject. "Are we on track for our launch tomorrow?"

Ronan's response was immediate. "We'll be ready to jump out of the solar system. We've taken care of any hiccups that have cropped up."

Frank smiled. "Captain Nikols will be pleased. I'll leave you to your work, but let's do dinner tonight."

Ronan gave Frank a thumbs-up. "Sounds great, Commander."

Frank patted his friend on the shoulder again and headed out of engineering.

After heading down the corridor and stepping onto the empty lift, his holographic DAT beeped. "Incoming transmission for Commander Rola on a civilian line."

Frank wasted no time activating his DAT and answering the call. He didn't recognize the older man's face, but the data feed stated it was Rich Melicoast, a name Frank did recognize. It was the former captain of the AURORA.

"Hello, Commander Rola. Thank you for answering my call."

Frank was perplexed. What would Melicoast want with him? "Is there something I can help you with?"

"I'd like to meet with you to discuss Captain Nikols. You should be aware of some things that I believe will help you as you serve under her."

Frank became immediately suspicious. He suspected it had to do with the former captain's dismissal from TERRA. After the Battle of The Solar System, he had been court-martialed and dishonorably discharged. Although details of the proceedings were kept confidential, Frank knew that as soon as Melicoast was expelled, Annette had been promoted to captain of the AURORA. It didn't take much to connect the dots and conclude Melicoast probably held a grudge against his former XO.

In the past, it hadn't been unheard of for officers to undermine their superiors if they saw an opportunity to take their place. Frank didn't think Captain Nikols had engaged in underhanded tactics against Melicoast, but had merely taken advantage of his misfortune in order to get promoted. She'd spent most of her career on the AURORA. It made sense for her to point to herself as the logical choice to replace her former captain. Frank saw nothing wrong with that.

"I don't think that would be appropriate," Frank stated.

Melicoast was insistent. "I wouldn't contact you if I didn't feel this was important. I've watched your career and have great respect for you. I don't want you to lose all you've worked so hard to achieve."

Melicoast had piqued the commander's interest, but Frank was still unconvinced. "I've got a lot to do before the INFINITY's launch . . ."

"Just listen to what I have to say. I'll be at the Amica Bar this evening at 2030 hours. It'll be worth your time." Before Frank could respond, Melicoast ended the transmission.

The commander wasn't sure what to do. He should ignore this request and not meet with the disgraced captain. But something within Frank was curious about what Melicoast might have to say. What could he know about Captain Nikols that was so important that it could affect Frank's career?

The commander didn't have time to debate the subject. He had duties to attend to and dinner plans with Ronan. If he got everything completed by this evening and felt up to it after dinner, then maybe he'd consider meeting the man.

CHAPTER THREE

Rich was seated in a booth, furthest from the entrance of the Amica Bar. He'd chosen this establishment because it was in the Indigo District of Infinity City. Very few TERRA officers frequented this part of the city, as it was furthest from headquarters. TERRA provided stipends for officers to stay in residences near HQ. When Rich lost his commission, he'd relocated to the Indigo District rather than moving to Earth or Mars. He'd hoped to do some civilian contract consulting relating to TERRA operations, but his dishonorable discharge made it all but impossible to find such work.

Luckily, Earth Security had been all too happy to hire him. His job was to help ES officers become acclimated to TERRA procedures. It was far from his glorious days as a captain, but it paid good money and allowed him to remain on Luna.

Rich flicked on his wrist hologram and checked the time—almost 2100 hours. It looked like Commander Rola wasn't going to show up.

As he was finishing his beer and getting ready to leave, he saw a tall young man in dark civilian clothes walk in. He recognized the man: Frank Rola.

Rich motioned him over to the booth. Soon both men were seated and facing each other. A waiter bot came by to see what Rola wanted to drink, but he waved the bot away.

"Thanks for coming," Rich started.

"I almost didn't. I can't imagine what you have to say to me."

"I meant it when I said I've admired all you've gone through in TERRA. You epitomize everything an officer should represent."

Frank was suspicious. "Don't try to appeal to my ego. Tell me what you want."

Rich could understand Frank's doubts and decided it was best to start talking. "It's Captain Nikols. You need to be careful around her."

"If you're trying to undermine my relationship . . ."

"I'm not," Rich insisted. "I know how she operates. It was because of her that I was expelled from TERRA."

Frank figured this might be his opportunity to learn what had happened during Melicoast's court-martial. He realized it would be a one-sided story, but at least he would learn the details. "What happened?"

"During the fight against the Screen near Mars, the capital ships were relegated to the back of the fleet and provided protection by those Ni ships."

"You're telling me nothing new. That's common knowledge."

"What isn't known is that I tried to maneuver the AURORA into the heart of the fight. I wasn't about to let TERRA's flagship be sidelined in such a historic battle. When we tried to move, we found the controls had been taken over by an external force. We did everything we could, but the AURORA wouldn't respond." Rich's body tensed up as he recounted the event. It was clear he still harbored anger over how things had happened. "After the victory, we were recalled to Luna. I was taken into custody and told I would be court-martialed. They had documented evidence I tried to maneuver the AURORA into the fight against the advice of my XO, evidence provided to them by Nikols."

The explanation made sense to Frank. "I don't understand the issue. Sounds like she did her duty and reported your attempt to circumvent orders."

"She was the one that proposed we should participate in the fight," Rich said. "She came up with a tactical plan to get us involved. When she was summoned to testify, she claimed she didn't agree with my plan and actively tried to convince me to reconsider. She even provided doctored logs that supported her false claim. I told them to check the AURORA's computer for her battle plan, but it was gone. Annette had erased it."

The revelation jolted Frank. He had dealt with officers who weren't above undermining others to further their own careers. He'd personally experienced that himself. But to hear that an officer would lie to the command council in official court-martial proceedings was unfathomable.

Frank had to remind himself to not get caught up in this story. Was any of this even true? Melicoast could be making all this up as petty revenge to undermine Captain Nikols's new command. Was he so bitter after all these years, he was willing to try and sabotage her?

"Do you have any proof?" Frank asked.

"If I had proof, you think I'd be sitting here talking to you?" Rich replied sarcastically. "Any evidence I might have, I would have used to expose her deception and get my command back."

"You're telling me Captain Nikols went through all this effort to get you booted out of TERRA so she could become captain of the AURORA? I know officers can be zealous in their career ambitions, but this sounds a bit much."

"It wasn't just to get promoted, but also to get revenge," Rich said. "A few years before, the captain of the SYRIA was getting ready to retire. Annette learned of this and put her name in to replace him. When PHOENIX was stolen, he debated whether to retire. I convinced him to stay, since we needed his expertise in case the Screen invaded the solar system in retaliation for PHOENIX's escape. I thought it only right to tell Annette of my conversation with him. She didn't take it well. She had been my executive officer for almost ten years and felt she was entitled to a promotion. In her mind, I blocked her chance to become captain."

It wasn't hard for Frank to draw the logical conclusion. "So, she plotted a way to get you out of TERRA so she could get promoted on the AURORA." When Melicoast nodded, Frank leaned back in the booth. "Excuse me for being blunt, but that's one messed-up story."

"You're right, it is. But you're about to embark on an exploration mission of former Screen territory. Anything can happen out there. If something goes wrong during your mission, I just want you to be aware of who you're serving under. Annette likes things to go perfectly and expects this first mission to go off without any problems. If something does happen out there, she'd be willing to shuffle any blame onto others to save herself, including you."

Frank had heard enough and got out of the booth. "Look, I'm sorry about what happened to you, but Captain Nikols's record speaks for itself. I see no reason not to trust her."

Rich shook his head and stood. "I'm just advising you to keep your wits about you. If you don't want to listen, then I wish you luck. Take care, Commander."

Frank watched as Melicoast left the bar, thrown off balance by his words. The former captain's last statement hadn't seemed to indicate he was plotting revenge, but rather looking out for Frank's best interest. He wasn't sure what to think.

Frank left the Amica Bar and slowly made his way back to the shuttle port, reviewing everything he knew about Annette Nikols. She was an officer with over thirty years of service to TERRA. Nothing in her biographical file or anything Frank had heard through the rumor mill indicated she was deceptive or underhanded. Her service record was unblemished and there was nothing that indicated any problems between her and Melicoast.

He also reminded himself that she'd had her pick of anyone in the fleet to serve as her executive officer. If she wanted perfection, or even the appearance of perfection, wouldn't she have chosen someone she knew on the AURORA versus an officer who hid his genetic status? No, the person who Melicoast had described was someone who would do anything to further her career while maintaining the illusion of perfection. He'd only just met the captain, but he didn't get the sense she was that sort of person.

He left the bar and headed back to the shuttle port, choosing to put this meeting behind him.

——— ——— ———

It was past 2200 hours before Frank got to the INFINITY's mess hall. Calling it a mess hall was an understatement. The kitchen alone was twice the size found on a capital ship. This allowed more food to be stocked and offered twenty-four hours a day, rather than three times a day. On top of that, bots could prepare and deliver food to officers' quarters, as they were all designed like apartments, with full kitchen setups. It was a nice new option for officers: they could eat in the mess hall while socializing or enjoy meals in their quarters.

Even though it was late, Frank was hungry. He hadn't had time to put a food delivery order in for his quarters, so he came to the mess hall for a late meal. He hadn't eaten much during dinner with Ronan, as they spent most of the meal catching up on things. This also gave him an opportunity to engage with the crew.

"Good evening, Commander Rola," the red service bot greeted as Frank approached the counter. "This unit's designation is G100. How are you this evening?"

Frank was taken aback by how human it sounded. "You must be one of the new galaxy line bots from Robonetrix."

Several of the private robotics firms had acquired some of the alien technological schematics from TERRA to develop a new generation of bots. Robonetrix was the first to release a new line of bots using those schematics. For now, they were only available to sell to TERRA. With such advanced artificial intelligence (AI) software in them, the military wanted to compile real world data on how they operated before authorizing their sales to civilians. The executive board of Robonetrix had tried to argue otherwise, but had to relent or risk losing the lucrative, and exclusive, multibillion-dollar contract with TERRA.

"That's correct," the bot replied in what almost sounded like an enthusiastic voice. "Again, how is your evening going so far?"

Frank couldn't help but smile. He was so used to issuing commands to bots he owned or worked with, it was difficult having an actual conversation with one. But he decided to go along and have fun with it. "It's fine. How are you doing?"

"This unit's operating systems are all within acceptable ranges. Thank you for your inquiry. What would you like for dinner?"

Well, it seemed the new artificial intelligence hadn't completely removed all traits of typical robot chatter from these new units. But from what Frank read about them, their AI software learned from experience and were adaptable. Maybe over time, the bot would converse in a more human-like vernacular.

The commander looked over the menu to see what might appeal to him. Another nice perk about this new mess hall was that officers had selections of meals to consider. On a capital ship, an officer was stuck with whatever had been made for breakfast, lunch, or dinner.

It didn't take long for Frank to decide what he wanted to eat. "I'll do the stuffed bell pepper with asparagus and chopped carrots."

"And to drink?" the bot inquired.

"Just ice water."

The bot quickly retreated to the cooking area in the back, prepared the meal, and returned. "Please let this unit know if the meal is not satisfactory," it said as it handed the tray to Frank.

"I'm sure it'll be fine. Thanks."

"That looks pretty good," said a voice behind him. "I almost ordered it myself." Frank turned to see Dr. Myers. He recognized the elder African-American with his distinctive white hair. "I know you from your bio file, Commander Rola. I'm Dr. Jeremy Myers."

Frank smiled as he shook the doctor's hand. "It's good to finally meet you. I've heard a lot about you."

Dr. Myers pointed to a table with a food tray sitting on it. "I just sat down myself. Join me?"

"I'd love to." Frank followed the doctor to the table. "I was excited to hear you'd be training our medical staff. Your years of experience on the PHOENIX will be a great help to them."

"I didn't think I'd be serving on another starship. They've kept me busy building the interspecies medical database at headquarters."

Since leaving PHOENIX, the doctor had been acquiring medical data from both the alliance and non-alliance races. The purpose was to gain a better understanding of alien physiology and their medical techniques. He was also working to identify any diseases that could potentially jump between alien species. With more and more alliance aliens participating in the military interspecies exchange program, TERRA felt it critical for their medical division to be well-versed in alien anatomies.

"It's a nice change to be serving on a starship again, if only temporarily," the doctor said. "Please don't hesitate to ask me anything."

Frank took an instant liking to the doctor. "I have a ton of questions about your travels on the PHOENIX."

"I'd be happy to share my experience with you. I only request that you don't ask about John Roberts," he said, referring to the captain of the PHOENIX.

Frank was perplexed. "Why?"

"People ask me these personal questions about him. I knew the man and considered him a good friend, but I don't have a deep psychological knowledge of him."

Frank chuckled. "Oh no! I'm more interested in the aliens you dealt with. I've never worked with an alien before and feel it's a handicap."

"You'll do fine, Commander. None of us had any experience when PHOENIX left the solar system. My best advice is to keep an open mind. In a lot of respects, the aliens in the alliance are not too different from us."

Frank was impressed by the doctor's confidence. If Myers believed he could get through the learning curve, then Frank would be confident as well.

"I've read the biography on Kordif . . ." Frank started.

Myers interrupted him. "He's a fine officer of the Onixin military. I met him a couple of months ago on Luna. He's done well in the interspecies exchange. Just be aware that Kordif has an affinity for *guao*. He'll drink it until he passes out if you let him."

That term sounded like sludge to Frank. "What's *guao*?"

"It's an Onixin drink, equivalent to human alcohol."

"Are you saying our chief navigation officer is a drunk?"

Jeremy shook his head. "No, no. If you tell him to stop drinking it, he will. He just needs a reminder when he's in casual social situations."

Frank found the notion of an alien having a possible drinking problem odd. Then again, aliens would have their own individual quirks, no different than humans. "Does it taste good?"

"No. I haven't met a human who likes it. It's best to avoid it, unless you want the taste of charcoal lingering in your mouth for days."

Frank laughed. "I'll make sure to warn the crew."

The doctor switched the subject away from alien drink concoctions. "Are you looking forward to being XO of this ship?"

"Very much so. It's a rare privilege to get this assignment. I have you to thank for helping me get here."

Myers had a confused look on his face. "How so?"

"You were on the committee who ruled that mutes could live off Earth and serve in the military. It was your exhaustive research that swayed the other committee members, and the command council, to drop the ban."

Dr. Myers had conducted research on mutes when it was discovered several PHOENIX crew members had genetic defects stemming from their Nuclear Holocaust heritage. He'd documented their medical histories and demonstrated their genetics didn't necessitate any more medical care than someone without such a history. Even after leaving PHOENIX, he'd continued his research. He'd testified before Parliament, the TERRA command council, and Earth Security about his findings, until the government and TERRA struck down the ban.

"I appreciate your gratitude. What I did was for the good of everyone," Myers said.

Frank smiled. "Well, I just wanted you to know what your efforts did for me."

The doctor nodded and looked around the mess hall. "I must say they've done an impressive job building these new ships. I was worried they wouldn't take advantage of the new alien technologies that had been acquired."

"You didn't think they could do it?" Frank assumed Myers was referring to the engineers' abilities to figure out how the alien technologies worked.

"No, it wasn't that. I was concerned TERRA would resume its old ways and isolate itself from the realities of our new world."

Frank couldn't imagine TERRA continuing on like it had for so many years. "Everything changed when PHOENIX came back. We couldn't resume business as usual. The capital ships can't compete with the other alliance ships, and we have the threat of the Cresorians looming over us."

"You and I both know that, but many in command were rooted in the old ways of thinking. They were more concerned with status and power than the good of the human race. Why do you think so many of them have been removed from their positions?"

Although Frank conceded Myers was correct in that most of the high-level officers in TERRA had been removed after the Screen's defeat, he was still uncomfortable with the subject. It wasn't his place to talk badly about his superiors, even if they were no longer active officers.

Myers likely saw the apprehension on Frank's face, because he gave an apologetic shrug. "I know it's impolite to talk about admirals, even former ones, in such a way, but at my age I've learned it's best to be transparent."

Frank agreed. "You're right. It's my training. Respect your superiors and accept that the decisions they make are in the best interest of the public."

"Usually, that's the case. But it's okay to question your superiors, especially if you're an executive officer," Myers pointed out. "Remember, a good XO questions their captain to ensure he or she has looked at all the possibilities."

Frank had been given that advice several times by fellow officers. He was tempted to tell the doctor about his meeting with Rich Melicoast, but held back. Doing so would give legitimacy to Melicoast's claims about Captain Nikols, and Frank was unwilling to give him that credibility.

"Have you met with the captain yet?" Frank asked instead.

"I did. I'm impressed with her. She'll do a fine job commanding INFINITY."

"You don't think her lack of interstellar experience will hinder her?"

"No amount of training or experience can fully prepare a captain. There are so many unknowns out in space. It's impossible to know what you'll encounter. Every captain, regardless of their years of experience, is in the same boat when it comes to space travel."

Frank appreciated the doctor's point of view. He'd been concerned that, with the exception of Dr. Myers and Kordif, none of the crew had space travel experience. The commander had felt that would put them at a distinct disadvantage. Talking with the doctor put his mind more at ease.

CHAPTER FOUR

Kordif was in his quarters, putting away his personal effects. He had arrived on the INFINITY three hours ago and been greeted by Commander Rola.

The reptilian Onixin had noticed the commander seemed awkward around him in their initial meeting. Kordif had read Rola's biography and knew he had no experience serving with aliens. It was something the Onixin was accustomed to. His time in the exchange program had found him working with TERRA officers who had never laid eyes on an alien before they met him.

It was a sentiment Kordif shared with the Quix and Senfo officers he'd met in the exchange: Humans were known for bringing races together, but many seemed unable to properly interact with aliens. It was an odd contradiction, one that Kordif had a hard time reconciling. But he found that after spending time with individuals, they became used to him. He concluded that humans needed to become familiar with an alien before they accepted them into their community.

The Onixin pulled a black pendant out of his bag. His yellow eyes glistened with moisture as emotion welled up within him. This was a *fupucha,* a soul commitment pendant exchanged between Onixins when they mated. Kordif's mate, Sente, had visited him in Infinity City. *Trusta genpu* later, Sente had called to inform Kordif she had laid seven eggs. The last inspection by their *entru* revealed two of the eggs were viable to make it to end-stage hatching. It was rare occurrence. Almost always, Onixin clutches resulted in a single viable egg. It would be a celebration for Kordif when he returned home to have two hatchlings waiting for him.

"Senior staff meeting in fifteen minutes," the computer announced.

"Translate into Onixin time measurements," Kordif requested.

"Fifteen minutes is *grunico.*"

Kordif had become adept at converting human metrics, but still checked the computer from time to time to make sure he was gauging time correctly. It would not be good for him to show up late for his first senior staff meeting, especially as a senior officer on a human starship.

The viv'r had spent two years in the interspecies program, far longer than most of the other participants. He wanted to garner as much experience as possible before returning to the Onixin military, to teach his fellow military officers as much as he could about how humans operated. Luckily, his interactions with a variety of humans had been mostly pleasant.

Since the Onixins had been free to conduct space travel en masse after the Screen's defeat, Kordif had volunteered to serve on a ship. He enjoyed space travel and could see a life in space. But his priorities had changed once he learned he would have hatchlings. It was his intention to return to Plein once he completed his first rotation on INFINITY, then remain there and participate in rearing his young ones with his mate. His service on INFINITY would be his last assignment in space for a long time.

The reptilian alien looked at himself in the mirror and checked that his bright-scaled green uniform was in good order. He placed the *fupucha* in the front waist pouch of his uniform and headed out of his quarters.

Captain Nikols was already seated at the head of the table in the briefing room when her senior staff started to file in. She nodded to each as they came through the door and took their respective seats. The only staff member she had not met was Kordif. She wasn't too surprised when he came in. He looked similar to other Onixins the captain had seen during her time at the shipyards.

When everyone was seated, the captain began. "I'd like to officially welcome you all on board INFINITY. I take it you have read each other's biographies, so we'll dispense with the introductions and get right to business. We're scheduled to depart the solar system at 1530 hours. I assume we're on track for that?"

Commander Rola took a look around the table and noticed someone was missing. Security Chief Hiroshi Ito was not present. Typically, the security chief was part of the senior staff and here it should be no different. However, Frank knew that the chief had been appointed to the INFINITY without Captain Nikols's consultation, as he was originally an ES officer. The captain did not hold him in high regard, as the chief had never attended the Academy and only wore a TERRA uniform due to the merging of both divisions.

Annette had made it clear to Frank that she did not consider the chief's presence at senior staff meetings necessary unless there was a critical security issue to address. He didn't agree with her stance, but had decided it was a battle not worth fighting. He'd made it a goal to facilitate a good working relationship between the captain and chief so she could see the latter's worth.

Frank cleared his throat. "Yes, sir. All final reviews have been done on our main systems and everything's checked out. We still have the problem with the tractor beam, but it's not an impediment to launching."

"Have you consulted with the DISCOVERY or SOLARIS about the problem?" Annette asked.

"I've consulted with the engineering teams on both ships," Ronan replied. "They haven't been able to resolve the phase variance in their beam's energy emission. Each time it's deployed it loses cohesion, preventing it from locking onto an object. They're working on a solution and have got the engineering bureau involved."

"PHOENIX left on its mission without a tractor beam system," Annette pointed out. "We'll just have to rely on Repos for retrieval operations." Repos were shuttles specifically designed to retrieve objects in space. INFINITY was stocked with four in the event the tractor beam was offline.

Annette looked over at her comm officer, Lieutenant Martin Singer. "Have you become acclimated to the new communications system?"

"Yes, Captain. We've adapted the system to the new protocols the alliance has established. All tests have come up clean and I anticipate no problems."

Annette expected nothing less. The lieutenant had served under her during her years on the AURORA and was adept in his abilities. She knew he was a perfect fit to serve here.

She turned to Lieutenant Ingrid Erikson, who had also served on the AURORA. "Anything to report regarding operations?"

"No, Captain," Lieutenant Erikson said. "As Commander Rola has already stated, with the exception of the tractor beam, all systems are good to go. All supplies have been loaded on INFINITY and all departments report ready."

Frank decided to make a proposition. "Captain, we've completed our launch preparations ahead of schedule. We could bump up our departure time."

"I'm glad to hear that, Commander, but there's no need to rush. If the crew's ready, they can spend some extra downtime relaxing. Once we leave, we're all going to be very busy." Annette looked over to Kordif. "And I'd like to give our new navigation officer time to become acclimated to his station."

"Thank you, Captain," Kordif replied. "I have reviewed all the specifications of the INFINITY navigation system. I am ready."

"Nevertheless, we are in no hurry for launch, so let's take the opportunity to reflect on our accomplishments." Annette looked over at Dr. Myers. "I have yet to receive a report on medical's status."

"I'm still evaluating medical. As Lieutenant Erikson has said, we have all the supplies we need. Training of the medical staff will be ongoing during the next couple of missions."

"I'll expect regular progress reports," Annette said. "I want medical best prepared to handle anything we may have to deal with out there."

"Do you anticipate we'll run into anything?" Martin asked.

"I don't think so. Our mission is to survey the space formerly claimed by the Screen. The database on their homeworld indicated all outposts and installations were abandoned for the invasion of the solar system. The alliance has located and verified those installations were abandoned. TERRA feels that conducting surveys of planets in former Screen star systems is necessary to ensure that we have not missed anything."

"They don't want any surprises," Ronan concluded.

Annette nodded. "The alliance has been preoccupied with providing defensive support to TERRA while we build our fleet. They're also trying to diffuse the Cresorian situation, so they've been too busy to conduct surveys of former Screen systems. This will give us an opportunity to see how one of our new ships does on a survey mission."

"There's probably nothing to find," Ingrid said. "If there were any leftover Screen, we would have known by now."

"Don't assume," Myers cautioned. "The Screen may be gone, but they may have left things behind. The archives on their former homeworld have provided a lot of information, but there's still a lot we don't know. We can't assume their records are complete. They did have time to alter or erase them before we occupied their world."

Captain Nikols respected the doctor's opinion, as he was the only one here with any experience with the Screen. "Dr. Myers is right. I don't want us conducting this mission resting on our laurels. We should be prepared for anything. Commander Rola, I want to have regular battle drills with the crew."

"Yes, Captain. We have several scenarios we can put them through."

"You bring up a good point, Doctor," Annette said. "Perhaps you should get the medical staff familiar with Screen physiology, just in case."

Myers agreed with the suggestion. "I think that's an excellent idea."

Annette was pleased by how fluidly the meeting had gone. "Good. If there's nothing else, then this meeting is adjourned."

The staff got up and slowly exited the briefing room. Dr. Myers approached Kordif and got his attention. "Excuse me, Viv'r Kordif. Do you have a moment?"

The Onixin's hidden mouth became evident as he smiled, his bright yellow teeth glistening in the room's light. "I appreciate you addressing me by my official title. *Flu'we.*"

Myers recognized the Onixin term for gratitude. "I'm here serving as chief medical officer temporarily until I get the staff trained on alien medical care. Given that you're the only non-human on board, I wanted to ask if you'd be willing to help me train them."

"I would be willing to help you in your efforts," Kordif replied. "What do you need of me?"

"Nothing invasive. All I need is for you to go through bio-scans, get the medical staff accustomed to treating an alien as a patient."

Kordif found the proposition acceptable. "I am at your disposal."

"Thank you. Also, be sure to come in to medical before launch to get your injection." Onixins required an enzyme that originated on their homeworld to regulate their biological functions. Those serving on non-Onixin ships needed regular injections of the enzyme; otherwise, they would slip into a coma.

"I will, Doctor."

Frank approached Captain Nikols as she got up from her seat. "I'll send a status report to you before the launch once I make another round with the departments."

"No need. I've read all your status reports and am satisfied the ship's ready. You've done well since coming on board. Take the next few hours off and let the crew not on duty know I expect them to enjoy a little downtime before we launch."

Frank was grateful that the captain was showing confidence in him. "I will, sir. Thank you."

——— ——— ———

Shortly before noon, Annette summoned Commander Anvil and Lieutenants Singer and Erikson to her quarters. She had opened a bottle of sparkling cider and poured it into four champagne glasses. When the officers arrived, she handed each a glass.

"I want to take this opportunity to toast our success on this mission and a bright future for all of us on this new starship."

"Cheers!" the group said collectively.

"We've all been through a lot together on the AURORA," Annette added. "I consider each of you the best that ship represented. I couldn't imagine taking this command without you."

Martin spoke up first. "We're grateful for your faith in us. It's good we're all together again."

"We'll always perform at our best for you, Captain," Ingrid added.

Annette smiled. "What do you think of the rest of our senior staff? You can speak freely."

Ronan started first. "I'll be honest, I didn't want to like Dr. Myers. I still consider him a traitor like those others," he said, referring to the first crew of the starship PHOENIX. "But he's made a good impression on me. His space exploration experience will be a great asset to the ship."

Martin spoke up next. "I thought I'd have a hard time with that Onixin, but he doesn't seem that different from the rest of us. I found it easy to talk to him. He's made an effort to fit in here."

Ingrid found his statement odd. "Are you kidding me? How can you say that with that scaly skin of his?"

"I'm just saying that I've found it easy to work with him."

"Remember, there are differences between us and him," Annette reminded them. "Make sure you've read up about his culture. We don't want to have any misunderstandings. It could interfere with ship operations and I won't have that. You'll want to make your experience with Kordif a good one so you can apply it to any other alien that might serve here in the future."

"You think TERRA will assign more aliens to INFINITY?" Ronan asked.

"I'm certain of it. The exchange program has been successful. TERRA's considering expanding the program."

"Makes sense," Martin said. "So far none of the crew here have objected to the notion of an alien being their superior officer. I think people will get used to the idea of aliens serving in TERRA."

Annette agreed, but she felt officers would accept aliens in TERRA because they had no choice. In the last few years there had been a lot of changes in the military, and the command council had made it clear that any officer not on board with these changes would find themselves out of TERRA.

"What do you think of our XO?" Annette asked the group. This was an important question for her. How her senior officers felt about Commander Rola would dictate how well the crew would function.

Ronan spoke up first. "He's a good man. I've worked with him before. He's a dedicated officer and is always eager to learn."

"He seems to trust our experience," Ingrid added. "He's been open to my suggestions."

Martin echoed their sentiments. "Same here. He complimented me on some of the new communication protocols I came up with for the ship."

Annette was pleased to hear this. She was confident her senior staff would be an effective command. With her curiosity satisfied, she decided to switch subjects. "I don't expect anything significant to happen on this mission. The alliance has reported no unusual activity detected in Screen space. I expect this will be nothing more than a survey mission."

"Maybe we'll find some life-supporting planets that could be colonized," Ingrid said hopefully.

"If this turns out to be a standard survey mission, we can take the time to refine INFINITY's systems," Ronan suggested.

"We'll be ready for whatever we come across," Martin said.

That was exactly the sort of confidence Annette wanted to hear from her staff. She knew they were ready. They had been planning this launch for months. It was time to show TERRA what the crew of the INFINITY could do.

——— ——— ———

"Come in," Security Chief Hiroshi Ito said as the door chime sounded. He looked up to see Commander Rola enter his office.

"Commander Rola," he said as he started to stand up. He'd been hoping to have an easy day and not have to deal with any TERRA officers. Well, he would try to keep this conversation short.

Frank held up his hand. "At ease, Chief. No need to stand on ceremony for me."

Hiroshi reclined in his seat. "I thought you TERRA officers loved your ceremonial rituals."

"Only if it involves an admiral who can demote me," Frank joked as he sat down.

It seemed this commander had a sense of humor. Hiroshi was still on guard. "What can I do for you?"

"I sent you a summary of the senior staff meeting. Nothing was discussed about security, but I thought you'd want to know what we talked about."

Hiroshi activated his holographic DAT and pulled up the file. "I appreciate it, Commander, but you shouldn't waste your time. Captain Nikols doesn't feel I need to know the daily happenings here."

"I don't agree with that. You're a senior officer and therefore entitled to know what's discussed at staff meetings, even if it doesn't apply to your department."

It seemed Hiroshi had gotten the commander all wrong. He'd assumed Rola was a typical TERRA officer who didn't hold much respect for ES officers. He was pleased to see his initial assumption had been wrong. "Thank you for extending the courtesy to me. To be honest, I expected to be kept at arm's length by the entire senior staff."

Frank knew where Hiroshi was coming from. ES officers were not held in high regard by TERRA officers. They enlisted into service, unlike TERRA officers, who competed for a spot to attend the Academy. A lot of individuals who applied but did not get into the Academy wound up enlisting in Earth Security as their fallback, which perpetuated the notion that ES officers were not of the same caliber as TERRA officers.

When Earth Security and TERRA officially merged, a lot of TERRA officers were bitter. Many found themselves suddenly reporting to an ES officer. Frank had heard from others several times how ES had taken over and TERRA was going downhill. In his personal experience, he'd found ES officers to be capable and just as dedicated to duty.

Frank wanted to assure the security chief that he wasn't holding a grudge. If he could establish trust with the chief, it would go a long way toward facilitating a good working relationship between Hiroshi and the captain. "I know how ES . . . *former* ES officers are perceived. Your record is impressive and the work you've done on INFINITY getting your security team in place is commendable."

Hiroshi nodded. "Thank you. I was hesitant taking this assignment, but not because of how I would be treated. I've spent my entire career serving in various positions on Earth. This is my first assignment in space." ES was strictly Earth-based, as the organization's purpose was to provide protection for Earth, while TERRA handled security on Luna and Mars, along with overall military operations.

"I read your service history," Frank said. "You served all over Earth in about twenty-three territories."

"Twenty-seven," Hiroshi corrected. "I was trying for the record, but that got scuttled when TERRA went rogue. Then I was tasked with coming up with a plan for the government to get control of TERRA again. I was all over Luna and Mars getting familiar with operations."

Frank knew that Hiroshi had been part of the ES group who had made recommendations as to which TERRA officers need to be expelled and who should stay. That alone wasn't going to endear him to many people.

"I would have thought your time doing that would have gotten you a high-level position," Frank said.

"I could have become a commander or captain. But I figure some of us need to be on the frontlines making sure this whole transition goes smoothly. I'm not worried. I'll get my promotion when I'm ready." Hiroshi decided to capitalize on the commander's presence and brought up another topic. "Since you're here, I want to ask you something. You know that my entire security team are former ES officers, which Captain Nikols isn't happy about. I hope you don't have a problem with it."

Frank knew that the chief had been given complete latitude to build his own security force. He assumed it was one of the perks Hiroshi requested when he took this assignment. "From what I've read, I'm sure you built a competent team. As long as they do their duties, it's irrelevant to me that they're ES."

"Thank you, Commander."

"I hope to see you on the command deck when we launch," Frank added.

"I wasn't planning on it. Now that I know one senior officer will welcome me up there, I think I'll be there."

"Great. See you then, Chief," Frank said as he left the security office. It was important to him to have a good relationship with every senior staff member. He was disappointed that Captain Nikols wasn't willing to give Hiroshi the benefit of the doubt. The commander intended to change her mind.

——— ——— ———

It was 1500 hours and the entire senior staff had assembled on the command deck. Final checks on all systems had been done and they were ready to go.

Annette emerged from her office and the command deck staff stood at attention. "Captain on deck," Frank announced from the operations table, where he was standing next to Lieutenant Erikson.

"What's our status?" Annette asked as she took a seat in her command chair. She didn't acknowledge Chief Ito, who was sitting in his seat adjacent to the command chair. She'd assumed he wouldn't be up on the command deck during the launch and was disappointed by his presence. But even though she didn't want him there, she accepted that he was doing his duty and ensuring no security issues cropped up during launch. She couldn't fault him for that.

"Luna Station is waiting to hear from us before officially sending us off," Frank said.

Ingrid did a final review of all ship systems. "All systems are at the ready."

Annette nodded as she looked over to her Onixin navigation officer. "Have you plotted our course out of the solar system?"

"Yes, Captain. Once we move out of the human star system, we will be ready to jump to the Jemyu system. It should take two days at factor four." The command council had decided to keep the designations the Screen made to the star systems in their territory. This was done to avoid confusion with the ongoing research that was being conducted by the alliance on the Screen's homeworld, which included documenting how they designated the star systems they used to control.

Years of construction, planning, and recruiting the right officers had come down to this moment. Captain Nikols had never imagined her service would include traveling beyond the solar system. This would be a new phase of her career, one that she was looking forward to.

The captain looked at her XO. "Well, Commander, I see no reason to delay."

Frank nodded and motioned to Lieutenant Singer. "Open a channel to shipyard control."

Martin inputted some commands in his console to open a communications link. "Luna Station control, this is TCS infinity, requesting permission for departure."

"This is Dockmaster Ai Vantine. All traffic has been cleared. Umbilical connections have disengaged. You are free to depart. Good luck out there."

"Thank you, Dockmaster," Annette replied. "infinity out." She appreciated that the dockmaster himself was present to see them off. It was a gracious sign of respect. "Kordif, fire maneuvering thrusters and back us away from the station."

"Thrusters are online," Kordif announced after he confirmed the ship was detached from the station.

The INFINITY slowly moved away from Luna Station. Dock workers and officers raced to the nearest windows to watch TERRA's newest starship move away. The blue-and-silver ship looked magnificent as she maneuvered out and away from her two sister ships. Many agreed that humanity had entered a new age as now a second starship had left to explore the stars.

"We have cleared the station and are in open space," Kordif announced.

"Bring sub-light engines online," Annette ordered. "Set the ship's speed to one half. If everything is in the green, punch it to full speed." There was no need to baby this ship. She wanted to explore INFINITY's capabilities.

"Yes, Captain," Kordif replied as he entered the commands in his console.

Frank leaned over to Ingrid. "The n'quadrin may spike a little hot going into the engines. It shouldn't be a problem."

"Thanks for the heads-up, sir."

"How's the energy network looking?" Frank asked. He could have quickly checked it himself but wanted to start cementing a cohesive working relationship with the operations officer.

Ingrid checked the readings. "The n'quadrin network is within tolerances."

The executive officer looked out the command deck windows. Luna was already nothing more than a dot as the ship moved through the solar system. He could hardly believe they had made it to this point. He felt a sense of euphoria at realizing they were heading out. Had the crew of the PHOENIX felt this way when they left the solar system?

After a few minutes of traveling, Kordif spoke up. "Captain, I am not detecting any stress in the sub-light engines. We should be able to push them to maximum speed."

"By all means, Kordif, you have my permission to go to full speed."

The captain monitored their acceleration from her command chair display. This ship was remarkable. They were going faster than the AURORA ever could and were using one tenth the energy to do so. There was no shuddering of the deck plates that she had become accustomed to on the AURORA whenever it exceeded over half of sub-light speed. The INFINITY was gliding smoothly through space. Having a ship with different alien technologies was already turning out to be advantageous.

The real test would take place when they left the solar system and jumped to faster-than-light travel. The hyperdrive was of human design; however, the INFINITY was the first starship to have a human hyperdrive interfaced with systems from multiple alien worlds. All simulations conducted showed no issues, but the crew would be nervous until the ship finally jumped.

"Nikols to engineering."

"Anvil here."

"Bring the hyperdrive online."

"Yes, Captain."

"INFINITY has cleared Pluto's orbital path," Kordif announced.

Annette found no reason to delay the jump. "Lay in a course for the Jemyu system, factor one."

Frank appreciated the captain's display of confidence. If she was nervous about INFINITY's first jump, she was hiding it well. Her calm demeanor would alleviate any worries the command deck staff had about jumping. He decided he needed to focus on his duties and push aside any nervousness he was feeling.

"Hyperdrive online," Kordif reported.

"All systems are within normal tolerances," Ingrid added.

It was time. The captain calmly folded her hands, as if she was about to embark on a leisure cruise. "Initiate jump."

The hum of the hyperdrive could be heard ramping up as Kordif activated it. Seconds later, INFINITY jumped out of the solar system and was hurtling towards the Jemyu system. "We are holding at factor one," the Onixin announced.

The command deck staff were all glued to their respective station monitors, looking for any hint of a problem. So far, none of the systems reported anything critical.

"There's some minor bleeding of the Dubois particles off the rear hull," Ingrid said.

"Adjust the hyperdrive's emission geometry by .04 percent," Frank advised. "That should clear the problem."

"Will that affect our ability to increase speed?" Annette asked.

"No, Captain," Frank replied. "Dubois saturation levels are still at acceptable levels, even with the bleed-off."

"The computer estimates it'll take about forty minutes to resolve the issue," Ingrid reported.

Annette was pleased by how well the launch had gone. She stood up and looked around at her staff. "Congratulations to all of you for this achievement. Lieutenant Singer, send a message to TERRA that we've successfully jumped and are en route to our mission."

"With pleasure, Captain."

"Kordif, if engineering is reporting no issues, you're authorized to increase our speed to factor three."

"Yes, Captain."

Frank moved away from the operations table and approached Annette. "Captain, going to factor three will mean that it takes us four days to get to the Jemyu system."

"We're under no timetable to reach our destination. I don't see a reason to needlessly push the ship. We can take the time to conduct additional checks on systems and revise some operating procedures."

Frank saw the merit in her thinking. "Yes, Captain. I'll inform the crew."

"I'll be in my office." Annette headed off the command deck.

Frank returned to the operations table. "So, what do you think?" he asked Ingrid.

"About the ship? I'm surprised we didn't have any issues. The construction teams did a remarkable job building her, but I expected we'd have some problems."

Frank smiled. Even though he hadn't been part of building INFINITY, he felt pride that his fellow officers could step up and build a vessel that was completely different from the old capital ships. "I'm taking this as a good sign that the ship will serve us well."

"It'll let us focus on the mission without worrying about systems breaking down," Martin added.

Frank agreed. "I'll be in engineering. You have the deck, Lieutenant Erikson."

——— ——— ———

"Remarkable," Ronan muttered to himself as he turned a white crystal over in his hand.

"What's remarkable?" came a voice behind the chief engineer. Ronan turned to see Commander Rola approaching him.

Ronan held up his hand. "These data crystals. The science behind them still amazes me."

Frank recognized the crystals. They were Aldarian in origin. They had replaced traditional fiber-based microchips used on the capital ships. The crystals had superior processing and data storage capacity. Even more remarkable was the fact they had self-healing properties. If cracked or damaged, they could heal themselves.

The crystals took many years to grow; luckily, there was an overabundance of them on Aldaria. The Aldarians were willing to share the crystals with the alliance, as they only used a small section of their underground city.

"I remember going through the training to learn about them," Frank recalled. "It took two weeks to learn how they function."

"Did you have Menthal?" Ronan asked.

Frank shook his head. "Drena was our teacher. But there were some hiccups in her schedule and they almost held the training on Aldaria."

Ronan's eyes widened. "I would have loved to visit their homeworld. I hear their city is a sight to behold." The Aldarian city was composed of crystals of various shapes and sizes. Visitors to their world agreed that it was an architectural wonder.

"I've only seen pictures," Frank admitted. "Maybe INFINITY will have a chance to visit Aldaria."

Ronan relished that thought, but knew the commander was down here on business. "I take it you came down here to see how things are going?"

Frank nodded. "XO prerogative. I know it's not necessary as everything up on the command deck showed all systems are good. I just feel it's better to touch base with departments in person whenever possible."

The chief engineer appreciated the personal touch. "Well, I can tell you that things are operating without a hitch down here. Except for some minor variances in the n'quadrin network, everything is functioning as we expected. INFINITY's a pretty remarkable ship."

Frank agreed. "Unless something changes, we'll reduce our status briefings to daily. I'll let the other department heads know."

"Sounds good, Commander," Ronan said.

"Well then, carry on," Frank said as he left engineering.

——— ——— ———

It was 1900 hours and Frank was in the captain's quarters. She had invited him over for dinner as an opportunity to better get to know each other. Both were still dressed in their black uniforms. Even off hours, Annette expected her officers to represent the military.

"I had the bots prepare the food," Annette said as she and Frank sat down at the dining room table. "I've never been much of a cook." AURORA's officers' quarters lacked kitchens, forcing the crew to eat in the mess hall. As Annette had spent the majority of her career on that ship, she'd rarely had the opportunity to prepare meals.

"It looks great, Captain," Frank said as he looked at the servings of sliced ham and mixed vegetables. A red service bot came around and poured sparkling water for the pair.

Annette raised her glass and made a toast. "To a good first day."

Frank raised his glass. "A very good first day."

After sipping her water, Annette spoke. "You were still in the Academy when PHOENIX left Earth, correct?"

Frank nodded. "I remember that day. I was home in Beirut

when I saw the news. I couldn't believe when they reported that two cadets were commanding it."

"Did you know John Roberts or Julie Olson?" Annette asked, referring to the cadets who were recruited to help steal that ship. "They would have been a year ahead of you."

"I didn't know either of them and I was grateful. Anyone who knew them was questioned extensively by security."

Annette wasn't surprised to hear that. The launch of that ship had created such upheaval that TERRA security had zealously tried to uncover how the ship had launched without the council's knowledge. "Understandable. It was an embarrassment for TERRA to have their secret ship stolen from underneath them."

"Didn't the AURORA try to stop them?" Frank immediately regretted asking that question. He didn't want the captain to take any sort of offense.

"We did. We were shocked when we found PHOENIX had shield technology. I think we were all stunned that she got away from us. Don't get me wrong, the crew was mad, but we realized we had gone up against PHOENIX blind, unaware of her capabilities. But things worked out in the end. We obtained new technologies that allowed us to build this ship and we're free to explore space."

Frank was relieved the captain didn't mind recounting AURORA's encounter with the PHOENIX. "I always dreamed of exploring space. With the Screen hovering over us, I assumed it would never happen. I did try to get a post on a capital ship when I graduated, but TERRA wouldn't have it."

Annette remembered those orders from the command council. They had placed a moratorium on new officers being posted to a capital ship. With that mandate, it was nearly impossible for officers to rotate to other facilities or ships. Essentially, everyone was stuck where they were for over three years. "TERRA wanted only seasoned officers on their ships in case the Screen decided to invade the solar system."

"I was assigned to the maintenance crew of the fighter and shuttle groups on Luna," Frank recalled. "Once the Screen were defeated, I was able to transfer to the JORDAN."

Annette fiddled with her water glass. "A lot of things changed. I lost a lot of good friends and fine officers."

Frank knew that she was referring to the mass expulsion of officers from the fleet by Earth Security to reassert control of TERRA for the government. Most of the high-ranking officers were removed, but lieutenants and commanders weren't spared either. Anyone who protested the changes made by ES found their commissions terminated. Frank had been told by the incoming captain of the JORDAN that the only reason he got onto that ship was because of all the vacancies that had occurred. It wasn't an illustrious way to get the post, but Frank wasn't picky about it. It had been his chance to gear his career in the direction he wanted it to go.

"The nice part of serving on the AURORA for so many years was that I made a lot of lifelong friends," Annette said. "I don't expect that here."

Her comment caught Frank's interest. "Why do you say that?"

"TERRA's rebuilding the fleet from the ground up. We're scuttling the capital ships for new ships. Over the next few months, they'll be launching a lot of these new starships. I anticipate they'll transfer officers from here, SOLARIS, and DISCOVERY once the crews are trained and can be moved to new ships as they come online."

Her reasoning made sense. TERRA would want to staff new ships with some experienced crew members to help train the new officers that would fill the crews on all the new ships. For now, that experience could only be acquired from those serving here and on INFINITY's sister ships.

But he also sensed some sadness in the captain's voice. "You don't want to lose anyone, do you?"

Annette gave a weak smile. "I like consistency in my life. I was fortunate to serve with the same group of officers for so many years. I won't have that here, and that's okay. I can remember my time on AURORA fondly as I move forward. Eventually, I'll be promoted to admiral and relocate back to Luna to work from headquarters."

Frank considered bringing up Rich Melicoast but decided

against it. It didn't seem to be the right time to dredge up some unpleasantness in the captain's past. The more Frank talked to the captain, the more he was convinced she hadn't done what Melicoast claimed. Captain Nikols was a fine, upstanding officer. He was convinced she didn't need to resort to underhanded tactics to move up the ranks.

After finishing dinner and chatting a bit more, Frank called it a night and left the captain's quarters for his own to get some sleep. Annette was tired, but there was one more person she wanted to talk to before she went to bed. She contacted the command deck and requested the on-duty communications officer make some arrangements for her. She waited patiently, perusing through personal photos on her DAT as she sipped some more water.

"Command deck to Captain Nikols. I have Captain Swenson on the line for you."

"Thank you, Lieutenant." Annette got off the couch and approached the wall monitor. "Put him through."

Seconds later an image of a TERRA officer appeared on the wall monitor. "Annette," he smiled, seeing his former captain.

"Hello, Dennis. It's good to see you. I thought I'd check in and see how things are on the AURORA."

"It's I who should be checking in on you, given you've left the solar system on a new ship."

Dennis Swenson had been Annette's executive officer on the AURORA. She held him up as an example of what a TERRA officer should be. He'd started his career on the AURORA, and she'd watched him work his way up the ranks on that ship. It was a no-brainer for her to make him XO when she was promoted to captain, as they worked well together.

Before she transferred to the Luna shipyards to help with INFINITY's construction, she had promoted him as AURORA's new ship commander. She would have rather brought him over to serve with her on INFINITY, but Dennis was ready to command his own ship. She couldn't deny him his own command, as Captain Melicoast had once denied her. Once the AURORA was decommissioned in a few months, he'd take command of one of TERRA's new starships and be out here exploring space with her.

"We jumped with no issues," Annette said. "INFINITY has operated beyond expectations."

"And how's your new XO working out?"

"Young, but I've been impressed with him. He shows good leadership skills and the crew have taken a liking to him. He's a fine addition to the ship. But I didn't call to talk about me or INFINITY. I want to hear how things are going with you and the AURORA."

Dennis expected that inquiry. Annette had a soft spot for the AURORA. After she'd transferred, she checked in on Dennis monthly to see how things were going.

"We're conducting orbital patrols of Mars. I don't expect AURORA will ever leave Mars again. We've got some civilian historical archivists on board taking videos and photos of the ship."

With all the capital ships being decommissioned, TERRA had decided to hire historians to document everything, from the technologies used, living arrangements, and interviews with the crew. TERRA had tried to obtain funding to build a fleet museum on Luna to house one or more of the capital ships, but public opinion was against it. There were still hard feelings about TERRA's actions in the recent past. No one in the government was willing to sponsor a bill to fund such an endeavor.

"How's the crew handling civilians being on board?" Annette asked.

"It's a tough reminder that we won't be together much longer. Some are looking forward to serving on another ship, but many would rather stay here, including me. AURORA may be old, but she's served TERRA well."

Annette was surprised to hear him say that. In past conversations, he'd reiterated how much he was looking forward to commanding a new starship. "I thought you'd be looking forward to helming a new ship?"

"Part of me is, but a big part of me wants to stay here. Sure, she's out-of-date, but she's never failed us. Just because something's old doesn't mean you get rid of it. I'm sure once I transfer, I'll be too busy to be sentimental."

Annette appreciated that sentiment. Despite commanding a

new starship, it was the AURORA she always thought of when she started and ended each day. She was convinced even the passage of time wouldn't diminish her fondness for her old capital ship.

"There's a Quix ship not too far from the solar system," Dennis added. "Word is TERRA is trying to arrange for us to conduct joint military exercises with them. Should change things up a bit for the crew. They've never worked with seven-foot slugs."

Annette chuckled at his remark. She'd met a couple of Quix before, and Dennis's description of them wasn't too far off. "Keep in mind they have this weird notion that we're all one military group working together. They call it protectionism, or something like that."

"I'll keep that in mind," laughed Dennis before getting serious again. "I'm glad things are going well for you. I mean that. You've always had my greatest respect."

"And you've had mine," Annette replied. "I never regretted leaving the AURORA in your capable hands."

"Maybe when you get back, you can visit us one more time before decommissioning. I've already dropped that suggestion to a couple of admirals."

It was something for Annette to look forward to when this mission was completed. Having a final walkthrough on the AURORA before it was put out to pasture would be a nice way to reminisce about her years on that ship one last time. "I'd like that." She wanted to say more to him but thought it best to end the conversation. "I better let you go. Have a good night, Dennis."

"You too, Annette. Good night."

The wall monitor flickered off as Annette smiled. It meant a lot to her to hear that her former crew was getting along okay without her. It would be a sad day for all of them when AURORA was taken out of service.

She vividly recalled her first day stepping foot on that ship. She was assigned to the operations group and was eager to prove her worth to the captain. She remembered going up to the command deck for the first time to meet with the senior operations officer. Annette couldn't remember what they talked about, as she could only stare at her superior officer and think, *One day I'll have your job.* And she did. From the senior operations officer, she was promoted to executive officer. Even though competition for those senior positions were fierce, Annette felt there were never any hard feelings from the officers who lost out to her. She truly believed that AURORA had the finest crew out of all the ships in the fleet.

Annette yawned, realizing she was tired. She pushed any more thoughts of the AURORA out of her mind as she headed to her bedroom.

CHAPTER FIVE

The INFINITY was on the second day of its journey to the Jemyu system. Except for some minor hiccups, the ship was operating better than anyone expected. With the starship operating so well, the crew took the time to make some revisions to their operating procedures.

Dr. Jeremy Myers was busy training the medical staff and conducting simulations. Kordif had been helpful, volunteering on his off time to be scanned by the doctors and nurses. The staff was becoming well-versed in Onixin physiology. Kordif had told them about his mate laying eggs back home, and the medical staff had quizzed him extensively about Onixin procreation. Kordif was more than happy to answer all their questions. Onixins had no cultural hang-ups about discussing their mating practices, as they considered it a natural biological process.

Myers had just concluded the latest training simulation, showing the staff how to analyze and conduct blood transfusions between species. When the class concluded, he went to the chief medical office with his colleague, Dr. Tao Noble, to discuss the staff's progress.

"They're handling the training pretty well," Myers remarked

as he sat behind the desk. "They asked a lot of questions, which tells me they're absorbing what's being taught to them and are curious to learn more."

Tao took a seat opposite him on the other side of the desk. "What you've taught us so far has been almost overwhelming, Jeremy. How were you able to handle learning all this while on the PHOENIX? I can't imagine what it must have been like treating your first aliens."

"A lot of research and some trial-and-error," Jeremy admitted. "But I had twice the staff on PHOENIX compared to INFINITY, so there were more people to spread the work around. Your staff here is very capable. They will get through the learning curve."

His phrase caught Tao's attention. "My staff? A little presumptuous, Doctor."

"Doctors Black and Ishmati have spoken to me and don't want to be considered for the CMO position. They feel they need more time and experience treating alien species before leading a ship's medical department."

"I don't blame them. It's going to take a lot of time to learn about the physiology of the alliance races, not to mention the other races not in the alliance."

"I've been watching you," Jeremy said. "You seem to handle what I've been teaching quite well. You've even stepped up to assist medical personnel during the instruction."

"This has all been fascinating to me. I find the information compelling."

"That's what you need to be an effective chief medical officer on an interstellar ship. I see no reason why you shouldn't be CMO."

"I appreciate your confidence in me."

Suddenly, the captain's voice came over the office speakers. "Dr. Myers to the command deck."

It was unusual for the captain to request anyone's presence without stating the reason. "This is Myers. Is there a problem, Captain?"

"We just picked up a distress call from a Senfo freighter that's under attack."

"I'm on my way." Jeremy looked at Tao. "Have the staff go to emergency readiness. Make sure they review all biological information we have on the Senfo."

"Understood," Tao nodded as both doctors exited the office.

——— ——— ———

Jeremy arrived on the command deck and found Captain Nikols, Commander Rola, Chief Ito, and Lieutenant Erikson around the operations table. He quickly joined them to get up to speed on the situation.

"Doctor, we received a distress call six minutes ago from a Senfo vessel," Annette said. "They're under attack."

"Have they said if they have any casualties?" Jeremy asked.

Frank spoke up. "No. The message was pretty garbled. We're still trying to triangulate their exact position. We know they're in this part of the sector." He pointed to the holographic chart on display over the operations table.

"Kordif, adjust our course to the general area of the distress call and increase speed to factor 5," Annette ordered.

"Yes, Captain."

"I've read up on many of the ships used by the alliance," Hiroshi said. "Senfo freighters are pretty resilient and could last awhile in a fight against most military ships."

"Are they normally armed?" Annette asked.

The security chief pulled up a general schematic of a Senfo freighter. "Since resuming their commerce operations, the Senfo have equipped their freighters and transports with yoagula beam weapons." The Senfo was the only race in the alliance that equipped their civilian vessels with weapons, out of fear of losing more of their kind. The Screen had decimated their homeworld's planetary atmosphere, resulting in the deaths of most of the Senfo population.

The term wasn't familiar to Ingrid. "Yoagula?"

"Similar to ruialon beam weapons, but with only half the output," Hiroshi explained. "Senfo freighters and transports don't have the necessary power requirements to handle military-grade weapons."

The explanation made sense to Annette. Ruialon weapons were strictly used for military ships in the alliance. As the Senfo was the only race that armed their civilian vessels, they were stuck with a less potent variety of weapon. It wouldn't do for a civilian ship to match a military vessel's armaments.

"It looks like their shield output is too low to take fire from beam weapons for an extended period," Ingrid pointed out as she reviewed the schematics.

"Correct, but their hull is composed of an unknown metallic compound, something the Commonality hasn't shared with the alliance," Hiroshi said. "It's pretty resilient to direct energy beam impacts."

"Captain," Martin called from his communications station. "I've isolated the source of the distress signal. It's in grid 9-2-7."

"Adjust our course, Kordif," Annette ordered. "Any idea who might be attacking them?"

Jeremy looked at the local star chart. "There are four life-supporting planets in the area, but we only know of one that's inhabited. I believe it's the Gercol. The planet's in the furthest part of the sector."

Annette was unfamiliar with that race. "Could they be attacking the Senfo?"

"Unlikely," Jeremy said. "Gercol rarely leave their homeworld. As far as we know, they don't have a military force, and none of their civilian vessels have weapons."

"Three minutes to destination," Kordif reported.

Annette went to sit in her command chair. "All hands to battle stations. Raise shields and standby ruialon emitters." Going into battle was the last thing she'd expected, but she wasn't worried about INFINITY's ability to handle itself in a fight.

The battle klaxons blared as the crew prepared for a possible confrontation.

"Arriving to location. Exiting jump," Kordif announced.

The INFINITY emerged from its jump. It only took a few moments for its scanners to pick up the activity that was occurring.

Frank quickly reviewed the sensor data on the operations table. "We're picking up the Senfo freighter and . . . three Cresorian ships."

"Bring up a visual," Annette ordered.

A holographic image appeared over the operations table. It showed a purple, oblong Senfo vessel trying to evade the attack of three black, diamond-shaped Cresorian ships.

"What the hell are they doing way out here?" Frank wondered aloud.

He had read the tactical reports on the Cresorians. No one had encountered them beyond the area of space near their homeworld. They'd broken off relations with the alliance a few years ago and declared war against it shortly afterwards. The alliance wasn't overly concerned about the declaration of war, as there was constant infighting between the Cresorian factions. It seemed every other week there was a new government.

"We'll worry about that later," Annette said. She looked to Martin as Hiroshi took his seat next to the captain. "Open a channel to the Cresorian ships."

It took no time for Martin to establish a communications link with the three enemy ships. "Channel open."

"This is Captain Annette Nikols of the TERRA starship INFINITY. The civilian Senfo vessel is under our protection. Break off your attack or we will engage you."

Her response elicited no verbal response from the Cresorians. Hiroshi reported their actions as he tracked them on sensors. "Two Cresorian ships have broken pursuit of the freighter and are heading towards us. Their weapons are hot, and they're targeting us."

Ingrid was surprised by their brazen action. "They're nuts to try and take us on."

Jeremy had an idea what they might be thinking. "They're not familiar with this ship's design. They may think it has the same capabilities as our old capital ships."

The Cresorians would be sorry, as Annette was more than willing to demonstrate the ship's capabilities. "Target both vessels. If they fire on us, you're cleared to respond in kind."

"Yes, Captain. Targeting both ships." Frank was impressed by how quickly the targeting system acquired the hostile ships.

"Kordif, send a message to the freighter," Annette instructed. "Tell them to head toward us. We can maneuver to provide them cover if they're closer to us."

"Yes, Captain."

"Hostiles are firing!" Hiroshi announced.

Multiple weapons fire from the two attacking Cresorian ships pummeled INFINITY as they passed by the starship. INFINITY responded by firing several red ruialon beams at them, striking both.

"Effect?" Annette asked.

"We've damaged the engine on one, the other's shields are down to 60 percent," Frank reported.

"What about us?"

"Shields holding at 98 percent," Ingrid replied. "No damage to hull or systems."

The command staff was impressed by how INFINITY had handled its first oncoming attack. It appeared that the Cresorians were no match against a SOLARA-class starship. With enough starships online, TERRA's fleet would be the equal of the other alliance militaries.

"Cresorians are coming around for another pass," Hiroshi announced. "The third ship has disengaged from the freighter and is coming after us."

These Cresorians didn't know when they were outmatched. "Fire starburst on third ship, and continue with ruialon fire on the other two," Annette ordered. "Load plasmatic torpedo tubes one and four."

The starburst was one of the alliance's best weapons. It drained a ship of all power, rendering it inert. That's exactly what happened when INFINITY fired its starburst and struck the approaching Cresorian ship. The energy burst passed right through the alien ship's shields and drained power from all systems.

"Cresorian ship disabled," Hiroshi reported. "Ship one has lost shields and ship two is at 23 percent shield strength."

"Fire torpedoes on ship three," Annette ordered. It was time to show that the INFINITY meant business.

INFINITY fired two plasmatic torpedoes. Both struck the drained Cresorian ship and destroyed it. Although the other two ships were at a disadvantage, they continued to attack. After several more exchanges of weapons fire, the other two ships were destroyed. The battle was over.

Annette leaned back in her seat. "Stand down from battle condition. What's our status?"

"Shields at 94 percent," Ingrid reported. "Hull is intact and no damage to systems."

"Well, we can safely say this was a successful test of INFINITY's battle abilities," Annette said. The command staff smiled, some nodding in agreement. Everyone was impressed how the ship handled its first battle.

Frank wanted to confirm everything on the ship was in good order. "Command deck to engineering. What's your status?"

Ronan's voice came over the command deck speakers. "We've done a quick check of systems and everything looks good."

The captain was appreciative of her XO's initiative and nodded at him in approval.

"We're getting a communication from the freighter," Martin reported.

"Put it up," Annette ordered.

A holographic image of a gray Senfo appeared over the operations table. He was wearing a hat that looked similar to a fez perched on his head. Senfo culture dictated that they wear their fez-looking hats at all times. In situations where they could not wear them, they were to at least hold them. No one had quite figured out why this was a cultural requirement. Even the Senfo couldn't explain it, as the reason behind it appeared to be lost to time.

Annette was aware of this cultural idiosyncrasy , but it was still humorous to her to see an alien wearing a hat. Still, to show her amusement would be rude, especially given what had just transpired. "I'm Captain Annette Nikols of the TERRA starship INFINITY."

"Cumondant Deel of the freighter WEALT. *Revib* for coming

to our aid."

"What's your status?" Annette asked.

"We have severe structural damage to *wonkis gui naf* of the hull. We will be unable to travel at faster-than-light, but we do not have the resources to make repairs of this magnitude."

"What about your crew?" Jeremy asked.

"There are *nupo jarf* of us. *Naba jurx* are hurt."

Frank converted the Senfo metrics to human standard on his console. "Captain, there are six aboard with two injured."

"Cumondant, we can tow your ship into our hangar and make repairs. You and your crew are welcome to remain on board INFINITY until your ship is space-worthy again," Annette offered.

"I have never met a human before, but your generosity is known among my people. *Revib* for helping us."

"Disengage your engines," Frank instructed Deel. "We'll send out shuttles to bring you in."

Deel tipped his hat as the holographic display turned off.

"Two Repos should be enough to tow them in," Ingrid advised Frank.

"I'll have medical stand by to receive Senfo casualties," Jeremy said to Annette. "I'll head to the hangar to assess the injured."

"I'll join you," Hiroshi offered.

"Apprise me of the situation when you get down there," Annette told the pair as they left for the hangar bay. "Commander Rola, we'll need an engineering team to go over the damage to the freighter."

"I'll let Commander Anvil know."

"Lieutenant Erikson, assign quarters for our guests," Annette requested. "Make sure to keep them together. I don't want to upset them by separating them. Coordinate with Chief Ito."

"Yes, Captain."

Frank approached Captain Nikols. "What about the Cresorians? This is the first time we've recorded them so far from their home system. This could be an indication that they're preparing to infiltrate alliance territories."

"I'll contact TERRA and apprise them of what's happened. They may have some intelligence about the Cresorians they're willing to share." Annette found it highly unlikely she would learn anything new. During her mission briefing, there had been no mention of the Cresorians being an imminent threat. With the alliance heavily occupying the former Screen homeworld and providing protection to the solar system, the Cresorians seemed unwilling to try and enter alliance territories.

Annette headed to her office as Frank returned to the operations table. He noticed that Ingrid was smiling. "Something funny, Lieutenant?"

"Don't you think INFINITY did well in her first battle?"

Frank looked around the command deck. "Yeah, she did pretty well."

CHAPTER SIX

"Does this look right, Doctor?" Nurse Romnie asked, pointing to the data on the medical display above the bed where one of the injured Senfo, Crorx, lay. "I administered the mixture you directed."

Jeremy looked over the data. "Yes, the readings indicate his circulatory system has stabilized." He looked down at their patient. "How are you feeling?"

"I feel much better, *revib*." Crorx clutched his hat in his hands. Myers knew better than to ask Crorx for his hat and let him hold onto it.

"If your vitals remain stable, we'll release you to quarters," Jeremy promised.

Crorx had a perplexed look on his face. "Quarters?"

"Living areas for you to rest and relax while you're on board."

"You humans are very kind. It is fortunate you answered our distress call." Crorx lifted his head and looked at his colleague lying on the main surgical bed. "How is Flebe?"

"She suffered severe radiation burns on nearly half her body," Jeremy said. "Our treatment is healing her wounds, but we're keeping her under sedation for now so she won't be in pain."

"She remained in the engine core trying to continue repairs, even after the cumondant ordered her to evacuate. If it was not for her, the Cresorians would have boarded us." Crorx was visibly upset.

Jeremy was quick to reassure his patient. "She's being well cared for. We'll make sure she gets everything she needs."

The Senfo laid his head back on the bed. He believed Dr. Myers when he said Flebe would be alright. From everything he'd been told about humans, they looked out for the welfare of others. He was relieved he and his crewmates were in safe hands.

Jeremy approached the main surgical bed where Drs. Black and Ishmati were reviewing their patient's progress. "How's she doing?"

"Her vital signs are stable," Ishmati reported. "She's in a deep sleep and not showing signs of distress."

"Keep an eye on the lacerations," Jeremy advised. "Senfo skin is resilient, but once it's been compromised it takes a long time to heal."

"Is she at risk for infections?" Black asked.

"No. They are pretty resistant to infections native to their world. But I want to limit her exposure to any non-Senfo bacteria until her cuts have closed up. We don't know how she'll handle any non-native bacteria."

"I'll set the computer up for continuous monitoring," Black said. "That will limit our need to come near her."

Jeremy nodded in agreement. "Good idea. We'll check on her progress in twelve hours to see how she's healing."

――― ――― ―――

Ronan was in the hangar and finishing his analysis of the WEALT's damage. He walked around the freighter, prioritizing what repairs needed to be done, while his team familiarized themselves with the freighter's systems with the help of two of the Senfo crewmembers. Meanwhile, Hiroshi did a walkthrough of the vessel's interior to make sure there wasn't anything on board that could pose a danger to the INFINITY's crew.

Cumondant Deel stepped off the freighter and approached the chief engineer. "We have sealed off all leaks to the power network."

"According to my analysis, we should be able to repair most of the primary systems," Ronan concluded. "The hull's another issue. From what I've reviewed, the xeranium we use won't bond with your ship's hull. The makeups of both alloys prevent proper integration."

Deel pulled up an inventory manifest on his circular handheld computer module. "We do not have sufficient procrium on board to seal all the cracks to allow WEALT to travel faster than light."

Ronan offered Deel some good news. "We've transferred your perishable cargo to our climate control storage area. It'll remain in good condition until we can meet up with an alliance ship heading towards Flutori," referring to the Senfo homeworld. "I'll talk to Captain Nikols when I give her the damage report, but you're welcome to remain on board until we figure out the arrangements."

"I must admit I was worried when your vessel arrived," Deel said. "We are familiar with all types of alliance vessels. Your ship is unknown to us."

"We just launched a couple days ago. But don't worry, you'll be seeing more of these ships out here."

Deel looked around the hangar in amazement. "I would hope to see many more ships like this one. It would guarantee no further attacks from the Cresorians. Rumor had it you humans were incapable of defending yourselves against aggressors. It appears that notion is unfounded."

Ronan chuckled. There was some truth to that. As TERRA worked to build new starships, they were reliant on the alliance to help protect the solar system.

"It is not an imposition to have us here, is it?" Deel asked.

"We've got plenty of room, and the alliance charter stipulates we must render aid and shelter to any member ship. Helping you will not impact our mission."

"May I inquire what your mission is?"

Ronan didn't have a problem sharing that information, as it wasn't deemed classified. "We're going into former Screen space to verify none of the planets have installations we're not aware of."

Deel had a look of disgust on his face. "I thought they were eradicated?"

"They are. We just want to be sure we haven't overlooked any outposts that might be on one of these worlds. Their homeworld records clearly show that whatever Screen didn't participate in the battle near Mars were on their homeworld. This survey is just a precautionary measure."

Deel adjusted his hat. "I hope that information is correct. If you should come across any remaining Screen, I expect you would eliminate them. They have committed too many atrocities against our races to be allowed to exist."

Ronan didn't know how to respond to Deel's angry reaction. Humans and the Senfo had not suffered equally at the hands of the Screen. The Screen had only killed a few hundred humans, whereas the Senfo homeworld had been decimated. This mission was mainly to iron out any kinks in INFINITY's systems, and he was certain it would turn up nothing. But what if they did find Screen still alive?

No, that was a silly thought. If there were any Screen around, the alliance would have seen signs of them.

Ronan shifted the topic back to Deel's ship. "Let's do another walkthrough and make sure we've captured all the damage."

"Excuse me, Commander," Hiroshi called out as he approached the pair. "Can I talk to you for a moment?"

"Sure." Ronan turned to Deel. "I'll meet you inside your ship."

Deel tipped his hat and went back inside the WEALT.

"I caught some of your conversation and thought you could use a bit of saving," Hiroshi said.

"The conversation was getting a bit too heavy for my liking," Ronan conceded. "There's no point in promising to eradicate a race that's already gone."

"They got the brunt of what the Screen were capable of," Hiroshi said. "I wouldn't be surprised if Deel lost friends and family. Only about 30 percent of the Senfo population survived what happened to them."

"I don't have much experience dealing with Senfo," Ronan said. "I didn't want to say anything to offend him. I figured it was better to change the subject."

"Smart idea. These Senfo may be small but they're probably very tough."

Ronan didn't think of the Senfo as tough. They were short in stature and, with the hats they wore, came across as living dolls rather than sentient beings. He needed to remind himself to be more aware when talking to them.

"I'm going to assign two security officers to the WEALT," Hiroshi said. "If you can provide them with your engineers' repair schedules . . ."

Ronan held up his hand. "I'll make sure they're kept in the loop."

Hiroshi was glad he wasn't getting any pushback from Commander Anvil. At least some officers on this ship weren't holding a grudge against him. Then again, there was nothing like a crisis to make people put aside their petty differences.

There was one more thing Hiroshi wanted to discuss with Ronan. "Did the cumondant tell you what sort of cargo they're hauling?"

"No, why?" Ronan asked.

Hiroshi pulled up his holographic DAT. "My security team did a scan of their cargo pods and one of them contains complex biological matter."

Ronan reviewed the data. "Readings indicate the composition is more complex than typical foodstuff, but the readings are inconclusive."

"That's because the pod is lined with some sort of material that scatters our sensors," Hiroshi revealed. "We can't say for sure what the pod holds, but it's more than just nuts and berries."

"Cumondant Deel didn't indicate they're carrying any sort of hazardous material," Ronan said. "As long as INFINITY's not in danger, it's none of our business. Our obligation is limited to rendering aid, not investigating what they're hauling."

"I only bring it up because I reviewed their flight plan. It shows they're scheduled to rendezvous with a private merchant freighter from Earth."

Ronan found that bit of news interesting. "I wasn't aware private companies were actively trading with alliance members."

"Me neither, hence why I'm bringing this up," Hiroshi said.

"I'll bring this to the captain's attention. She can decide if she wants to handle this."

Hiroshi had no problem letting Ronan delegate this issue to Captain Nikols. He had covered himself by fulfilling his security duties in identifying a possible issue with the Senfo freighter. Whatever the captain decided to do with the information held little interest to the chief.

"By the way, I wasn't aware you were permitted to look at the WEALT's flight schedule," Ronan said.

Hiroshi cracked a slight grin. "No one said I couldn't, either."

——— ——— ———

Captain Nikols was in her office, awaiting a call. She had reported INFINITY's encounter with the Cresorians to TERRA. The captain had requested real-time communication to see if there was any new information TERRA could provide them.

"Captain, we have an incoming communication from TERRA," Lieutenant Singer announced over the office speakers. "It's Admiral Terry Winston."

"Put him through," Annette requested. Admiral Winston was the fleet liaison assigned to the INFINITY, SOLARIS, and DISCOVERY. He was also a member of Earth Security. She was not enthused to have to deal with him, but there was nothing she could do about it. Resigned, she reminded herself that he might be ES, but was still a military officer, same as her.

The holographic image of the admiral appeared over her desk. "Captain Nikols."

"Admiral Winston. Have you read my report?"

"I have, and so has the command council. The discovery of Cresorian ships so close to the solar system has caught us all by surprise. The council is consulting with the alliance on the matter."

"The alliance has no record of Cresorian ships expanding beyond their territory?" Annette asked.

"Correct. The Cresorians have limited their attacks to non-military ships passing near their space. This is the first verified encounter of them so far from their star system. The alliance had no indication of the Cresorians moving further from their home system."

"Could it be rogue ships?" Annette asked. The Cresorian government had mandated their people return home to help with rebuilding efforts. There had been resistance to that mandate, as rumor was the conditions on their world was harsh, with work camps forcing citizens to work under deplorable conditions. Those Cresorians refusing to return home were being hunted down by those who believed reconstruction was a top priority.

"Who knows," Winston admitted. "We don't have reliable information. None of the alliance governments have been able to maintain diplomatic ties. The Cresorian leadership is constantly changing. It's because of that constant upheaval that they haven't been able to follow through on their declaration of war against the alliance.

"But the bottom line is, this encounter with them doesn't affect your mission. Your fight with them shows our new starships can easily handle them. INFINITY is to continue with its survey mission. We want to ensure the Cresorians won't try to claim Screen space as belonging to them. Your presence there will mitigate that risk."

"Understood, Admiral." When the Screen was defeated, the alliance had agreed to cooperatively manage former Screen space. No one member's race could claim a world without the consent of the entire alliance. With the Cresorians out of the alliance, they had no claim to Screen space.

The admiral had additional information for Annette. "We're planning to reroute SOLARIS to conduct follow-up patrol duty around where you encountered the Cresorians. Notify us if INFINITY comes across any more enemy ships."

"Understood. I do have one more item I want to bring up with you. The Senfo freighter we saved had damage to their cargo environmental systems, so we're storing their containers in our cargo bay. Ship's security conducted safety scans and found some unusual readings in one of the containers, the details of which I'll transmit to you. I only bring this up because we've learned the freighter is scheduled to rendezvous with a freighter from ARB Industries. I was not aware private companies were conducting trade with alliance worlds."

"Stand by." Annette watched the admiral hit a couple buttons on his console. His holographic image disappeared for a few moments. When it reappeared, her own console alerted her that the transmission was now on a classified secure channel.

"I was hoping we could have apprised you and the other SOLARA ship captains together. ARB Industries has been contracted to conduct exclusive trade with the Senfo, the details of which I'm not at liberty to divulge. All I can tell you is the cargo poses no threat to INFINITY. You're to notate in your log that this matter is considered resolved. You and your people are not to discuss this with the Senfo freighter crew."

The admiral had piqued Annette's interest. "Admiral, I understand if this is a classified matter, but can't you tell me anything?"

Winston shook his head. "I'm afraid not. The matter is highly sensitive and involves both our government and the Senfo Commonality. Only the command council and select individuals in TERRA are privy to the information. I can assure you that your ship is safe and this matter is for the benefit of our people."

Annette realized she wasn't going to get any more information out of the admiral. If he said INFINITY was safe from whatever the freighter was hauling, it was good enough for her.

"Understood, Admiral. I'll make a notation in my log and inform my people not to discuss the matter with the freighter's crew."

"Very good, Captain. Winston out."

That discussion had gone smoothly. Despite being from two separate divisions, Annette had found it easy to talk to the admiral. ES officers often treated TERRA officers as incompetent, but Winston had appeared to treat Annette as an equal. It was nice that they could hold a civilized conversation. It proved that, despite the differences between TERRA and ES, officers from both sides could focus on the importance of whatever mission was being conducted.

As for the cargo container with the strange biological readings? Well, it seemed that would remain a mystery. Annette could accept that it was classified, but she still speculated what it could be. The admiral indicated it would benefit them. She wondered what exactly that meant.

INFINITY had resumed its course to the Jemyu system. The Senfo, with the exception of Flebe and Crorx recovering in medical, were settled in their quarters. Commander Anvil's engineering team was busy repairing the WEALT.

Both Captain Nikols and Commander Rola had discussed the presence of the civilian Senfo on board and how it might impact their mission. They collectively decided on a course of action and headed over to meet with Cumondant Deel in his quarters to see if he would be agreeable to their plan.

Frank pressed the door chime. "You may enter," came Deel's voice.

Both TERRA officers entered and found the cumondant approaching them from the living room area. "Welcome."

"Cumondant, I'm Commander Frank Rola. This here is Captain Annette Nikols."

Deel smiled as he tipped his hat to them. "It is agreeable to finally meet you." He looked at the captain. "I thank you for saving us."

"It was fortunate we were in the area and picked up your distress call."

Deel looked around his quarters. "I was not aware human vessels were this opulent."

Frank took that compliment as personal and couldn't help but smile. "INFINITY is one of our newest starships. We designed it to make space travel as comfortable as possible."

Annette wasn't interested in talking about INFINITY's aesthetics. She wanted to get down to business. "May I ask what you were doing out here?"

"With the Screen gone, our merchant guild has elected to expand its trading routes. We were returning from a trade session with the Larcmines."

Both the captain and commander were confused by the word. "Larcmines?" Frank asked.

"An alien race," Deel clarified. "We were initially heading to the Gercol homeworld but came across a Larcmine merchant ship. After *poelqui* of communication, we were able to conduct trade with them."

Annette canvassed her memory for any non-alliance races that had been discussed in the meetings she'd attended, but came up empty. "We haven't heard of these Larcmines."

"I transmitted our encounter to the Senfo Commonality," Deel said. "I am sure they will share the details of the encounter with the alliance."

Frank never considered that a civilian ship could have a first-encounter scenario instead of a military vessel, but it made sense. Except for humans, the alliance had a lot of civilian and military ships out in space. Civilian ships were just as likely to encounter a new alien race.

"We look forward to learning more about these Larcmines, but Captain Nikols and I are here to discuss a proposition with you."

Deel was intrigued. "State your proposal."

"The INFINITY is conducting a survey mission of former Screen space," Annette explained. "We're currently heading to one of their star systems. My understanding is we don't have the materials to properly repair your ship's hull. We would conduct the survey of the Jemyu system, then return you to Flutori."

"The goods we acquired from the Larcmines will maintain their integrity in a cool environment, which your head engineer has already taken care of," Deel said. "My crew and I are used to being away from home for a long time. We would enjoy a chance to spend time on a human vessel and learn more about your people."

Annette was pleased he was amenable to their offer. "Then it's settled. You and your crew will have free access to non-critical areas of the ship." Although the Senfo were part of the alliance and some of their technology was embedded in the ship, the captain wasn't about to have civilians running around, getting into sensitive areas.

"You can consult the computer about Crorx and Flebe's condition in medical," Frank added. "Last I checked, they were responding to treatment and recovering fine."

Deel was happy to hear his crewman was recovering. "*Revib* to your medical officers for helping her."

"The computer can guide you around the ship," Annette reminded him. "If there's anything you need that the computer cannot answer, contact Commander Rola."

"I would like to spend the time repairing my vessel," Deel said. "I found working with your Commander Anvil a most enjoyable experience."

Just then the captain's holographic DAT beeped. "Command deck to Captain," came the voice of Lieutenant Singer.

"Go ahead."

"Captain, you wanted to be notified when we made the updates to your command chair."

Captain Nikols had not been happy with her command chair console layout during the encounter with the Cresorians, and had requested specific changes be made to it to better review information in a crisis situation. "I'll be right up. Nikols out."

She looked at Deel. "It was nice meeting you. Again, please reach out to Commander Rola if you need anything." She nodded to Rola before leaving the quarters.

"Are you settling in alright?" Frank asked Deel.

"Yes, these accommodations are pleasant. It amazes me how similar human structural design is to Senfo architecture."

Frank found that to be an odd statement. He had never visited Flutori, but thought that it would be a challenge for any human to visit, as he'd assumed everything there would be as small as the

Senfo, who were barely a meter tall. He imagined trying to crawl through tiny buildings on their world or cramming into whatever transportation vehicles they used.

"Is this your first time away from your home star system?" Deel asked.

"Is it obvious I'm new to space travel?"

"It is my understanding that very few humans have traveled outside their star system. Based on probability alone, I assumed this is your first trip through space."

Frank had no problem admitting to being new to interstellar space. "It is. Dr. Myers is the only one on board who has any space travel experience. This is all new for the rest of the crew. What about you? How long have you been in space?"

"I have traveled as a trade merchant for *piosux*," Deel replied. "When I was awakened from cryostasis, I immediately went back to working as a merchant."

Frank found it odd that Deel, or any Senfo, would want to leave their world. The Screen had destroyed Flutori's atmosphere, forcing them to enter cryostasis. But there hadn't been enough stasis pods for the entire population. Given the loss of so many lives, they had done a remarkable job of rebuilding their world.

Frank was curious why Deel was so quick to leave Flutori. "Why wouldn't you want to stay on your world?"

"The Commonality asked that I return to conducting interstellar trade to help restart our economy. I was willing to fulfill that request. Seeing the destruction of the natural beauty of Flutori was too painful for me. I had also lost *shaviba* mates, so there was nothing left for me to do but return to my duty as trade merchant."

"I'm sorry you lost family." Frank did not personally know anyone else who'd lost a loved one to the Screen.

"Did you lose any mates because of the Screen?" Deel asked.

"No, I was fortunate. My whole family lives on Earth. I'm the only one who's in TERRA."

Deel adjusted his hat. "The Senfo suffered the most at the hands of the Screen. Although the alliance is safe now that the Screen are gone, many of us feel we were robbed of justice. They should have suffered just as equally as we did."

Frank wanted to point out that the Cresorians had suffered more than the Senfo. Flutori's natural landscape had been destroyed with the destruction of the atmosphere, but at least their infrastructure had remained intact and their atmosphere had eventually recovered. The Cresorians' entire world, including their buildings, had been wiped out. Senfo society had been able to resume without too much difficulty, but the Cresorians had degenerated into infighting and civil upheavals.

Frank decided to change the subject to something more uplifting. He pulled a small square, translucent data chip crystal from his pocket. "I brought something that might make your stay here more enjoyable," he said as he handed it to Deel.

Deel manipulated the square crystal with his three-digit hand. "What is it?"

"A selection of music from my world."

Deel's eyes beamed with delight. "Chris Anne?"

Frank chuckled. "No, we have many musical artists back home. I picked a wide selection from Earth and Mars."

"*Revib*." Deel clutched the chip as if it was a precious gift. "You are most gracious to share this with me."

"That data chip is for you to keep when you leave. I figure you and your crew can enjoy it when you're back on your ship. In the meantime, INFINITY's computer contains a huge array of music for you to enjoy."

"I will take advantage of that luxury while I am here," Deel promised. The Senfo was anxious to share this gift with his other crewmates. They only had an opportunity to listen to Chris Anne's music through broadcasts from Flutori. Now he'd been given music of other human musical creators to hear. He would share it with his fellow Senfo back home, but only after he and his crew had listened to the entire collection.

——— ——— ———

On the command deck, Captain Nikols was enjoying the new layout of her command chair console. Although the battle with the Cresorians had been an easy victory, it had also provided an opportunity to make some changes to her chair layout to better access information she needed during a battle.

"This will work quite nicely for me," the captain said to Lieutenant Singer.

"If you want, we can always load up a few templates that you can switch between," Martin said. Annette nodded in satisfaction.

"Captain," Ingrid called from the operations table. "Can you join me a moment?"

Annette got up from her chair and went over to Ingrid. "What is it?"

"I'm getting some readings from the probe we sent out ahead to the third planet in the Jemyu system. It's picked up some unusual readings in the northern hemisphere."

Annette checked the sensor data coming in from the probe. "There's a lot of atmospheric interference coming from the planet. We should be able to penetrate the distortions with the ship's new sensors."

"We'll have to be in orbit for INFINITY's sensors to cut through the interference," Ingrid said.

"Any chance you could modify the probe's sensors to get through?"

"The probe we sent out is one of the old capital ship variants. It simply doesn't have the ability to cut through all this interference."

The INFINITY had been loaded with a few leftover probes from TERRA's capital ships. The capabilities of these probes were inferior to the new ones designed for the SOLARA-class ships. "Why would you use an old probe instead of a new model?" Annette asked.

Ingrid had an answer ready. "This was the first test of our probe launch system, which is separate from our torpedo system. I decided it was best to use an old probe in case the system malfunctioned."

That made sense. They didn't want to needlessly test the probe launch tube with a new probe if an old one was available. "I understand. What's got your attention?"

Ingrid brought up a holographic image of the third planet and zeroed in on a small segment of the northern hemisphere. "It's this land mass. I'm picking up increased energy emissions from it but can't identify the source or type. The probe can only verify that there's increased energy being displayed there."

"What do you think it could be? Feel free to speculate if you like." The captain always used opportunities like this to challenge her officers.

"It could be a natural phenomenon. Perhaps a fissure in the area emitting gases from the planet's core. It could also be a malfunction with the probe. These old X-1 probes are prone to calibration problems."

The lieutenant magnified the area on the holographic display. "If this was a natural phenomenon, I'd expect to find similar areas around the planet, but it's isolated to a twenty-five-square kilometer area. My gut's telling me the anomaly may be artificial."

"Perhaps something originating from a technological source," the captain mused. "Are the energy emissions Screen in nature?"

"We won't know until we use INFINITY's sensors to scan the planet. From what we know, the Screen used outposts and space stations sparingly due to their decline in population. Anyone working away from their homeworld did so usually on a ship."

"The PHOENIX did find a planetary garrison of Screen during their mission," Annette said, recalling what she'd read in one of the ship's mission logs.

Ingrid had read the same log. "That garrison wasn't listed in the Screen's homeworld database."

Annette dismissed the idea that the anomaly detected on the planet was Screen in origin. If it was a garrison or planetary outpost, they would have left their base once they stopped receiving visits or transmissions from their homeworld. No, this had to be something else.

"Send this information to Lieutenant Singer," Annette instructed. "Have him send a message to the occupation team on the Screen's homeworld requesting they recheck the planetary database. Have them verify no Screen base was established in the Jemyu system. And send a copy to all senior officers. I want everyone prepared when we arrive at the third planet."

"I've reviewed the planet's unique atmospheric properties. In addition to the ship's sensors, we can use one of our newer bot probes to penetrate the atmosphere and determine what's down there."

The captain was pleased to have an alternative option. "Let's wait to launch the probe until we arrive at the system. If there's anything down there, they may have picked up our first probe. I want to see if any new activity occurs between now and when we get there."

"Understood, Captain."

Annette stepped away from the operations table and returned to her command chair. This was an interesting development.

It could be the Cresorians. The INFINITY had just encountered their ships not too far from Screen space. It wouldn't be a stretch to think they could have set up a secret base somewhere in the Jemyu system. The alliance had been effective at patrolling areas under their control, but even with the combined resources of the Onixin, Senfo, and Quix, the patrols were still stretched thin. Humans were just releasing their first batch of new ships, and the Aldarians had no starships to offer. Until TERRA built up their fleet to a sizable level, there was a risk that the Cresorians, or any other hostile race, could enter alliance space undetected.

CHAPTER SEVEN

"We're exiting jump," Lieutenant Kelly Nalus announced as the SOLARIS slowed to sub-light speeds.

Jacob sat up in his command chair. "Any signs of ships out there?"

Fotell, their Senfo operations officer, checked the ship's sensors from the operations table. "No active ships are in our vicinity; however, I am picking up debris. The metallic pieces are consistent with Cresorian ships."

"Extend long-range scanners to see if they're any Cresorian ships hiding out there," Jacob ordered.

"You looking to get us into a firefight?"

Jacob turned to see his executive officer, Michelle Gimron, exit the lift onto the command deck.

"INFINITY may have proven itself against the Screen, but I don't want SOLARIS's first interstellar mission to turn into a fight as well. Been there, done that."

Jacob chuckled at her remark, knowing she was referring to their adventure on their old vessel, the capital ship SOLARA. They had taken it on its first mission away from the solar system to another galaxy and barely made it back to the Milky Way.

"If we pick up any jumpgates, I'll be sure to get us out of here," Jacob joked.

Michelle rolled her eyes as she headed to the operations table. The word jumpgate made her skin crawl. She was happy to learn that their first assignment didn't involve any sort of weird technology that could send them to another galaxy. With word that the INFINITY had taken out a couple of Screen ships, she felt comfortable knowing the SOLARIS could handle a Screen attack as well.

"Cresorians I can handle, weird aliens from another galaxy . . . no," Michelle muttered.

"Then this should make you feel better, Commander," Fotell said. "I am detecting a single Cresorian vessel on long-range sensors heading our way."

"Fuck!" Michelle blurted, regretting her words. *Sure, no weird aliens from another galaxy, but let's throw some known hostile aliens in the mix.* She was certain the universe was out to get her.

"Battle stations," she said. "Raising shields and arming rui-alon and starburst weapons."

Jacob found it premature to be going to battle alert, but appreciated Michelle's sense of caution. This was the crew's first interstellar mission together since their travels through the Screen jumpgate. None of them wanted to be caught off-guard again.

The captain checked the data on his command chair console. "Looks like we can send them a message from this range."

"Yes, sir," Lieutenant Brayden Marco reported from the communications station. He had replaced the previous senior communications officer, David Block, when David accepted a position back on the Mars communications facility in Crimson City. Jacob had recruited the lieutenant on the advice of Captain Nikols, who had worked with Brayden on the AURORA.

"Open a channel to the Cresorian ship," Jacob ordered.

Lieutenant Marco nodded, indicating the channel was open.

"Cresorian vessel, this is Captain Jacob Diego of the TERRA starship SOLARIS. State your intentions."

The crackling sounds of a response came over the command deck's speakers. Apparently, the Cresorian captain refused to open a visual display. "Human vessel, we do not recognize your authority here. Either vacate the area or prepare to be boarded."

Michelle looked at Jacob and mouthed, "Are you fucking kidding me?" It amazed her how the Cresorians were willing to throw out threats they clearly couldn't follow through on.

Jacob cleared his throat. "You have no authority here. The stellar map we sent your government clearly shows this sector as alliance space."

"That was sent to a government no longer in power. We do not recognize your claim here or any other space. Leave or be destroyed."

It was clear that there was no reasoning with this particular Cresorian. Jacob's response was calm and direct. "Very well, we'll proceed to intercept and destroy you. Lieutenant Nallus, plot a course to the Cresorian ship." He then looked at his security officer sitting next to him. "Chief Auguston, as soon as we're in range, obliterate the Cresorian ship."

"Plotting intercept course." Kelly smiled as she directed the SOLARIS towards to the Cresorian ship.

"You risk an interstellar incident!" the Cresorian captain yelled.

"As your government clearly states repeatedly, we're at war," Jacob replied coolly. "This is what enemies do, destroy each other."

"Intercept in two minutes," Kelly announced loudly, so that the Cresorian captain would hear her.

"Ruailon emitters online and starburst is ready," Chief Auguston added. "I've also loaded plasmatic torpedoes."

"Human SOLARIS vessel. Halt your advance." The sound in the Cresorian captain's voice sounded more like a plea than an order.

"No," Jacob replied. "Lieutenant Nallus, maintain course to target. Chief, as soon as we're in weapons range, fire. I want nothing left of their ship."

"Captain, the Cresorian ship is powering up and moving out. Trajectory shows they're returning to Cresorian space," Michelle reported.

"Pursue them," Jacob ordered.

"Human vessel, we will retreat for now. But . . ."

Jacob cut him off. "When you get back home, tell your superiors that if any Cresorian ship enters alliance space again, they will be destroyed on sight. No talk, no negotiation."

"They've cut off the communications," Brayden reported. "But they heard you."

Jacob looked over to Kelly. "Match speed to the Cresorian vessel and keep pursuing. Let's make sure they make it back to their space."

"With pleasure, sir."

Michelle approached Jacob from the operations table. "I still think we should have blown them up, but whatever. They should get the message. Now you'll have a story to tell Chad when we get back to Luna."

Jacob appreciated her easygoing nature. It helped to defuse stress and tension in these situations. "Diplomacy hasn't worked with them. If we're going to keep the Cresorians at bay, we'll have to be aggressive."

"Which we can do now that our ships are superior to theirs," Kelly remarked.

"Lieutenant Marco, send a status report to TERRA and copy the INFINITY and DISCOVERY as well," Jacob ordered. "Kelly, how long until the Cresorians reach their territory?"

The lieutenant calculated the time. "At current speed, six days."

Jacob smiled. "Let's see if we can encourage them to go faster. Increase speed to factor three."

"Maybe we should fire off some weapons in their direction," Michelle jokingly suggested. "Just for show."

Jacob chuckled. "Maybe, if they refuse to speed up."

Chief Auguston spoke up. "Captain, it goes without saying we'll need to remain in the area to ensure the Cresorians don't return."

"You're right. We'll continue on pursuit course until the Cresorian ship is back in its territory, linger close to their border, then head back."

Michelle agreed with his thinking. "That should piss them off."

Jacob got up from the command chair. "Fotell, you have the deck. Commander Gimron, join me in my office."

Michelle followed her captain as Fotell transferred the command chair controls to her operations table station. It took too much effort for the Senfo to climb down from her seat, head over to the command chair, and climb up into it. So Chief Engineer Walters had programmed her station to display needed command operations when she was in command of SOLARIS.

"It didn't take long for our ships to find action," Jacob said as he and Michelle entered his office.

"Maybe we'll get word from DISCOVERY that they've engaged the Cresorians."

"I hope not. DISCOVERY is still in the solar system." Jacob poured two glasses of water and handed one to Michelle. "I want you to check with the counselors on board, see if any of the crew are having difficulty with our near-encounter with the Cresorians."

"Civilians or officers?" Michelle asked.

"Officers. This is the first time we've been in a hostile situation since the Triangulum Galaxy. I want to be sure none of them are suffering any stress."

The SOLARA's adventure in the Triangulum Galaxy had been a horrific experience for the crew. Many officers were killed, and the ship barely made it back home. Because the mission was deemed classified, TERRA ordered that any officers who remained in TERRA would have to be kept together to minimize the chance of their mission details being leaked. Jacob had been fine with that arrangement, as he felt a strong bond to his fellow crewmates. He'd arranged for counselors to reside on SOLARIS so his officers could have access to mental health services if necessary.

"I doubt any Cresorian ship would rattle our officers," Michelle said. "But I'll let our counselors know to do a pulse check. Since we're on the subject of the crew's well-being, how are you holding up?"

Jacob found her question odd. "Me? What makes you think I'd be rattled by that Cresorian ship? I'm fine."

"Things were different back on the SOLARA. You didn't have

Chad back in your life."

"Oh." Jacob hadn't considered his son while dealing with the Cresorians. He thought about him every day, but never when he was on duty, running the ship. "I don't think about Chad when I'm working. I don't think much of anything in a crisis situation. I'm focused on trying to make sure we survive whatever situation we're in."

"Fair enough. I just wanted to check, that's all."

"Now that you brought him up, I guess I'm glad that he's looking to pursue a career at the engineering bureau and not on a starship."

"Because of the dangers involved in space exploration?"

Jacob took a seat behind his desk. "We saw firsthand on the SOLARA the dangers that lurk out there, and I saw it multiple times on the PHOENIX. I remember all the friends I lost after the fight in the Ni system. It was tough, but I tried to tell myself at least I didn't lose any family members."

"I'm glad I don't have any family in TERRA," Michelle said. "I couldn't imagine losing one in the line of duty."

"There will always be something out there that poses a danger to us. With Chad planning to stay on Luna . . . well, it's one less thing I'll have to worry about."

"If he starts thinking about serving on a starship, send him my way. I'll tell him stories that'll scare him enough that he'll never want to leave the solar system."

Jacob laughed at the notion. "I have no doubt you would."

CHAPTER EIGHT

The INFINITY senior staff were assembled at their stations on the command deck as the ship entered the Jemyu star system. Everyone had been apprised of the discovery made by the X-1 probe. With no unusual activity coming from the planet since the initial finding, Captain Nikols had Lieutenant Erikson launch a new bot probe as soon as they entered the system.

Annette had shared her concern that they could uncover a hidden Cresorian base with Commander Rola. Both agreed that if that was the case, the base could not be allowed to remain. It would encourage the Cresorians to try and make further inroads into alliance-controlled space.

If the base existed, whether it would be removed by diplomacy or force remained to be seen. Captain Nikols was willing to try diplomacy, as it would be her first time negotiating with an alien race. Given the Cresorians' past behavior, it was more likely force would be needed, but she remained open-minded.

"We're on course to the third planet," Kordif reported from the navigation station.

"Probe should be orbiting the planet within a minute," Frank added.

"Captain, we should raise shields and arm weapons," Hiroshi recommended.

"No, the increased energy emissions might be picked up by whoever might be on the planet. Lieutenant Erikson, have the probe start scanning the planet when it reaches orbit. Program it to start transmitting to INFINITY when we get into orbit. That should reduce the chance of the transmission being picked up."

"Yes, Captain." Ingrid wasted no time sending the programming instructions to the probe.

A few minutes later, the INFINITY arrived in orbit of the third planet and was hovering over the northern hemisphere, where the increased energy emissions were coming from.

"We're getting data from the probe," Ingrid announced.

She and Commander Rola began reviewing the data. They were amazed by how much information the probe had already gathered. It gave them a complete picture of what was down there, and what was down there took them by surprise.

"That can't be right," Ingrid muttered in disbelief.

Frank reviewed the sensor readings. "Let's confirm the data. The probe isn't malfunctioning, is it?"

"Diagnostics show no malfunctions. The probe's fine. The data's correct."

"What is it?" Annette asked.

Frank gave the captain a disturbed look. "The probe's identified the energy source. Captain, it's Screen in origin."

The command staff looked at one another in disbelief. How could humanity's deadliest enemy be down there?

Annette was the first to break the uneasy silence that had descended on the deck. "Are you sure?"

Frank triple-checked the sensor readings. "There's no doubt. Energy emissions match Screen parameters. The probe has also picked up multiple vocal communications on the planet. It's confirmed they're Screen."

"I thought the Screen masked their language so no one could understand them," Kordif said.

"I can't explain why we're able to discern what they're saying," Frank admitted. "Lieutenant Singer, start analyzing the communications and verify they're Screen."

"Battle stations. Raise shields and arm all weapons," Annette ordered as she got up from her command chair and approached the operations table. She'd thought it possible they would find a Cresorian base, or another threat. But Screen? This was something she'd never expected. "Can we identify their offensive and defensive capabilities?"

"The probe's picked up a fleet of three hundred Screen fighters," Ingrid confirmed. "I'm not detecting any land-based weapons platforms or a shield system."

"We should pull the probe back and go into higher orbit," Hiroshi suggested. "We don't want to risk them picking us up."

"I don't think they can," Martin said from the communications station.

"Explain," Annette said.

"I'm monitoring their communications. They're definitely Screen, but so far I'm not finding anything that would indicate they're aware of us."

That didn't make sense to the captain. "If we can detect them, they should be able to detect us."

Frank thought it over. "It's possible they don't know we're here. The INFINITY is comprised of multiple different technologies, as well as the Ni," referring to the now-extinct gaseous alien race that helped defeat the Screen. "Our sensor system is much more advanced and therefore able to penetrate this planet's unique atmospheric properties."

"The Screen put a military outpost on a planet with no ability to detect what's in orbit?" Annette questioned.

"It's possible, Captain," Frank said. "We need more data."

Hiroshi had his own thoughts. "Having a base on a planet where the atmosphere can distort most sensors would be a tactical advantage for them."

The captain thought it over. So far, neither the first probe they'd sent out nor the bot probe had triggered any response from the Screen. Secondly, Lieutenant Singer had indicated the Screen's communications showed they were unaware of INFINITY's presence. It seemed plausible the Screen couldn't actively monitor anything in orbit.

Commander Rola was right; they needed more information. "We'll remain at battle alert status," Annette said. "Lieutenant Singer, I want our communications officers to monitor all transmissions on the planet. Lieutenant Erikson, compile as much information as the probe and INFINITY's sensors can gather. See if there's a way to access their main database without alerting them to us. Chief Ito will assist you. I want summaries of all findings in eight hours and submitted to Commander Rola for review. Commander, we'll reconvene the senior staff after you've reviewed their findings."

"Yes, Captain," Frank nodded. Along with the rest of the command deck staff, he watched as Captain Nikols went to her office. He assumed she was going to contact TERRA and alert them to the INFINITY's discovery.

"I can't believe we found Screen alive," Ingrid said. "I thought they were all extinct."

"You think the outpost sent some of their people out when they stopped receiving communications from any ship or their homeworld?" Hiroshi wondered.

"If that was the case, I wouldn't think the rest of them would just remain here and stay in hiding," Martin said. "That seems to go against their aggressive nature."

Frank put a halt to their conversation. "It doesn't do us any good to speculate. Let's gather what information we can and come up with some definitive answers."

In her office, Annette sat at her desk. "Computer, bring up all information about the Screen. Display on my desk console."

"Information on the Screen is extensive," the computer replied. "Is there a set of search parameters you would like to input to narrow results?"

"No, display all information." Annette leaned back as the information popped up. She intended to learn every detail about the Screen: every encounter, every weakness. If they needed to strike at them, she intended to be swift and decisive.

——— ——— ———

Frank walked at a rapid pace down the corridor. He was going to grab a bite to eat in his quarters before heading to engineering. Commander Anvil had some ideas about improving the ship's n'quadrin output and wanted to go over it with the commander. Given the discovery of a Screen outpost, Frank wanted to take advantage of anything that could give them an edge in case the situation turned hostile.

Frank could still hardly believe it. TERRA had said the Screen became extinct shortly after their defeat by the alliance, after suffering a massive environmental disaster on their homeworld. Since then, the alliance had occupied their world and was going through every piece of information on the planet. Never once had TERRA insinuated that there might be Screen living on other worlds. Lieutenant Erikson had gotten confirmation from the lead TERRA officer on the Screen's former homeworld that they'd rechecked all databases, and none showed the establishment of any outpost in the Jemyu system.

Frank did recall that the PHOENIX had found an outpost on another planet. That also hadn't been listed in any Screen database. Did they make a habit of not cataloging their planetary outposts? If so, it was an odd intelligence move.

"Commander Rola," a voice called from behind Frank. He turned and looked to see Cumondant Deel racing up to him. "I must speak with you."

"I'm a little busy." Frank continued walking, albeit at a slower pace so the three-foot-tall Senfo could keep up with him.

"I want to know what you intend to do with the Screen on the planet."

So much for keeping that bit of news concealed from their guests. Then again, it was hard for the crew to keep something like this quiet. "No decision has been made. We're still gathering data."

"What data do you need to take action? They are our enemies. They must be wiped out!"

That was a dramatic proposal. "So far, they're not aware of our presence. They don't pose a threat."

Deel grabbed Frank's arm with his three-digit hand, forcing

the commander to stop walking. He was surprised by the strength of the Senfo's grip.

"They killed most of my people!" said Deel, visibly upset. "They must be destroyed."

"And become just like them?" Frank blurted out. It was a gut reaction.

Deel released his hold on Frank and looked at the commander with disbelief. "It is *vobata* that you would compare the Screen to any of us. Our people are nothing like them."

Frank realized he wasn't going to win an argument with Deel. He needed to end this conversation and get back to his duties. "Look, we're meeting with Captain Nikols. She'll make the final decision on what to do with the Screen. When she does, I'll let you know."

Frank knew full well that the last thing the captain would do was kill all the Screen on the planet. He expected TERRA would be notified, and a garrison of alliance ships dispatched to handle the situation. Within a matter of days, INFINITY would either participate in the operation with the other ships or continue its exploration of former Screen territory.

"I expect that your captain will not fail us," Deel concluded before walking away.

"What the hell is that supposed to mean?" Frank muttered to himself.

——— ——— ———

Cumondant Deel was not happy about the conversation he'd had with Commander Rola earlier in the day. He'd expected the commander to be more open about getting rid of the Screen. If the second-in-command wasn't committed to eliminating the Screen on the planet, he was worried that the other humans on this ship would follow the commander, and captain's, lead. The Senfo merchant wasn't willing to sit by and risk having the Screen be captured. That race was too dangerous to allow to live. Luckily, he had one person on this ship he could try to sway.

The ship's computer directed him to his destination. He

arrived at a set of quarters and stretched his diminutive arm to reach the door chime. After a few moments, he heard a voice say, "Enter."

The door opened, and Deel stepped through, greeting the reptilian creature that stood on the other side. "You are Kordif of the Onixins."

"I am. Is there something you need assistance with?" Kordif asked.

"I would have words with you. It is regarding the matter of the Screen on the planet."

"I am expected on the command deck in *corkundaj*. I can speak to you about this matter." Kordif motioned Deel to follow him to the living room area. "Is there some subsistence I can offer you?"

"No. This situation with the Screen is most upsetting. I am *oogbuti*. I come here as a fellow kindred. Both our people have suffered at the hands of the Screen."

"I must respectfully disagree with you on that statement. Your homeworld was decimated by the Screen, whereas my world was left untouched."

"They prevented your people from exploring space," Deel argued.

"I sense you are attempting to sway me to your perspective before you have presented your argument. Present your case."

"I spoke to Commander Rola and was surprised to learn that they are considering capturing the Screen. I expected they would simply destroy the outpost."

"They are considering all available options."

Deel was surprised by Kordif's matter-of-fact tone. "You are not upset? I would think you would want the Screen destroyed."

"I am a v'vir of the Onixin military. My obligation is to follow the orders of my superiors."

"You are serving on a human vessel," Deel pointed out.

"Under the terms of the TERRA exchange program, I am to follow the orders of my superior officers. It is no different from how the Onixin military operates."

"Surely, you have an opinion on this matter. If you have a

difference of opinion . . ."

Kordif interrupted him. "My opinion does not matter. My role is to carry out the orders of Captain Nikols and Commander Rola in my capacity as navigation officer. It serves no purpose to offer them my point of view, only to assist them in whatever path they choose to pursue."

"And if they choose to capture the Screen?"

"As I already stated, I will fulfill my role as navigation officer to assist them in whatever decision they make."

Deel couldn't believe that Kordif was willing to go along with whatever the humans decided. To say he was outraged was an understatement. This was an insult to the entire Senfo race. Did no one on this ship recognize the threat the Screen represented?

"Is there anything more you wish to discuss?" Kordif asked.

"No. I am sorry I wasted your time, and mine." With that, Deel left Kordif's quarters.

The Senfo felt helpless, unable to do anything but sit by and let the humans dictate how the Screen would be handled. If his freighter was flight-worthy, he'd take his crew and leave this human vessel. He wanted no part in whatever plan they came up with that did not involve eliminating the Screen. But for now, he was stuck here.

CHAPTER NINE

It was early evening when the senior staff gathered in the conference room. Annette had shown up early and sat patiently at the head of the table, waiting for her officers to arrive. No one said anything as they filed into the room, each lost in their own thoughts about the Screen.

When everyone was seated, Annette turned to her executive officer to start the meeting. "Commander Rola."

Frank had memorized the reports Lieutenants Erikson and Singer had given him. "We were able to hack the outpost's computer system and pull everything we needed. The Screen established this outpost in order to facilitate the containment of the human race. All the Screen fighters that destroyed ships trying to leave the solar system came from here."

"That means the outpost was established over a hundred years ago, when the ISA HORIZON tried to leave," Ingrid concluded.

Kordif was unfamiliar with human space history. "The HORIZON?"

Annette spoke up. "Before TERRA existed, there was the International Space Agency, the ISA. They commissioned the construction of a ship, the HORIZON. It would have been the first human vessel to venture out into deep space. The ship was sent to Pluto, where it was to deploy a jumpgate device to travel to Alpha Centauri. The ISA lost contact with her during the mission. It was later learned that the HORIZON was destroyed by the Screen. From that point on, any ship trying to leave the solar system was destroyed by a Screen fighter." She nodded to Frank that she was done with her history lesson.

"Two Screen cruisers were stationed near the solar system and deployed a fighter whenever it detected a human ship was moving past Mars's orbital boundary," Frank said. "The outpost was established to provide fighter and supply replenishment to the cruisers. Since no fighter was destroyed until the PHOENIX, the cruisers and outpost rotated their fighter groups."

"Those must have been the cruisers PHOENIX destroyed before leaving the solar system," Jeremy remarked, recalling that battle. "I'm surprised the outpost didn't get concerned when they stopped hearing from them."

"The Screen had very regimented rules," Frank explained. "The outpost was under strict orders not to reach out to the cruisers under any circumstances so as to minimize the risk of discovery. The cruisers and outpost would sometimes go years without communicating with one another."

Ronan was surprised by this arrangement. "So that was the outpost's sole mission? Provide fighter support to the cruisers monitoring us?"

Frank nodded. "It would appear."

"What's the complement of the outpost and its capabilities?" Annette asked.

"The outpost isn't equipped with any offensive or defensive systems," Frank said. "They only have the three hundred fighters on the ground to provide protection. As for the population . . . there are six hundred thirty-four Screen down there."

Grumbling erupted in the conference room. That was a much larger number than anyone had expected.

Annette remained calm. "Well, it seems we have a problem to take care of," she said. "I've been reading up on all the information we have about the Screen. They're a violent, aggressive race that was bent on subverting or destroying other races. I've listened to some of the communications going on down there. It seems the outpost is continuing operations to support the suppression of the human race."

Frank confirmed what the captain was saying. "That's correct. As far as the outpost goes, it's business as usual. They have no idea their people were wiped out."

"It took the effort of many races to defeat the Screen," Annette said. "We're lucky the environmental disaster that occurred on their world solved the problem of containment for us. We have no such luxury here."

Only Dr. Myers knew the real truth about what had happened on the Screen homeworld, as he'd personally witnessed it on the PHOENIX. It hadn't been an environmental disaster, but something more sinister. The truth had been suppressed, so as not to incite panic among the alliance and other local races. The doctor saw no need to reveal the truth to the INFINITY staff, as it was not critical information they needed for the current situation.

"We'll need to formulate a plan for how to eliminate the Screen down there," Annette said.

Frank was taken aback. He'd assumed the alliance would coordinate a plan to capture the Screen and secure the outpost. He'd never expected that she'd propose eliminating them, and was so shocked, he was rendered speechless.

Jeremy had no problem voicing his opinion. "You can't be serious, Captain."

"I am."

"These people aren't a threat to us. Whatever crimes their race committed against us don't warrant exterminating them. We have an opportunity here . . ."

Annette interrupted him. "Doctor, this discussion is not open for debate. If you have a different opinion, we can discuss it in private." She looked at the rest of her staff. "We have the advantage that they don't know we're here. I want to capitalize on that. Tomorrow, each of you will come up with ideas on how to eliminate the outpost inhabitants. Commander Rola will coordinate with each of you. By the end of the day, I want a plan for how to take care of our adversary once and for all. Dismissed."

The senior staff, including Frank and Jeremy, departed the conference room. The commander wanted to speak to the captain, but felt it best to hold off. Now wasn't the time to make his case. Emotions were running high, and he wanted to give the captain time to think about her intentions. He was glad when she didn't ask him to stay behind to talk.

"Dr. Myers, wait up," Frank said as he caught up to the doctor. "Are you okay?"

Jeremy waited for the other senior officers to be out of earshot before he spoke up. "I'm not okay with exterminating an entire race. I want no part of this."

"I agree. I assumed the captain would want a plan to capture the Screen. I never expected her to want to eliminate them."

"Nothing good will come of this," Jeremy said. "All this will teach the crew is that it's better to take the more convenient path. I'm not blind to the fact that a lot of people would want these Screen eliminated, but it's not up to us to decide the fate of a species."

"If they were a threat, I'd be arguing with you," Frank admitted. "But we're in a much stronger position now than we were a few years ago. We should make a plan to capture them."

"Then I suggest you talk to Captain Nikols and let her know how you feel."

Frank was hesitant to share his personal opinion with the captain. He had cemented a good working relationship with her and didn't want this situation to ruin that. He was willing to offer her alternatives, but wanted to do so without letting her know how he personally felt.

"I'm going to give it some time before I talk with her," Frank said. "I think all of us need to take a step back and let things settle down."

Jeremy gave him a look as if he wasn't convinced. "You do what you feel is right, Commander." He said nothing more as he walked away.

Frank got the sense that his decision hadn't impressed the doctor. He liked Jeremy and didn't want to do anything to upset him, but he reminded himself that he couldn't please everyone. This was a difficult situation, and it would only get worse if people started taking sides.

Alone in the conference room, Annette brought up the files on the Screen once more, intending to learn everything possible before initiating any sort of engagement. She continued her work, bent on knowing everything about humanity's mortal enemy.

It was 1940 hours and Annette was relaxing on her living room couch in her quarters. She appreciated the sprawling living space that this new class of starship provided. At first, she hadn't paid much attention to the lectures of the psychologists who claimed larger quarters would provide better mental health for the crew. But after moving onto the INFINITY, she was inclined to agree with their assertions. It was nice having such a large living area for herself. It was a pleasant change from the AURORA's cramped quarters, where she'd lived for so many years.

She was reviewing the data on the Screen on her DAT, trying to figure out how to destroy the outpost in a way that would minimize the risk to her crew. TERRA had studied Screen technology extensively, so the INFINITY was more than a match for anything the outpost might throw at them. The challenge would be ensuring every Screen on the planet was killed. Ideally, she wanted to accomplish this from orbit and avoid sending anyone to the planet. She was confident that could be done. If orbital bombardment didn't work, they could always send fighter bots down into the atmosphere.

The door chime rang, distracting the captain from her studies. "Come in."

The door opened and Dr. Myers came in. "Good evening, Captain."

Annette turned off her holographic DAT and sat up. She assumed he'd come to discuss the Screen situation. "What can I do for you?"

"It's about the outpost. I'd like you to reconsider your plan of destroying it."

The captain realized this was going to be a long discussion. She was firmly resolved in her decision, but elected to hear his reasoning. Given his extensive experience with the Screen, it would be prudent to hear what he had to say.

"Go ahead." Annette got up and went to the kitchen. She poured two glasses of water from the dispenser.

"Destroying the outpost doesn't benefit us. Even if they were a threat to us, they are no match against INFINITY, or the alliance. We have an opportunity to establish peaceful relations with them."

Annette reemerged from the kitchen and handed him a glass. "Is that even possible? From everything I read about PHOENIX's encounters, the Screen refused to open any sort of dialogue. Why would now be any different? As far as the outpost knows, nothing has changed."

"But it has. They've been out of touch with their homeworld for years. If we explain and prove to them what's happened to their people, they may be willing to talk. They're the last of their kind and I don't think they'd want to risk being wiped out."

Annette conceded the doctor made a good point, but she still wasn't convinced. "That's a big assumption. The Screen military was trained to treat aliens as enemies who cannot be trusted. Even if they did surrender to us, how long before they'd betray us? They'll hold us responsible for the loss of their people and eventually will want to exact revenge. There's also our own people to consider."

"How so?"

"Many of our people may not want to show leniency to the Screen, even if it's only a few hundred."

"Captains aren't in the business of winning popularity contests. Would you really let other opinions prevent you from doing the right thing?"

Annette grinned. "Destroying the outpost doesn't constitute a mistake in my opinion. You still haven't convinced me to reconsider. But you're right, I'm not concerned with others disagreeing with me. I'm simply doing what I feel is in our best interest."

"Compared to the Aldarians, Senfo, and Cresorians, we lost very little life to the Screen," Jeremy pointed out. "They have more of a reason to exterminate the Screen than we do."

"Doctor, this outpost was responsible for trapping humans in the solar system by killing anyone trying to leave. It could have been used for more aggressive actions against us, like a staging ground to invade us, maybe even exterminate us. I don't care if they only killed hundreds of our people versus the millions they killed with the other races. Their aggression towards us was clear."

Jeremy didn't want to engage in a hypothetical scenario with her. "But they didn't, and we prevailed. We have an opportunity to show that we're better than them. The Screen down there aren't a threat. They should be spared. Tactically, it makes no sense to eliminate an enemy whose technology is no match for us. This will give us a chance to really learn about them instead of interpreting the information from some leftover databases on their world."

Annette appreciated the doctor's attempt to reason with her from a military perspective. Tactically, it wouldn't benefit her to wipe them out. They were no match for INFINITY or any other alliance ship. And she could obtain some valuable information from interrogating live Screen. Such interrogations could even help with uncovering secrets on the Screen's homeworld that the alliance had not yet discovered.

The more she thought about what Jeremy had said, the more it resonated with her. "If we do this, we're going to need a means to contain them. Our brig isn't big enough to hold six hundred Screen, and I'm not comfortable with only taking a few and leaving the rest behind."

"We could request the assistance of other alliance ships."

Annette didn't like that idea. Whatever way they went about capturing the Screen, she wanted INFINITY to do it alone. It would be an enormous boost to her reputation if she was able to capture them with just the resources of her ship and crew. "I don't want to risk any other ship. You've done extensive studies on Screen biology. Certainly, you have a means by which to sedate them."

Jeremy saw what she was getting at. "That can be easily done.

We have enough compounds on board to synthesize sedatives to subdue all of them."

"We can use one of the cargo bays to hold them," Annette said. "We can get Commander Anvil to install emitters for security fields." Yes, she believed that would work nicely. "Nikols to Commander Rola."

"Rola here."

"Commander, there's been a change in plans regarding the Screen. We'll be making contact with them tomorrow and making arrangements to bring them on board as prisoners of war. Dr. Myers will explain our plan to you. Include Security Chief Ito and Commander Anvil in the discussions."

"Yes, Captain. Rola out."

"Thank you, Captain," Jeremy said.

"I'll expect a detailed plan by late morning tomorrow. I don't want to delay this any longer than necessary."

"We'll have one for you. Good night, Captain. Again, thank you." Jeremy left the captain's quarters.

Annette hoped she was making the right move. It'd be unfortunate if something went wrong. But she reminded herself that the doctor was correct; they had the advantage here. She was commanding an advanced starship that could handle any Screen technology thrown at them. She didn't anticipate any major issues in taking the Screen into custody.

CHAPTER TEN

Frank got up at 0600 hours to start his day. He quickly cleaned himself up, grabbed some food out of his fridge, and met Dr. Myers and Chief Ito in medical to go over their plan. On his way, he received an update from the communications department with a summary of their findings from eavesdropping on the outpost's communications.

There was one disturbing revelation that caught Frank off-guard. He decided to wait until he, Jeremy, and Hiroshi had finalized their plans before sharing the information with the doctor. He was grateful Captain Nikols had changed her mind and elected to make contact with the Screen rather than eliminate them, and suspected he owed her decision to Jeremy.

The captain had mentioned the doctor last night when she'd contacted Frank. He suspected Jeremy had gone to Nikols to change her mind. Frank should have been upset that the doctor had gone around him to the captain, but he wasn't. As far as he was concerned, all that mattered was that she had abandoned her plans to destroy the Screen.

Plus, Jeremy had a lot of experience with the alien race and could provide valuable input to ensure they were taken into custody safely. Frank could put his ego aside for the greater good.

The three men hunkered down in the CMO office and spent the next two hours hammering out their plan to safely bring the Screen on board. As they brainstormed, Frank became increasingly sure they were doing the right thing.

"I think we have something to present to the captain," Jeremy said as they did a final review of the proposal they'd drafted.

"I'll personally go over this with her," Frank said as he uploaded the plan into his DAT.

"I'm assuming she'll approve it, so I'll get my team to work on clearing out cargo bay three and putting security procedures in place," Hiroshi said. "Shall I contact Commander Anvil or will you?"

"You can go ahead and reach out to him to coordinate the security details," Frank said. "I'm glad the captain changed her mind."

"You weren't in agreement about wiping out the Screen?" Hiroshi asked.

"Not really. I know the people who lost loved ones to them would disagree. Yes, they did try to wipe us out, but this outpost is the last of their race. It wouldn't be right to kill them."

Hearing this gave Jeremy a lot more respect for the commander. The doctor had met too many officers who merely reiterated their satisfaction that the Screen had been wiped out. He'd gained compassion for the Screen after being privy to a classified meeting with the command council. A Screen jumpgate had been discovered and a capital ship was sent through it to the Triangulum Galaxy. The council had learned that the Screen originated from that galaxy, where they'd lived as slaves, and had fled to the Milky Way to escape their oppressors. It was understandable they were fearful of other races and had taken drastic action to protect themselves. He wasn't excusing their actions, but he'd gained a better understanding of their motivations.

"Maybe once they learn their people are gone, they may be receptive to establishing relations with us," Jeremy said.

Frank agreed. "I hope so, because it's not just military lives at stake." He pulled up some transmission snippets from the outpost and showed it to Myers. "In monitoring their communications, we learned there are children down there."

Jeremy was shocked, and quickly reviewed the comm logs. "It was nearly impossible for them to have children."

"This does change things," Hiroshi said. If this outpost had only military personnel, then they could be justified in destroying it. But military rules dictated avoiding targeting areas with civilians.

"It does," Frank said. "Those on the outpost spent time trying to tackle their breeding issue. They were able to successfully reproduce thirteen offspring."

"This is unbelievable," Jeremy said, more relieved than ever that Nikols had reconsidered eliminating the outpost's inhabitants.

"I wouldn't think a military outpost would have the scientific equipment to do that sort of research," Hiroshi said.

"They may not have needed such comprehensive equipment," Jeremy replied. "From what we know, the Screen blamed their reproduction problems on the pollution of their homeworld's atmosphere. This planet is clean of any harmful pollutants and could have remedied the population's reproduction abilities. We can verify this by examining the inhabitants. This could mean their race can be saved."

"Probably best not to advertise that possibility," Frank cautioned. "I don't think it would sit well with a lot of people."

"If we do save this race, that means we'll be giving them a chance to rebuild their population," Hiroshi said. "Would the alliance be willing to accept that possibility?"

"That's something for our leaders to decide," Frank said. "It's not our place to make those types of decisions. Let's carry out the plan we came up with and get them on INFINITY. Once they've been transferred to the appropriate facility, TERRA and the alliance can decide what to do next."

Jeremy saw the wisdom in the commander's thinking. Many people would be opposed to the notion of trying to save the last of the Screen race, let alone the idea that the Screen could reproduce. The INFINITY would do what they needed to do, and let the alliance take it from there.

——— ——— ———

Annette had spent the past hour walking around the ship, trying to clear her mind as she contemplated recent developments. Despite her conversation with Dr. Myers, she was still weighing the pros and cons of letting the Screen live. In the absence of the Screen, TERRA had made real progress toward space exploration. Why did a leftover group of Screen have to exist? Why did she have to be the one to find them?

It was a situation she did not want to be in, despite the accolades she expected to receive for capturing them. Maybe it would be easier to eliminate the Screen and be done with it? She was confident that the command council, and most officers, would support her if she destroyed the outpost. But the doctor had brought up a good point: In rules of war, one did not attack an opponent who could not defend themselves.

Annette reminded herself it wouldn't hurt to try to establish relations with the outpost. The worst-case scenario would be they would refuse to negotiate, INFINITY would be forced to destroy the Screen fighters, and the aliens would be forcibly taken into custody. The captain saw little risk to her crew if things played out that way.

The captain reached the door of her intended destination—engineering. She'd come down to talk to the one person she trusted the most among the crew.

As the door opened and she stepped inside, she spotted Commander Anvil at the hyperdrive console station. "How's the hyperdrive?" she asked as she approached the chief engineer.

Ronan smiled as he looked over to see his captain. "In tip-top shape. It handled our jump flawlessly. I'm just double-checking that it's still within operating specs."

Annette only nodded as she looked at the hyperdrive. Ronan knew that when the captain said nothing, she had something important on her mind. "Is there something I can help you with?"

"It's about our situation with the Screen. As you know, I'll be making an official announcement about our plan to try and make contact with them."

Ronan was already aware of that plan, as he'd consulted with Chief Ito on installing additional security measures in cargo bay three. "You're having second thoughts about it?"

Annette was grateful that she had worked with Ronan for enough years that he recognized when she needed counseling. "It would be a simple matter to just eliminate them and be done with it. I don't think anyone would be bothered."

"I agree."

Annette did not expect that response. "Even knowing there are children down there? Some would argue they are innocent."

"We're treating them as if they're like human children. We know nothing about Screen offspring. For all we know, they're born with the full mental capabilities of adults and can serve in military operations."

Ronan made a valid point. They knew little of Screen culture, but Annette had a counterpoint. "We do know that only elder Screen served in the military. They purposely kept their young from serving."

"Only because of their procreation problem. If it wasn't for that, it's entirely possible their young would have served in their military. I've read up about PHOENIX's encounters with new races. What I learned is we can't always compare another race's culture to our own."

Ronan was right. Annette couldn't look at the Screen within the framework of human culture. It could lead her to make false assumptions. She couldn't base her decisions on what she thought she knew. "If our attempts to establish a dialog with them fail and taking them into custody fails . . ."

Ronan knew where the conversation was going. "It's only because the Screen is extinct that we're free. If things go south, no one will blame us for protecting ourselves. You've always put the well-being of the crew above all else. Whatever happens, we know it's in everyone's best interest."

Despite her years of command experience, Annette found it beneficial to bounce ideas off those she trusted. It had served her well before, and it served her now.

"Thank you, Commander. I'll see you at the staff meeting tomorrow."

"Always glad to help," Ronan said as the captain left. He didn't envy the position she was in. This was a complicated situation and he was glad he didn't have to make the choice. But he was honored she'd come to him for counsel. He hoped he had given her sound advice.

CHAPTER ELEVEN

It was 0800 hours the following morning. The senior staff had already gathered to discuss Commander Rola, Dr. Myers, and Chief Ito's plan to make contact with the Screen. Some staff members asked questions, but no one objected—primarily because Captain Nikols had endorsed the plan. If she approved of it, they were more than willing to go along.

Cummodant Deel, on the other hand, had made numerous attempts to meet with Captain Nikols to voice his opposition to contacting the Screen. Kordif had already informed her of his conversation with Deel, and Annette was not interested in having a debate with the Senfo. She had made her decision and was not accountable to him. She had Commander Rola communicate in very clear terms that she would not meet with him until their mission concluded.

Unsatisfied by her response, Deel had attempted to send a communication out to Flutori. Lieutenant Erikson had blocked it, as all non-essential communications were prohibited for the duration of the mission, then informed the captain and commander of what Deel had tried to do. They assumed he was trying to contact his homeworld to notify the Commonality of

INFINITY's discovery. Frank had informed Deel that communications would not be allowed until further notice, and the unhappy cumondant had gone on a rant—but that had done nothing to change the captain's mind.

With the senior staff at their posts on the command deck, Annette was ready to get the mission underway. "What's our status?" she said as she arranged her chair display.

"Systems are good to go," Frank reported from the operations table. "On your command, we'll take INFINITY into low orbit before sending a communications signal to the outpost."

The plan was to send a signal directly to the outpost's communication tower. To punch through the atmospheric interference, they would have to send a continuous signal. Hopefully, the Screen would be willing to reply to their hail. In the meantime, INFINITY would monitor the outpost fighters to ensure they wouldn't launch.

"Very well, Commander," Annette said. "Viv'r Kordif, activate thrusters and take us into low orbit above the outpost. Take it slow. We don't want them picking us up."

"Yes, Captain." Kordif activated the ship's thrusters. The staff monitored the descent on their respective stations. There was not so much as a shudder as INFINITY descended towards the planet.

Martin was monitoring the outpost's various communications, looking for any signs that the Screen had detected them. "So far, no indication that they've picked us up."

So far, so good. "Time to prearranged position?" Annette asked.

"Eighty-five seconds," Frank replied.

"As soon as we're in position, open a channel to their comm tower." Annette didn't want to delay contacting them. If the Screen somehow picked up the ship before making contact, they might react and attempt to attack INFINITY out of fear.

"We are holding position above the outpost," Kordif announced.

This was it. Now they would find out if the Screen would talk to them. Annette looked over at Martin. "Open a channel to the outpost."

"Sending signal." Martin activated the ship's communications array. "Boosting signal to 150 percent of normal." His console showed the signal penetrating the planet's atmosphere with ease and reaching the outpost's communication tower. "We've established a link to the outpost. You can go ahead, Captain."

"This is Captain Annette Nikols of the human starship INFINITY to Screen outpost. We want to speak with a representative of your outpost."

They waited for a reply to come back, but heard nothing.

"Signal is holding, Captain," Martin confirmed. "They heard you."

"Should we raise shields?" Hiroshi asked from his seat.

Annette shook her head. She didn't want to initiate an action that could be interpreted as hostile. "Screen outpost, we are communicating to you under a flag of peace. We have vital information regarding your people. We have no hostile intentions towards you." Again, there was no response. Annette looked over at her XO. "Are you picking up any activity on the surface?"

Frank checked the readings on the operations table. "I'm showing no activity with their fighters and no increased energy emissions anywhere on the outpost."

"They may not be able to understand us," Jeremy said. "The Screen have used inhibiting devices to prevent microns from working around them."

Martin had accounted for that when he sent the signal down. "I adjusted the communications to adjust for that contingency. They should be understanding the captain."

Suddenly, the operations table beeped an alert. Ingrid was the first to check it. "Picking up an increased energy emission." Her eyes grew wide as she saw the energy burst heading up towards them. "Cut the comm line, now!"

But it was too late. The energy burst struck INFINITY. Immediately, alarms went off as explosions ripped through the ship's energy network. Lights flickered and consoles turned on and off as the power flow fluctuated.

"Comm line cut!" Martin reported.

"Navigation is offline," Kordif said in a calm voice. "Attempting to restore thrusters to prevent orbital decay."

"We've got damage reports coming in throughout the ship," Ingrid said. "Our energy grid is severely compromised."

"Switch to auxiliary network," Annette ordered.

Frank glanced at the sensors and picked up another threat coming their way. "Captain, we're showing Screen fighters are launching. They're on a direct intercept course."

This must be the Screen's plan. Disable the ship, then destroy it. "Where are we at with weapons?" Annette said.

Ingrid checked the status. "Ruialon beam emitters at 50 percent, torpedo system's offline."

"Fighter bots are available," Frank said, relieved.

"Target fighters on the ground and open fire with ruialon weapons," Annette ordered. "Launch fighter bots and have them target any enemy in-flight."

Both Ingrid and Frank worked on those tasks, with Ingrid targeting the fighters still on the ground and Frank programming and launching the fighter bots.

The captain checked her chair display and saw the ship's shields were offline. "Kordif, we need to move INFINITY away."

"I am still trying to get the thrusters back online. Hyperdrive and sub-light engines are down."

"Command deck to engineering. We need engines," Annette demanded.

"We don't have enough power to jump or go to sub-light speed," Ronan replied over the speakers. "We still have blowouts occurring in the power grid we're trying to contain."

Stuck in position, INFINITY was an easy target. Luckily, their available offensive weapons were protecting the ship.

"Ruialon attacks have destroyed ground fighters," Ingrid reported. "I've also taken out their comm tower."

"Fighter bots have engaged enemy ships en route toward us," Frank said. Fortunately, the fighter bots far outnumbered the Screen ships. "We should be safe."

Annette checked her chair console and was satisfied they were not in any danger from the enemy fighters. They could focus on repairs. "I want a complete tally of damage we've taken and a report to me in the hour. Priority is to our shields and hyperdrive. Lieutenant Singer, can we send a signal out to the SOLARIS?"

"Negative, Captain. INFINITY's communications relay is completely destroyed. We have no means to contact anyone." The energy pulse the Screen sent along the communications frequency had decimated the ship's communications equipment.

Although the captain appeared calm, her blood was boiling. How could they have been taken out so easily by an inferior enemy? "I want a full report in an hour." She stood up from her chair, approached the doctor, and gave him a hard look. "I should have never listened to you."

Jeremy was speechless as she walked past him. What could he say? They had tried diplomacy and the Screen responded with violence. As the captain went to her office, the doctor left the command deck for medical to help anyone who had suffered injuries in the attack.

With the last of the Screen fighters destroyed, Frank directed their fighter bots to take a protective position around INFINITY. Ingrid prioritized repairs while Kordif tried to keep the ship afloat in orbit. Hiroshi deployed security teams to sensitive areas of the ship as Martin checked the communication sensor data—and saw something unusual.

"Commander Rola, I found something you need to take a look at," he said.

Satisfied the fighter bots had taken position around the ship, Frank joined the senior communications officer at his station.

"I checked our sensor logs and found what appears to be a secondary signal transmitted at the same time they sent the energy spike at us."

Frank checked the sensor data. Sure enough, it appeared that the outpost had sent a second transmission, separate from the energy spike they sent to INFINITY. "Do we know what it contained?"

"No, sir. We lost sensor resolution when we got hit by the energy spike. But I was able to triangulate where it was sent. Commander, they sent a signal to the solar system."

That made no sense to Frank. Why would the Screen send a

signal there? It worried him. There had to be a reason.

But there was no way to warn the command council. INFINITY's communications system was destroyed. They had no means to alert anyone back home.

CHAPTER TWELVE

It was early afternoon in Crimson City on Mars. Lieutenant David Block was busy attending to his duties at TERRA's communication facility, located adjacent to Crimson City's dome. For the last two years, he'd run the daytime communications shift, reporting directly to the head of the facility and his good friend, Commander Billy Pedia.

David enjoyed his work. They weren't just handling communications between TERRA's various facilities and ships, but also with alliance ships and outposts. Despite being stationed on Mars, David had befriended some of the Quix, Senfo ,and Onixins he spoke to regularly. In fact, his Onixin contact had made arrangements for David's mom and siblings to visit Plein and experience Onixin culture. With his position, David was able to afford a nice home in Crimson City, big enough for his family to live in.

At work, David walked between rows of consoles, occasionally checking with an officer at their station to help clarify any communications-related questions they might have. He'd come to enjoy being out on the floor rather than sitting in his office, even though he was naturally introverted and had a tough time engaging with people. With encouragement from Billy and a firm resolve, he'd become more confident and comfortable conversing with his fellow officers. Now, he was regarded with respect and officers regularly solicited him for advice. He had come a long way from a few years ago, when he'd felt completely ostracized by his peers.

"Lieutenant Block." An officer waved from her station.

He made his way over to her two rows down.

"Sir, I'm picking up a narrow beam transmission heading our way. It's coming from the Jemyu system."

"Could be a message coming in from the INFINITY," Block said. He had been briefed on the starship's mission to survey former Screen systems.

"The energy pattern doesn't conform to TERRA's. I should be able to identify the energy type once it gets closer."

They waited a few moments until the computer could identify it.

"Sir, readings show the transmission conforms to Screen standard."

That didn't make sense to David. How could a Screen signal be coming in when the race was extinct? But anything was possible. Maybe it was an automated signal. INFINITY might have set off a device at an abandoned installation while surveying a planet.

"Lieutenant Block to Commander Pedia. Please join me at station B-4." David leaned closer to his comm officer. "How long until it reaches the solar system?"

"Less than a minute. It looks like the signal is heading towards Mars."

Billy was already out of his office and joined his friend at the comm station. "What have you got?"

"A Screen transmission was sent from the Jemyu system. It's heading our way, to Mars."

"Do we know where exactly?" Billy asked as he looked at the data on the console display.

The comm officer triangulated the destination. "Computer estimates it's going to Olympus Mons."

"We don't have any facilities there," David pointed out. "And we don't have any military or civilian operations that are even close to that volcano."

"When's the last time we heard from the INFINITY?" Billy asked.

"About nineteen hours ago," David replied.

Billy tapped the shoulder of the comm officer in the adjacent station. "Send a signal to INFINITY. Let's see if they know anything."

"We should tap into the sensor drones monitoring Olympus," David advised.

Billy agreed. "The AURORA's also been doing survey runs around Mars. Apprise them and have them move in orbit over Olympus."

David nodded and went over to the nearest empty comm station to raise the AURORA as Billy pulled the sensor drones' feeds onto the large main display at the center of the circular room.

"Screen transmission has reached Olympus," the comm officer reported.

Billy focused his gaze on the large display. The volcano looked normal, and nothing seemed to change in sensor readings. Suddenly, sensors picked up seismic activity. "David, are you seeing this?"

After sending a message to the AURORA with instructions, David tapped into the sensor drones. "Picking up significant earthquake activity at the base of the volcano. Detecting significant shifts in the basaltic minerals in the area, particularly large movement of iron compounds. Billy, it looks like some large mass is emerging from the area."

Billy saw what David was referring to as he reviewed the sensors on the main display. He quickly opened a channel to the AURORA. "Commander Pedia to AURORA. Captain Swenson, are you seeing this?"

"We are. The mass is twenty-three kilometers below ground and is moving at a rate of 346 kilometers per hour."

"At that rate, the mass will reach the surface in less than four minutes," David calculated.

"We're not picking up anything more than a large compound moving up," Swenson said.

"I think we can all agree it's more than that. It was a Screen signal that prompted this activity. We have to assume it's hostile." Billy looked over at David. "Go to battle alert status. Notify Crimson City control to initiate emergency shelter procedures."

The battle klaxons blared as the communications facility went into lockdown. As David contacted the city liaison, Captain Swenson readied his crew.

"All hands, battle stations," Swenson announced as he took a seat at his command chair. "Commander Beam, bring weapons and shields online."

"Aye, captain," the XO replied. Moments later, the ship's plasmatic beam weapons and torpedoes came online. A low humming sound could be heard as the ship's shields activated.

"What's the status of the object?" Swenson asked.

"Less than two minutes before it emerges," Commander Beam reported.

"Target torpedoes and beam weapons on the area where the object will emerge," Swenson ordered. "But wait for my order before firing. I want to see what we're dealing with." He looked over to his communications officer. "Commander Pedia has most likely notified the command council, but send a signal to headquarters and apprise them of our situation."

"Yes, sir."

The officers on the AURORA and the Mars communications station waited in anticipation as the unknown object crept closer to the planet's surface. Although no one knew what it could be, they assumed that it wouldn't be good. Nothing from the Screen was ever good.

The object reached the surface and broke from the base of the volcano. From both the AURORA and in the communications center, they watched a greenish sphere punch through the surface. It had a smooth glassy surface that reflected the sun's rays. The sphere emerged about halfway above the surface before stopping.

"What the hell is that?" David muttered.

Billy reviewed the readings on the main display. It still reported a mass similar to iron in composition, but nothing else. "Modify the sensor drones and see if we can't penetrate that thing."

They were having the same challenges on the AURORA. "Sensors can't penetrate the sphere's interior," Commander Beam reported. "Wait! Something's happening."

Both groups watched as the sphere slowly split open. "Getting readings now," said Commander Beam. "Picking up a massive energy source inside. Captain, it's firing an energy burst."

A large green energy ball shot up from the sphere into the sky. Officers from both groups quickly reviewed the data to determine what they were dealing with.

"Energy burst conforms to Screen energy weapon," David reported. "It's on a direct course towards Earth."

Billy checked the composition of the energy ball. It contained enough energy to decimate a continent. "Captain Swenson, are you reading . . ."

"Already on it!" Swenson snapped as the AURORA's sensors reported the same devastating conclusion. "Fire all weapons."

The AURORA fired its complement of plasmatic beam weapons and unloaded all its torpedoes. The weapons did nothing to dissipate the energy ball.

"No effect on target," Commander Beam reported.

They couldn't let the energy burst reach Earth. The captain quickly realized the AURORA's shields might stop it. "Move AURORA into the path of the target."

"Sir?" his navigation officer questioned.

"Our shields might dissipate it. Just do it!"

The navigation officer complied and fired up the AURORA's engines. The capital ship moved into the path of the energy ball and waited.

"Route all power to shields, including life support," Swenson ordered. They would need every bit of power if they hoped to survive the energy's impact.

The energy ball reached the AURORA and struck it. The reaction to the shields was explosive, causing the energy ball to be disrupted and dissipate. Unfortunately, the energy disruption was too great, and the reaction ripped through the AURORA. Multiple explosions tore through its hull and ignited the ship's plasma energy network. When the explosions ceased, there was nothing left but charred fragments of the AURORA floating in Mars's orbit.

The officers at the communications center were in disbelief as they watched the capital ship being destroyed and then saw what remained of the AURORA on the sensor displays. The AURORA had stopped a deadly attack against Earth, but at a terrible cost.

Commander Pedia didn't need confirmation that the AURORA's entire crew was lost. There was no need to mount a search-and-rescue team. His attention turned back to the sphere. "Status of enemy weapon?"

David pulled himself away from the horror of what had happened and checked the sensors. "No power coming from it."

"Notify the command council. We're going to need help securing that thing," Billy said. "Tell them we need all the weapons they can provide. And notify Crimson City to remain under lockdown until further notice."

CHAPTER THIRTEEN

The INFINITY's senior staff gathered in the conference room. It had been over an hour since they were attacked by the Screen outpost. Repairs were well under way and the ship remained at battle status. Now, the captain would learn how extensive the damage to the ship had been and what exactly the Screen had done to cut through INFINITY's superior defenses.

Once everyone was seated, she motioned for Commander Rola to begin. "Commander, do we know how exactly the Screen attacked us?"

The commander sighed. "Unfortunately, they were genius in their attack. They were able to send an energy burst along the communications line we sent back to the ship. Once it struck, the energy spread through the ship's energy network."

"I didn't think it was possible to stage an attack through communications signals," Martin said. "If I had only known . . ."

Frank tried to reassure him. "None of us knew. There's nothing you or any of us could have done."

Annette wasn't interested in soothing the egos of any of her officers. "Continue with your report, Commander."

"The attack did a lot of damage. The safety systems in our

energy grid did a good job containing most of the breaches, but the n'quadrin network still took a beating. We're maintaining power through our auxiliary network, but we're only at 30 percent of normal. I've ordered decks nine, ten, and thirteen shut down to reduce power consumption."

"Weapons?" Annette asked.

"Torpedo system is back online, and we do have ruialon weapons, but at reduced power. Starburst is offline," Ingrid said.

Ronan chimed in. "Our engines have been affected. We have 40 percent sub-light capability, but the hyperdrive took some damage. We'll need to finish repairing it before we can jump."

"Is it possible to jump with limited power?" Kordif asked.

"It would take some effort, but we could do it," Ronan said.

Annette reluctantly turned to Dr. Myers, whom she held responsible for this entire situation. "What about medical?"

"Thirty-three injuries. Thankfully, no fatalities. Most are second- and third-degree burns. Three people suffered broken bones, which we're treating now. I expect they'll make a full recovery."

"That's your sole priority, nothing else," Annette said. It was her way of telling the doctor that his input on any matters beyond medical was no longer welcome. She turned to the senior staff. "Lieutenant Singer identified that the outpost sent a second signal towards the solar system at the same time they attacked us. We need to contact TERRA to find out the purpose of that signal and to apprise them of our situation. I know our communications relay was destroyed. Can we replace it?"

"We could poach the comm relays from our shuttles and try constructing a new relay for the ship," Martin offered. "But it would take time and there's no guarantee it would work."

"Why not keep those relays on the shuttles and just use them?" Kordif asked.

"The shuttles we have are from our old capital ships," Frank said. "None of them are equipped with interstellar comm systems. We're supposed to get new shuttles when we return for resupply."

The situation was unacceptable to Annette. "We need to have communications capabilities."

Ronan had an idea. "What about the Senfo merchant ship? Their comm system is still intact."

"I could talk to Cumondant Deel," Frank offered.

"Do it," Annette replied.

"What if he refuses?" Martin asked.

"He has no choice," Annette said. "We're using his equipment with or without his cooperation."

"Should we request additional support when we contact the command council?" Ingrid asked.

Annette turned to Martin. "Notify the SOLARIS. Let them know what's happened, but reiterate we have the situation under control and will request their support if we need it."

"So, what's the plan then?" Ingrid asked. "Are we going to finish repairs and leave the system?"

"No," Annette replied. "We have a job to do. Continue repairs for now. We'll reconvene after we've contacted TERRA and the SOLARIS. Dismissed."

The staff got up and left the conference room. Frank stopped at the door when he spotted a visitor. "Captain, Cumondant Deel is outside."

Well, now was as good of a time as any to talk to the persistent Senfo. "Let him in."

"You want me to stay?"

"No. We'll talk later."

Frank motioned for Deel to enter. As soon as the door closed and Annette was alone with the Senfo, the alien started up. "Captain, I thought you humans were accommodating. I have attempted to meet with you several times, only to be refused by your Commander Rola."

"On my orders. I have a ship to run and, given our current situation, my time is valuable. You have my attention now, so tell me what's on your mind."

"I was right. Trying to make contact with the Screen was a mistake. I do not wish any harm to you or your crew, but I hope this was a lesson to you. They cannot be reasoned with."

Annette didn't appreciate the lecture, but he was right. Her attempt to open a dialogue with the Screen had turned out to be disastrous. "What's done is done. I promise we'll take care of them, but in order to do that we need your help. Our communications system was destroyed in the attack. We need to use your ship to contact our home."

Her request was welcomed by Deel. "It is done. Use it to communicate with whoever you feel needs to be contacted. But I want to know what you intend to do about the Screen on the planet. They cannot allow to remain down there."

The captain did not hesitate to answer him. "After what they've done, there won't be a single Screen left alive down there."

Deel grinned. He had imagined what it would be like to exact revenge against the race that had killed so many of his people, but he'd never thought he could be a part of exterminating the last of the Screen. His race was recovering, but he could help make sure the Screen would never harm his people ever again.

The cumondant tipped his hat to Annette. "Whatever resources I have to assist you in this endeavor are yours. *Revib.*"

Annette reclined in her seat as Deel left the room. Her next action against the outpost would be swift and decisive. There would be no one left alive down there.

CHAPTER FOURTEEN

On Luna, Admiral Vespia convened an emergency meeting of the command council to discuss the situation on Mars. TERRA had been on high alert since the activation of the Screen weapon hidden on Mars and the destruction of the AURORA. Crimson City was still on lockdown, and ELM News was providing around-the-clock reporting of what had occurred.

Several alliance vessels had arrived in the solar system to provide support to the survey teams on Mars. They were monitoring the Screen weapon to see if it activated again. Other alliance vessels had been dispatched to conduct detailed scans of every planet and moon in the solar system and locate any more hidden weapons.

After sharing what the teams had learned on Mars with the council, Karla adjourned the meeting and headed to her office for a call with the president's chief of staff and planetary security advisor on Earth. She sent both individuals a report that she'd gone over with the command council and alliance representatives ahead of the call.

So far, there had been no finger-pointing regarding this incident, but Karla expected she'd have to defend herself against accusations of complacency. She anticipated that Michael Forsent, another council member and former ES officer, might use this incident to remove her as head of the council. He was always angling to take her place and made no secret of it.

As she approached her office, her bot assistant motioned to her. "The president's chief of staff is waiting on a secure line for you."

"Route it to my office," she ordered without halting her step. She entered her office, closed the door, and got seated at her desk. "Accept communications, voice authorization Karla Vespia."

The display flickered to life, hovering over her desk. On it was the president's chief of staff, Arnold Platus. "Admiral, I have to brief the president's security advisors in twenty minutes before they meet with President Butu prior to her press conference with the public. Make it quick."

"I've sent you a detailed report that I've already gone over with the council. We've confirmed the weapon is now inert. It was designed for a one-time discharge of energy it converted using the volcano's molten core."

By the look on Arnold's face, it was clear that he wasn't convinced. "How can you be sure it's no longer a threat? You weren't even aware of its existence."

"The Quix sent their own teams down into the sphere. They've assured us the weapon is no longer functional. They're already begun the process of dismantling it."

"That'll put the public at ease," Arnold said.

"I'm recommending keeping Crimson City on lockdown until the morning," Karla said. "The major components of the weapon will have been extracted by then."

Arnold agreed. "I'm sure the president will go along with that, despite Senators Tso Weng and Escobar's demands that the lockdown be lifted."

"Senators always put their self-interests before the public good," Karla said.

Both senators had been sending her personal messages demanding the city be reopened. Their concern was the negative economic impact of a lengthy shutdown. She'd responded by sending both senators a copy of the colony's accord, which stipulated that TERRA had the authority to shut down the colony at any time during a crisis. The accord was outdated, and had been drafted when the colony was first established. It hadn't been rescinded when Mars was designated its own territory, with all the same rights as territories on Earth.

Until the accord was voided, the admiral would continue to take advantage of it. She expected that after this crisis, the senators would introduce a bill in Parliament amending that directive.

Arnold had more questions. "How the hell did the Screen manage to plant a weapon that large on Mars without us knowing it? And how come we never detected it?"

Karla had answers for both questions. "Analysis indicates the weapon to be about a hundred years old. Our experts speculate the Screen must have planted the weapon after destroying the HORIZON, sometime around 2074."

"Which would have been before TERRA was established. I can't believe none of the planetary surveys of the volcano picked up the weapon."

"The interior of the sphere is lined with a metal unique to the Screen. It's similar to the type they used on their ships. The combination of that metal and Mars's natural elements concealed the weapon from being picked up on sensors. The Quix came up with a way to detect the weapon and have distributed that data to the teams surveying the other planets in the solar system. If there are other weapons, we'll find them."

"What about the INFINITY?" Arnold asked. "My understanding is the signal that activated the weapon came from the star system they're investigating."

Unfortunately, Karla did not have a concrete answer to provide. They had sent several communications to the ship's last known location, but so far had not received a reply. The admiral was preparing for the possibility that the ship might have fallen victim to some sort of calamity. "We're still trying to make contact with INFINITY."

"If she's not answering, then send one of the other new ships to check on them," Arnold said.

"I've ordered the SOLARIS to head to the Jemyu system to determine INFINITY's situation. But their hyperdrive is down due to a malfunction and won't be up for twenty-four hours."

"Then send the DISCOVERY," Arnold demanded.

Karla knew he was probably feeling pressure from the president, who wanted to know what was going on with the INFINITY and learn the details of the events that triggered the signal being sent to the weapon. But she disagreed. "DISCOVERY is our only starship here in the solar system. I won't risk our security by sending our strongest ship away. If you're intent on learning what's going on at Jemyu, I can always have one of our alliance members send a ship."

The admiral suspected Arnold wouldn't be eager to have an alliance ship check in on TERRA's missing vessel. She'd attended enough committee meetings to know that many government officials felt strongly that TERRA needed to show it was the equal of the other alliance militaries. They couldn't lean on them whenever a crisis arose. It was hard enough depending on them to defend the solar system while TERRA built its fleet up.

"No, we want to keep the alliance out of whatever's going on at Jemyu," Arnold said. "If something's going on there, TERRA should be the one to investigate it."

These government types were all the same: dedicated to keeping up appearances. "I agree. I'll notify you as soon as SOLARIS gets to the Jemyu system."

Arnold nodded. "In the meantime, you'll need to start coordinating personnel for construction of shipyards and installations in the solar system."

Vespia found his statement odd. She assumed that, given this incident, she would receive orders to speed up ship construction. "I've already directed additional personnel for ship construction."

"You misunderstand me, Admiral. In two hours, a bill will be presented to Parliament authorizing a significant increase in funding for the military. Shipyards, orbital defenses, outposts, you name it. The president wants to capitalize on this incident and get the funding we need to ensure we can protect the solar system. Given what happened on Mars, we can't take any chances.

We expect Parliament to pass the bill with ease."

Parliament had allocated more money to TERRA to construct new shipyards for ship construction after the Screen's defeat. However, with the Screen becoming a distant memory, the Cresorians not posing a threat, and the continued protection of the alliance, politicians had become complacent and hadn't seen the need to build additional military installations. Karla herself had met with several senators to try and convince them to fund TERRA to sufficient levels, but to no avail. Leave it to a crisis and loss of life for politicians to act.

It didn't matter. Karla would finally get what she wanted: a bigger and stronger military. "I'll notify the council and begin coordinating our people."

"Good," Arnold replied. "Expect a call from the president this evening. Good day."

The chief of staff abruptly ended the conversation, which suited Karla. They had a mutual dislike, as he'd served in ES and she was a TERRA career officer. It was a rare occurrence where they were both on the same page, as they were now.

As she began setting up another meeting with the council, her desk beeped. "Admiral, you have a guest waiting outside for you," her bot assistant stated.

The admiral checked her schedule and saw no meeting with anyone for the next two hours. "Who is it?"

"Admiral Michael Forsent."

Her adversary on the council. This would be a good opportunity to talk to him. It was important to figure out how he would use the current crisis against her. They had argued so much over matters big and small that it had become routine. She didn't mind their constant conflicts. It allowed her to keep a pulse on what he was up to.

"Let him in," Karla ordered.

A few moments later he walked through the door into her office. "Michael, what would you like to debate, or tell me what I'm doing wrong?"

Although they rarely agreed on anything, they'd come to address each other by their first names. It was a sign of respect.

Michael handed her some papers. "I took the liberty of drafting this proposal."

Karla expected it to state that she should relinquish leadership of the command council, and detail the transfer of power to Admiral Forsent. When the contents revealed something different, she looked at him in genuine surprise. "You wrote this?"

Michael nodded. "With everyone busy excavating the weapon site and ensuring security was beefed up, I didn't want to forget about the crew of the AURORA."

The papers outlined a proposal for a full military funeral for the AURORA's crew, including erecting a monument in their honor, naming a new starship to carry on the AURORA name, and full honors for the deceased.

"I never would have expected this from you," Karla admitted.

"Why? Because they're not ES officers? As far as I'm concerned, we're all one and the same. We wear the same uniform and have pledged our support to defend humanity. The AURORA's actions proved that."

"And here I thought you were going to recommend me stepping down as head of the council." She set the papers on her desk.

"Oh, I do want your job and I will get it someday. I promise you that." Michael sat down. "But not like this, not using this tragedy as a tool for my own ends. We're better than that, Karla."

"You haven't spent enough time with career TERRA officers. But you're right, using this tragedy to advance either of our careers wouldn't be right."

Michael smiled. "Why, I do believe we just agreed to our first truce."

"Then we better enjoy it while it lasts. Was there something else you wanted to discuss?"

"It's the INFINITY. I know we can't send DISCOVERY out to investigate her status. The security of the solar system is our top priority."

"All we know is that the communications signal that set off the weapon came from the system they're investigating," Karla said. "I won't speculate on INFINITY's current status. In twenty-four hours, the SOLARIS will arrive at Jemyu and find out what's happened. For all we know, they could have a malfunction in their communications system. These are new ships."

"New ships that the council was assured were ready to enter service," Michael reminded her. "But that's irrelevant. As soon as SOLARIS ascertains INFINITY's status, then both ships should return home."

"Barring any unforeseen circumstances, I agree."

Just then, Karla's desk beeped. "Admiral, there is a priority level transmission coming in from the Mars communications center."

"Route it to my office." Karla assumed it would be some updated information about the Screen weapon. She activated her communications link and saw Commander Billy Pedia on the screen. "Commander, I'm here with Admiral Forsent. What do you have for us?"

"Admiral, we have a live signal coming in from the INFINITY. Captain Nikols is on the line."

That was good news. At least the INFINITY hadn't been destroyed.

"Why aren't they contacting headquarters directly?" Michael asked.

"Their communications system is offline. They're using the comm system from a Senfo freighter they picked up."

TERRA headquarters hadn't updated its communications network to handle alliance vessels communications, so it was left to the Mars communications station to pick up and reroute any sort of transmissions that might come in. "Very well, patch the captain through," Karla ordered.

Billy nodded and routed the call through. Seconds later, his image was replaced by an image of Annette Nikols.

Karla had no interest in wasting time with pleasantries. "Captain Nikols, what's your status?"

Michael had come around the desk so the captain could see both council members. "Admiral Forsent, Admiral Vespia, the ship and crew are fine."

Karla was too experienced to buy this. She suspected the captain did not want to reveal the extent of any damage done to

INFINITY to avoid it reflecting poorly on her command abilities. "If the ship is fine, then why are you using a Senfo freighter to communicate with us? Now's not the time to be hiding things from your superior officers."

Annette paused, looking as if she was weighing her options. "We discovered a Screen outpost on the third planet in the Jemyu system. We attempted to make contact with them; unfortunately, they used our comm transmission to send an energy burst at us. It disrupted numerous systems and knocked out our communications system."

The admirals were shocked. Like everyone else, both had assumed the Screen were extinct. The only two remaining Screen alive were the two leaders TERRA had in custody after the race's defeat at the solar system. They had been extensively interrogated and never revealed that any pockets of their people still existed on a planet other than their homeworld.

"What's the status of the enemy outpost?" Michael asked.

"We destroyed their fighter fleet as well as their auxiliary craft. We're monitoring them to ensure they remain on the planet. While attacking us, they sent a transmission to the solar system. We weren't able to ascertain what it contained or why they sent it."

There was no reason to hide what had happened from the captain. Karla was blunt. "It was an activation code. The Screen had planted a weapon beneath the surface of Mars. It fired an energy burst directed towards Earth. If it wasn't for the AURORA, it would have caused significant destruction to the planet."

Annette stammered over her next words. "What happened . . ."

Michael interrupted her. "I'm sorry, Captain, but the AURORA was destroyed while blocking the energy burst. They gave their lives to protect the people of Earth. I know it's tough to hear, as you worked on that ship for years and knew most of the crew."

To learn that her old ship and her former crew had been destroyed by the Screen was unfathomable. It reinforced the regret she felt about trying to make contact with the outpost. "Admiral, we're prepared to bombard the outpost and eliminate the enemy."

"Negative, Captain," Karla said. "We need those Screen alive for interrogation. The outpost needs to remain intact so we can go through their computers to see if there are other weapons they hid in the solar system."

"The alliance teams on the Screen's homeworld can check the databases there," Annette said.

Michael had already contacted those teams. "They found no records on the Mars weapon. The outpost may have some information on it, or on other weapons they may have planted. We need the outpost intact and the inhabitants taken as prisoners."

"They're the enemy. We're at war with them and they should be treated as such." Annette's body tensed up and it was apparent she was trying to hold back her anger. "They need to be destroyed."

"As you were, Captain." Karla knew the captain was reacting to the news of the AURORA's destruction, but she was still an officer and needed to maintain composure and look at the big picture. "We need to ensure the safety of the solar system, and we can only do that by verifying the Screen haven't hidden any more surprises. You are to maintain position and monitor the outpost, nothing more. The SOLARIS will be en route to you and rendezvous with INFINITY in twenty-four hours."

"We don't need support," Annette stated. "We have the situation under control."

"We need as many of our people as possible going through their records and interrogating the inhabitants," Karla said, concerned that the captain might try to exact revenge. The presence of another starship with a second captain monitoring the mission would ensure that Captain Nikols would stick to her orders. "You'll continue making whatever repairs you need to your ship and take no further action until the SOLARIS arrives."

To make sure that Nikols wouldn't do anything stupid, Karla threw out one more order. "When the SOLARIS arrives, Captain Diego will take command of the mission. You'll report to him."

That did not sit well with Annette. "You can't sideline me. This is my mission!"

"Which you let go awry when you attempted to contact the Screen," Karla reminded her. She needed to get the captain in line, and being brutal would ensure cooperation. "As soon as you discovered the outpost, you should have contacted us instead of trying to handle it on your own. Captain Diego has experience that makes him uniquely qualified to handle this mission. Stay where you are and do nothing until the SOLARIS arrives. Do I make myself clear, Captain?"

"Yes, Admiral."

"Very good, Captain. We'll talk again soon." Karla turned off her comm link, confident she had ensured Captain Nikols's cooperation.

"I don't need to be a psychologist to see she's not in a good state of mind," Michael said.

"She just learned her old ship was destroyed and her former crew killed." Karla wasn't defending Nikols, merely stating an observation. She had no interest in the captain's feelings, only that she remained compliant.

"Understood, but we now have a critical mission to complete. Does Captain Nikols have the mental wherewithal to see it through?"

"She's a long-serving officer of TERRA with a unblemished career," Karla said. "I wouldn't expect her to take matters in her own hands, but just in case, that's why I'm hedging my bets with Captain Diego. He can keep Captain Nikols in line. She won't defy the orders of someone I've put in charge."

Michael had to give his rival credit for making that call. "Given his experience on the SOLARA, I have no doubt Captain Diego will handle this mission professionally. He knows how to handle difficult officers."

"It seems we have a lot of work to do." Karla handed the papers back to Michael. "Since you drafted this, would you mind handling the preparations? You have my full support."

"Of course," Michael said as he got up. "Don't take this as our relationship changing, but it is a breath of fresh air that we agree on something."

Karla was quick to assure him. "I'm sure when we talk next, we'll be arguing."

Michael chuckled. "I'll see you tomorrow."

Karla nodded as he left her office. There was one more thing she needed to do. She reactivated her desk comm system. "Priority communication to Commander Lewis. Encrypt to priority level one, voice authorization Karla Vespia."

"Stand by," the computer replied.

The admiral waited less than a minute before the image of Commander Lewis, who was in charge of the detention facility on Mars, appeared.

"Yes, Admiral?"

"I want you to begin interrogation of the Screen prisoners," she said, referring to the two Screen leaders. "I want to know about any facilities or weapons they may have hidden in the solar system." She leaned in closer to the holographic monitor. "Use any means necessary to get them to talk."

"Even at the risk of killing them?" the commander asked.

"Their lives are no longer important. You will interrogate them until they either give up the information or are no longer able to communicate. This will be the last time they are to be questioned. Understood?"

The commander knew exactly what the admiral meant. "I'll notify you of any information they provide us. What about the bodies?"

"Burn them. No one's going to miss them." The alliance worlds had squabbled for years over who had the right to put the Screen leaders on trial, but the Cresorians and other matters had made it less of a priority. It had been over two years since anyone asked the admiral or the command council about them.

"Create a cover story for how they died," Karla said. "I'll leave it to you to handle the details."

"I'll take care of it," Lewis promised.

Karla ended the transmission, got up, and went over to the side table by the window looking over Infinity City. She picked up the photo of her son Kory.

She had waited patiently to exact her revenge on the remaining Screen. Now she would have it. She had sealed the leaders' fates, and she would do the same to the Screen outpost inhabitants once they were taken into custody and brought to Mars.

She closed her eyes and relished the thought of torturing them. They would each suffer terribly before being killed. For the admiral, it would be an appropriate end to the Screen.

Karla looked at her son's photo with a heavy heart. "I hope you don't think less of me for doing this."

——— ——— ———

On the INFINITY, Captain Nikols returned to her quarters after talking with Admirals Vespia and Forsent. She had Cumondant Deel erase the transmission from the freighter's communication's log as well as giving him other instructions.

On her walk from the hangar to her quarters, she didn't acknowledge any of her officers. Her mind was preoccupied with memories of her former crew on the AURORA. When she entered her quarters, she went into the living room and picked up a picture frame, which rotated through various pictures of Annette with the AURORA crew that she'd taken in her twenty years aboard that ship. She smiled as she recalled some of the events surrounding the pictures.

Her smile disappeared as she realized she would never see most of the people in these photos again. The last remnants of the AURORA crew were on INFINITY, officers she had transferred to serve under her here.

If she hadn't tried contacting the Screen outpost, her colleagues and friends would still be alive. It was her fault for buying into the idea of diplomacy. There could never be peace with the Screen, whether there were six hundred or six billion. Captain Nikols had been naïve to think otherwise, and the crew of the AURORA had paid for her mistake with their lives.

No more. Captain Nikols would ensure the Screen would never harm another person.

CHAPTER FIFTEEN

Frank got up at 0600 hours to start his day. After showering and dressing, he remained in his quarters to eat breakfast. He wasn't in the mood to go to the mess hall and socialize. As executive officer, he knew he should go out and boost the crew's morale, but he wasn't up for it. He beat himself up for allowing the Screen to damage INFINITY. This was a new ship, with a composite of various alliance technologies. It should have been able to repel any attack, yet the Screen had found a vulnerability.

Frank reminded himself that they couldn't have anticipated all scenarios. He remembered a report written up by the PHOENIX senior staff, saying that no matter how much advanced technology you put on a ship, it would still be vulnerable to some unknown alien technology out there. All you could do was adapt and move on. That appeared to be the case here. The crew of the INFINITY hadn't thought anyone could use a communications system to launch an attack. Now they knew, and the communications and engineering groups were coming up with solutions to prevent a reoccurrence.

"Computer to Commander Rola. The senior staff meeting scheduled for 0800 hours has been cancelled."

That was odd. The captain was a stickler for routine and believed morning staff meetings were critical for smooth operations. It made no sense to cancel this meeting given their crippled state. "Computer, who cancelled the meeting?"

"Captain Nikols."

The commander was perplexed. Certainly, the captain had contacted TERRA to apprise them of INFINITY's situation and to request instructions. "Computer, location of the captain."

"Captain Nikols is on the command deck."

"Computer, has the captain made any other changes I should be aware of?"

"Your query is open-ended. Please specify."

Frank rolled his eyes. This was why they should have installed a Senfo AI. "Changes to mission orders, changes to personnel."

"Changes to mission profile are restricted. Please see Captain Nikols for any updates to mission parameters. One change to personnel assignment."

That caught his attention. "What's the change?"

"Dr. Jeremy Myers has been relieved as chief medical officer. Dr. Tao Noble has been designated as his replacement."

The captain should have apprised Frank of any changes to the senior staff. Why was he kept out of the loop? His instincts told him that he wouldn't get any answers from the captain.

"Rola to Dr. Myers."

"Myers here."

"Can we meet and talk? I just learned from the computer that you've been relieved of duty."

"Commander, it would be inappropriate for us to meet. You'll need to discuss this with the captain."

"I'm asking you. What the hell is going on?"

"I'm sorry, Commander. You'll need to discuss this with Captain Nikols. Myers out."

Frank threw his hands up, exasperated. He needed to get to the bottom of this mess. Getting up, he headed out of his quarters to the command deck.

—— —— ——

Captain Nikols was at the operations table with Lieutenant Erikson, reviewing tactical data. "Have you accounted for the variance in the atmospheric turbulence?" Annette asked.

Ingrid nodded. "I've narrowed our error rate to 5.3 percent. Both the high yield of the torpedoes and simultaneous launch of multiple warheads should mitigate the error rate."

"How long until the warheads are reinforced?"

Ingrid checked her display. "Last check with engineering estimated four hours."

The captain was satisfied. She spotted Commander Rola emerging from the lift. "Carry on, Lieutenant." Annette approached her executive officer.

"Captain, can we talk?" Frank asked.

Annette sensed something was bothering him and suspected it had to do with cancelling the staff meeting. "In my office," she gestured. Once they were inside and the door had closed, she continued. "My apologies for not notifying you ahead of time about cancelling this morning's meeting. I plan to have one this afternoon to go over TERRA's orders."

Frank breathed a sigh of relief at hearing that she had spoken to their superiors. "What did they say?"

"The command council was pleased to hear we suffered no fatalities. After apprising them of what happened to us . . . Commander, their orders are clear. We're to destroy the outpost and eliminate the Screen."

"Even knowing there are children down there?" Frank asked.

"The Screen represents a threat too great to allow to exist." She anticipated her XO was going to protest. "I don't like it either, Commander. Now that we know what the outpost is capable of, we can defend ourselves. But the command council doesn't want to risk allowing it to remain."

The explanation sounded plausible to Frank. He could see the council not wanting to have the Screen as an adversary again, even if the number was only six hundred. "What about Dr. Myers? Why did you relieve him of duty?"

"It was Dr. Myers who pushed to open a dialogue with them. He's been vocal about not doing any harm to the outpost inhabitants. The council felt that relieving him of duties would create less divisiveness on the ship. He'll be recalled to Luna when we return."

Frank found it strange that the council would make such a decision. He'd never heard of them relieving someone of command remotely. That was a commanding officer's prerogative. And why would the captain go beyond reporting the doctor's recommendation to establish contact and add that he was against harming the outpost? Was she trying to deflect responsibility for the attack and pin the blame on him?

"What about the signal the outpost sent to the solar system?" Frank asked.

"It turned out to be nothing but static. They concluded it must have been sent erroneously during the attack. It contained no data."

Frank didn't believe that for a second. He'd reviewed the sensor data, and it clearly showed a substantive data file was embedded in the transmission. She was lying to him. He was certain of it.

He was tempted to ask for the comm log with the official order file so he could authenticate the captain's claims, but he suspected it didn't exist, or she'd come up with an excuse not to give it to him. Besides, he didn't want to tip her off about his suspicions.

"What do you need me to do, Captain?" he asked.

"Make sure repairs are on track. I want INFINITY to be battle-ready by this afternoon."

"I'll coordinate with the departments. Do you need me to do anything else?"

"No, the repairs are our top priority."

That was another red flag for Frank. She was having him only coordinate repair efforts and not participate in any sort of tactical plan development.

"That'll be all, Commander. Thank you."

Frank nodded, left her office, and headed directly to the lift. "Hangar," he told the computer. "Commander Rola to Cumondant Deel."

"Yes, Commander."

"I need to use the comm system on your ship."

"My apologies, Commander. Captain Nikols requested that no one is to use it under any circumstance. She indicated we must remain under a communications blackout to conceal ourselves from the Screen."

Without the Senfo freighter, Frank couldn't contact TERRA and verify their orders. He didn't want to force Deel to let him use the freighter's communications system. He knew the Senfo was an advocate of destroying the outpost. If Frank forced Deel to let him use the comm system, Deel might go to the captain and protest. "Understood. Rola out."

Frank needed to figure out what to do next. None of this was sitting well with him. "Computer, deck six."

Frank recalled his meeting with Rich Melicoast. The former captain had told Frank that Captain Nikols had lied to get him booted so she could take over the AURORA. It seemed that she was repeating the same pattern here in order to get her way. He wanted to give her the benefit of the doubt, but couldn't ignore his feelings. He needed another perspective.

——— ——— ———

"I'm coming," Jeremy shouted as he hurried out of his bedroom. Someone was pounding on the door and refused to announce themselves. He punched the panel and opened the door. There stood Commander Rola. "Commander, we shouldn't be talking."

"We're way past that," Frank said as he pushed his way inside. "Do you know the captain's planning to destroy the outpost?"

Jeremy was disheartened to hear this. "I didn't know, but am not surprised."

"She's claiming she's under orders from the command council."

"I don't believe that. I've been to several council meetings where the possibility of the Screen still existing was discussed. They were clear each time that if any were found, they were to be captured."

"I want to contact the council, but the captain's ordered Deel to keep anyone from using his ship's comm system. With INFINITY's comm still offline, I have no way to verify that the captain is being truthful."

"What about the council's orders? Surely, she provided you a copy of that."

Frank slowly shook his head.

Jeremy was alarmed. "There's no reason for her to ignore that protocol." The doctor took a seat on the couch. "You may be right. She may be acting against TERRA's orders."

"I want to believe her," Frank insisted. "She's my captain, but I know something's not right. She also said it was the council who ordered you be relieved of duty."

Jeremy gave Frank a sympathetic look. "You have good reason not to trust her. When she relieved me of duty, she was clear it was her decision. She never mentioned she was acting on the orders of the council."

"I'm duty-bound to follow her, but if she's been lying about the council ordering us to destroy the outpost . . ." Frank felt he had to say it. "I'm obligated to stop her, even if it means removing her from command."

The commander gave the doctor a pleading look, hoping he had an alternative. No captain had ever been removed from command by their XO.

Jeremy gave him no such option. "It's clear she's elected to conduct a rogue operation without the council's approval."

"None of the crew were killed," Frank pointed out. "And INFINITY will be repaired. I can't accept that her ego is so bruised that she'd resort to lying to destroy the outpost. I need confirmation from the council."

"Are you sure the communications system can't be fixed?"

Frank thought about it. The comm equipment had been obliterated by the outpost's attack, but there was a secondary system everyone had forgotten about. "We did salvage SOLARA's old comm system before it was scuttled. The thought was to use it in case the new system didn't work. Since the new system has worked flawlessly, the SOLARA's was never installed."

"Is it still here?"

Frank activated his holographic DAT and checked the ship's inventory manifest. "It's in cargo bay two." He smiled, seeing the unit's status. "It's all hooked up. All we need to do is reroute power from a conduit and we're good to go."

"I need to advise you that if you contact the command council without the captain's knowledge, it would be considered insubordination. You'd be putting your career in jeopardy."

Frank didn't relish the idea of putting his career on the line. He had worked too hard to get this far to throw it away. From what Rich Melicoast had said, Frank was certain that Captain Nikols would nail him to the wall if she discovered he'd gone behind her back.

Jeremy could see the XO was struggling. "I may have an alternative. You could contact one of INFINITY's sister ships and, officially, get a status update. Compare operational notes, exchange ideas, that sort of thing."

"Captain Nikols ordered no one could use the Senfo's comm system, but she never issued an official communications blackout." Frank said it aloud, trying to convince himself he was within his rights to contact another ship.

"I believe the SOLARIS was to conduct patrol duty as part of their shakedown," Jeremy said. "You should be able to access their current location."

Frank was glad they had settled on a plan. "I'll head to the cargo bay and get the old comm system up and running, but we'll need to send the message encrypted, without alerting the rest of the ship."

"I believe Chief Ito is well-versed in hiding communication signals." Jeremy recalled that information from the chief's bio.

Frank wasn't concerned that Hiroshi would turn him in to the captain. The chief was a former ES officer and had no love for Captain Nikols. But he still harbored some nervousness about getting the security chief involved. The fewer people that knew about this, the less likely someone on the ship would find out.

"Do you know when the captain plans on attacking the outpost?" Jeremy asked.

"We have a staff meeting this afternoon, so I bet sometime afterwards."

"I wish I could offer more help, but it will create suspicion if you and I are seen together."

"I'll try to keep you in the loop of what's going on," Frank promised as he headed out of the doctor's quarters to visit Chief Ito.

——— ——— ———

The chief was in his quarters, listening to traditional Japanese hogaku music. With all security concerns taken care of, he'd chosen to spoil himself with a little time alone, listening to some of the music he'd enjoyed while growing up. Listening to hogaku music allowed Hiroshi to clear his mind and let go of all the obligations weighing on him.

When the door chime rang again and again, he didn't answer, lost in his imagination. Only when the voice of Commander Rola came over the speakers did he snap out of his trance.

"Commander Rola to Chief Ito. The computer says you're in there. I need to speak with you."

Hiroshi opened his eyes and looked around his quarters, trying to get his bearings. "Computer, restore normal illumination," he said as he got up from the living room couch. Checking that his uniform was in good order, he spoke up. "Come in."

"I'm sorry if I'm bothering you," Frank said as he rushed in. "But this is important."

"Is there a security issue?"

"Maybe. There's no way to sugarcoat this, so I'll just tell you."

Frank spilled everything that had happened between him and Captain Nikols, his suspicions, the lack of documented orders from the command council. When he was done, he watched anxiously as the chief paced the living room area with his hands behind his back.

Frank realized he had dumped a lot of information onto the chief, but it was still agonizing watching him pace and say nothing. "Well?"

Hiroshi stopped pacing and looked at Frank. "What makes you think I wouldn't take this to the captain?"

Frank's heart pounded. "You're former ES and the captain's treated you like you don't exist."

Hiroshi smiled. "I could try to ingratiate myself with her and tell her your suspicions. But you're right, she's treated me like shit. I'm on your side."

Frank's legs felt so weak with relief, he almost wanted to sit down. He considered telling the chief about what Rich Melicoast had told him back on Luna, but decided against it.

Hiroshi grabbed a glass from the kitchen and poured some cranberry juice into it. "I hope you have an idea how to handle the captain," he said as he handed Frank the glass. "We can't let her execute her plan."

Frank gulped his drink quickly. "We have an old communications system in cargo bay two. I can use it to contact the SOLARIS and inform them of our situation."

"Without her being aware?" Hiroshi asked.

"We'll have to encrypt it."

"Which is why you're here to see me."

Frank was impressed by how the chief connected the dots. "I don't have the expertise you do at encrypting transmissions."

"I have no problem helping you. If the captain carries out her unauthorized mission, we'll all be looking at court-martials. I've worked too hard to let her ruin my career. I only ask one thing."

"What's that?"

"If we do this, you need to see it all the way through. No questioning your loyalties to her or doubting your actions. We go all in or not at all."

Frank took a deep breath, then stood up and extended his hand. "I'm all in."

Hiroshi shook it. "Good, then let's get to the cargo bay."

——— ——— ———

Less than an hour later, Frank and Hiroshi arrived at cargo bay two. They found the SOLARA's comm system to be in good shape. Frank rerouted power to it as Hiroshi set up the encryption protocols on his DAT. He transferred them to the comm system and accessed the nearest relay satellite to locate the SOLARIS. Once pinpointed, the security chief sent a transmission out, marking it for captain's eyes only so that Captain Diego would reply.

Frank was nervous as they waited for the reply. How would he explain all of this to Captain Diego? He didn't want to come across as some petty XO trying to take his captain's place. He kept telling himself to stick with the facts as best he could.

The display flickered for a few moments before Captain Diego appeared. "This is Captain Diego of the starship SOLARIS."

"Captain, it's Commander Rola of the INFINITY."

"Commander, why are you using the SOLARA's old protocols? Haven't you repaired the INFINITY's comm system?"

Frank ignored his question about the comm system. "Captain, are you aware of orders issued to the INFINITY by the command council?"

Diego nodded his head. "The INFINITY is to maintain position around the planet and wait for our arrival to coordinate the capture of the Screen."

That was contrary to what Captain Nikols had told Frank. He felt a pit welling up in his stomach as he realized he'd just gotten the verification he needed that she had lied. "Sir, Captain Nikols told me that the command council ordered us to destroy the outpost and eradicate all the inhabitants."

The look of surprise on Diego's face reinforced that Frank's suspicions had been correct. "Are you sure?" the captain said.

"Yes, sir. Engineering is currently retrofitting most of our torpedoes. They plan to attack in just a few hours. I became suspicious when she didn't provide me a copy of the orders."

"Can you prevent her from carrying out her plans?"

Even though Frank had decided to remove Captain Nikols from command, he wasn't sure how to go about it. "I don't know."

Hiroshi interjected himself into the conversation. "Captain, I'm Security Chief Hiroshi Ito. Most of the INFINITY's crew served with Captain Nikols on the AURORA and are loyal to her. They may not support us if we try to stop her. We need reinforcements.

How fast can you get here?”

"Not fast enough. I can't go into details, but I'm not sure when we can get to the Jemyu system. Commander Rola, you're going to have to do whatever it takes to prevent Nikols from attacking the outpost.”

"What about the DISCOVERY? We could enlist her help.”

"She's ordered to remain in the solar system to provide defense because of the attack.”

Frank and Hiroshi looked at each other, confused. "What attack?” Frank asked.

"She didn't tell you? The outpost sent a signal to Mars and activated a hidden Screen weapon. It destroyed the AURORA.”

Captain Nikols's plan suddenly made sense to Frank. She had spent most of her career on the AURORA, worked side-by-side with the crew. She blamed the Screen for the loss of her compatriots and was going to exact revenge. It also explained why she'd removed Dr. Myers from duty. He was against attacking the outpost and she couldn't let him get in her way.

"Captain Diego, if Captain Nikols learned that her old ship was destroyed, she may be looking to get back at the Screen. I won't be able to stop her from carrying out her attack,” Frank said.

"If you can't convince her, then you'll have to remove her from command.”

"Captain, I need to remind you again that most of the crew here are loyal to her,” Hiroshi said.

"We can't allow her to kill the last of the Screen. There may be additional weapons they hid elsewhere in the solar system or at other alliance systems. The outpost may have such information. It's vital you stop her from carrying out her plans.”

Captain Diego was right. They needed survivors to interrogate. Frank wasn't sure how he would stop her, but he would come up with something. "I'll do what I can, sir.”

"We'll get to you as soon as we can. I'll contact Captain Nikols myself and see if I can convince her to abandon her plans without tipping her off that I learned about them from you.”

Frank wanted to say more, but he was already risking the

command deck picking up the transmission by talking this long. "I'll try to contact you somehow if things change."

"Negative. Don't attempt any further contact. We'll see you soon. Diego out."

As soon as the console display went blank, Frank shut off the communications equipment.

"You think you could convince Captain Nikols to abandon her plans?" Hiroshi asked.

"No." Her former ship was obliterated and the crew dead. He couldn't compete against that sort of anger.

"My security officers are all former ES," Hiroshi said. "They'll support us in removing Captain Nikols from command."

"Your security officers against four hundred sixty-three of the crew? Not very good odds." Frank shook his head. Without help from the SOLARIS, they were outmatched.

"We have the element of surprise on our side. The captain doesn't know we're aware of the council's true orders. She'd have no reason to suspect anyone would try to stop her."

"We need to come up with something that'll give us the best chance to take control of INFINITY." Frank thought of what their next steps should be. "Rola to Viv'r Kordif."

"Yes, Commander?"

Hiroshi was about to protest Frank contacting the Onixin, but the commander held his hand up to silence him. "Meet me in my quarters immediately. Tell no one where you're going. This is a sensitive matter."

"Understood, Commander. Kordif out."

"What the hell are you thinking, getting that alien involved?" Hiroshi demanded.

"He doesn't have the same loyalty to Captain Nikols as the crew. If I explain the situation to him, I'm confident he'll help us. Maybe an alien's perspective will help us come up with a plan."

"Big maybe. He may just go directly to the captain about us."

"It's a chance we'll have to take."

"Well, why don't we try to get those Senfo to help us while we're at it," Hiroshi suggested sarcastically.

The Senfo wanted the Screen dead. The last thing they would

do was help Frank and Hiroshi subvert Captain Nikols's plan. "Very funny." Frank motioned for Hiroshi to follow him. "Come on."

A strategy started to form in Frank's head as the pair headed out of the cargo bay. It wouldn't be enough to take over the ship. They would have to do it without hurting any of the crew. Frank would not have it on his conscience if his actions resulted in anyone being harmed.

CHAPTER SIXTEEN

After his conversation with Commander Rola, Jacob summoned his executive officer to his office and filled her in on the situation with the INFINITY. Her response was, as usual, direct.

"Are you kidding me? What the fuck is she thinking? She's a career officer. She has to know doing this will end her commission. I know no one loves the Screen, but we're military. There's tactical issues to consider."

"She may think she'll be hailed as a hero for destroying the outpost." Although he didn't know her intimately, Jacob had spent enough time with Captain Nikols at the shipyards to pick up on some of her motivations. He could tell she wanted to set herself apart from the rest of the officers in TERRA. She'd remarked more than once that her reasoning for helping build new starships was to make a name for herself. In a lot of ways, she was no different than the captain Jacob had served under briefly on the SOLARA during the jumpgate mission. People like that ignored logic to justify their actions in the pursuit of fame and glory.

Michelle wasn't interested in psychoanalyzing someone she barely knew. "I hate to say this, but what are we really losing if she carries out her plans? TERRA and the alliance are already doing detailed scans of the solar system. They're bound to find any other hidden weapons the Screen might have hidden."

"How's it going to reflect on us if one of our officers destroys a defenseless outpost, one that has young Screen? Military rules dictate you don't attack civilian targets if you can avoid it."

Michelle couldn't ignore his assessment. If the outpost only had adult military officers, she wouldn't be bothered by Captain Nikols's intentions. Children were another matter. She couldn't ease her conscience knowing innocents would be harmed.

"I checked with Jonas," she said, referring to their chief engineer. "It's going to be a few more hours before the hyperdrive is running."

That was news Jacob didn't want to hear. "A fine time to test a new propulsion system."

SOLARIS had not been stranded due to engine trouble. When the ship was commissioned, the story was that it would be conducting patrols of space outside the solar system. Its true mission had been a secret to everyone but TERRA's command council: SOLARIS was to test experimental technologies, from weapons to new forms of energy.

Given the crew's experience in the Triangulum Galaxy, the council felt they needed one ship dedicated to exploring the edge of scientific and technological advancements. Even the ship's crew makeup was hidden from the public. As far as the fleet knew, SOLARIS's crew was comprised strictly of TERRA officers. In reality, most of the crew consisted of civilians from various sectors of the scientific community.

"Get down to engineering and help Jonas with getting the hyperdrive back up," Jacob said. "Getting to Jemyu is our top priority."

Michelle nodded and headed out of the captain's office. She knew he wasn't about to let Captain Nikols carry out her plan if they could stop her. She felt bad for Commander Rola. He seemed like a good officer and didn't deserve the position he was in.

In the office, Captain Diego requested his communications

officer open a transmission to the INFINITY. Persuading Captain Nikols to sit by until SOLARIS rendezvoused with INFINITY was his only option. If he couldn't convince her to wait, then it was up to Commander Rola to stop her.

"Lieutenant Linstrom to Captain Diego. I'm unable to reach the INFINITY. I'm getting an automated reply that they're under a communications blackout."

Jacob tightened his fists. Was it possible Captain Nikols had found out her executive officer had contacted SOLARIS? Or maybe she had instituted a complete communications blackout to prevent any of her crew from finding out what had happened back at the solar system. "Patch a transmission through to Admiral Vespia, priority one."

"Yes, sir. Stand by."

If Commander Rola couldn't relieve Captain Nikols of command, it would be up to Jacob to do it. Removing her from command was something he wasn't looking forward to doing. They had established a good working relationship in their time at the shipyards and he wasn't fond of having a hand in ending her career. He hoped that she would reconsider her actions.

Lieutenant Linstrom's voice came over the speakers. "I have Admiral Vespia on the line."

Jacob quickly patched the communication through his office desk terminal. The holographic image of Admiral Vespia appeared. "Admiral, we have a situation with the INFINITY. Commander Rola contacted me a short while ago and informed me that Captain Nikols plans to destroy the Screen outpost."

The admiral looked surprised. "She's under explicit orders by me to take no action against the outpost. How does Commander Rola know her intentions?"

"She informed him personally, claiming the orders came from the command council."

"I'm assuming she didn't provide him with a copy of the orders for authentication."

Jacob nodded. "Correct."

"Have you tried reaching out to her?"

"INFINITY is under a communications blackout. They're not

accepting transmissions from anyone."

"How soon can you reach her?"

Jacob quickly referred to the SOLARIS's status on another screen. "We're still a couple hours away from getting our hyperdrive back up. Admiral, we may not reach her in time. I recommend we send an alliance ship to the Jemyu system to take command of INFINITY."

"Absolutely not! This is an internal matter. I won't have aliens, even alliance members, interfere on our behalf."

Jacob didn't agree with the admiral. Now wasn't the time to worry about TERRA's honor. "This concerns the Screen, which affects the entire alliance. There's also an alliance member serving on the INFINITY. We can't argue this is an internal issue."

Karla had a counter-argument. "That alliance member you're referring to is in no danger, as far as we know. This situation involves a career officer disobeying orders and taking matters into her own hands. I won't have that dirty laundry aired to the alliance. It could complicate matters for TERRA in our future dealings with our friends."

"Admiral . . ."

But Karla cut him off. "I know you credit the alliance for saving you and your crew during the jumpgate mission, but we need to look at the bigger picture. TERRA's been too dependent on the alliance. We have to show we can stand on our own two feet. Handling this sort of affair without their involvement is what we need right now if we're to be seen as equals."

Jacob hated that the admiral's point of view made sense to him. Relying on the alliance to protect the solar system had been an ongoing concern. What if one of the alliance races decided to turn against the others? It had happened with the Cresorians. As distasteful as it was for him to think such a thing, he had to be a good military officer and anticipate all worst-case scenarios. Humanity needed to prove it could stand alone.

"Alright, Admiral. I see your point. We'll keep the alliance out of this."

Admiral Vespia liked Captain Diego, who didn't let his personal feelings get in the way of his pragmatism. He could see the big picture. It was that sort of foresight that would get him to the admiralty. "Contact me as soon as you've secured command of INFINITY."

Karla ended the transmission and Diego referred back to the status display of the SOLARIS. He quickly swiped it away, realizing he couldn't do anything sitting in his office. No, what they needed to do was get to the INFINITY as soon as possible. He jumped out of his chair and headed down to engineering, intent on doing whatever he could to restore the SOLARIS's hyperdrive.

CHAPTER SEVENTEEN

Frank and Hiroshi waited in the commander's quarters for Dr. Myers and Kordif to show up. They didn't have much time. In a matter of hours, Captain Nikols would be ready to launch the strike against the Screen outpost.

When they finally arrived, Frank quickly filled them in on what he had learned from Captain Diego regarding TERRA's orders and about the hidden weapon on Mars. Dr. Myers wasn't surprised to learn that Captain Nikols was actively going against orders, but Kordif had a harder time with the news.

"Our military operates so that the orders of a superior officer are always followed," Kordif said. "I thought the human military operated under the same rules, but you are saying this is not always the case."

"We do," Jeremy admitted. "This is an unprecedented situation. We've never had a TERRA officer violate the chain of command like this."

"Captain Nikols has a valid reason for attacking the outpost," Kordif pointed out. "They did attack us and destroyed your ship back home. She must have a valid tactical reason to retaliate against them. Perhaps she has concluded that destroying the outpost will prevent them from activating another secret weapon they may have planted on one of your worlds."

Frank sighed, realizing Kordif needed some more convincing. "Captain Nikols is responding out of emotion. The ship that was destroyed, the AURORA, is where she served for many years. She lost a lot of friends and is looking to get revenge."

"There's no tactical reason to attack the outpost," Hiroshi added. "We destroyed their fighters and rendered them helpless. They're no threat to us. There's no reason to wipe them out."

"Have you questioned Captain Nikols about her plan?" Kordif asked.

"Yes," Frank replied. "I have."

"Then you have fulfilled your duty as a subordinate officer. If the captain feels destroying the outpost is warranted, then we should follow her."

Frank was getting frustrated with Kordif, but was determined to get him to see their side. "A good executive officer points out all available options, as well as telling the captain the merits and consequences of an action. Usually, such conversations are all that's needed to come to consensus. But in rare cases, it doesn't solve the disagreement."

"What is your protocol regarding such a situation?" Kordif asked.

Frank, Hiroshi, and Jeremy looked at one another. None were anxious to discuss what needed to be done. But the captain had put them in a corner. They needed to act quickly if they were going to stop her.

Frank finally spoke up. "When an officer is acting out of accordance with orders, they are relieved of their position. In the case of a ship commander, they are removed from command and the next senior officer takes control of the ship."

"Which is you," Kordif concluded. "The senior officer being relieved accepts this protocol?"

Frank wasn't sure what he was asking, but Jeremy realized what he was getting at. "No, the officer is relieved of duty against their wishes."

"This is an acceptable practice in your military?" Kordif asked.

"How can you operate knowing your command structure could collapse at any time?"

Hiroshi was surprised by his reaction. "You Onixins have never had to relieve a commanding officer of their duty when they go wacko?"

"As I have already said, Onixins may question a superior officer, but will always follow whatever orders stand. You humans may have this wacko disease, but my people do not."

Frank decided to approach the argument from the Onixin's perspective. "You said that Onixins obey the orders of their superior officers, no matter what."

"That is correct."

"That's what we're dealing with here. Captain Nikols is disobeying a direct order from her superiors in the command council. If she's unwilling to follow their orders, then it's up to us to carry them out."

Kordif considered the commander's words. "You do not think she will voluntarily step down if you tell her you are aware of the orders from your council?"

"Probably not," Jeremy said. "She has the backing of many of the crew here, as most served with her on the AURORA."

"Their backing?" Kordif asked, unsure of what the phrase meant.

"It means they would prevent us from relieving the captain of command," Frank clarified. "In all likelihood, we'd be thrown in the brig while the captain carries out her mission."

"We're going to confront the captain," Hiroshi stated. "We could use your help. Are you with us?"

Kordif always saw humans as a cooperative group, fostering collaboration amongst themselves and others. To hear that some were planning to go against one of their own was difficult to hear. "What do you propose?"

"I'll have to confront the captain directly and give her the chance to change her mind," Frank said. "We might as well see how the crew will react, so I'll do it on the command deck."

"And if they move against us?" Jeremy asked.

"I'll have my security teams posted in key locations throughout the ship," Hiroshi offered. "It shouldn't be hard to convince the captain that it's necessary in case the Screen try another attack and attempt to board us."

That was a good start, but Frank knew they needed to do more. "We need to shut down critical systems that would disable the ship in case she retains control. Shutting down the engines would be ideal."

"That may be difficult, given the security protocols around them," Hiroshi pointed out. "Only senior-level officers have a chance of breaking them, and I'm sure the captain doesn't consider me a senior officer."

"I could reprogram the navigational system," Kordif offered.

That piqued Frank's interest. "How so?"

"The computer on this ship is a combination of the best operating systems from each of the alliance races. Onixin programming is compatible with the computer. I could insert a program that would steer the ship away from the outpost regardless of the navigational inputs."

Frank had some exposure to Onixin computer programming language. It was so complex that no non-Onixin could grasp the fundamentals of it easily. There were TERRA officers who had spent over two years immersed in learning it in order to gain some intermediate knowledge.

"It'd certainly delay them from attacking the outpost," Jeremy said. "But the torpedo firing sequence would compensate for the ship's change of course to hit the target. The weapons systems need to be disabled."

"I could do that," Hiroshi said. "I could preprogram the computer to put the weapons' systems into a recurring diagnostic cycle. That way, we're not constrained by time."

"Once they discover your access code put the weapons into diagnostic, the captain may realize what's happening," Jeremy warned.

"We should also knock out internal communications so they can't coordinate capturing us if things so south," Hiroshi said.

Frank wasn't worried about the time factor. He was confident they could take over the ship before the captain or her allies realized what was happening. "It sounds like we have a good plan. We'll make the preparations and reconvene at the staff meeting." The commander looked over at the doctor. "Except for you. We'll need to keep you in the loop about what's going on."

"I can keep the doctor apprised," Hiroshi said.

"How long for you to create the navigation program?" Frank asked Kordif.

"*Pes'du'vi.*"

Frank checked his DAT to translate the Onixin time to human measures. "Twenty minutes. Okay, then let's get to work. I want everything in place by the time we meet with senior staff."

——— ——— ———

Frank walked down the corridor, trying to appear normal.

He was committed to going through with the plan, but still felt an obligation to Captain Nikols. To hell what Rich Melicoast had told him. Captain Nikols was a long-serving TERRA officer with a distinguished career. He had to give her the benefit of the doubt. He hoped she would listen to reason, but he couldn't tip his hand too much in case she refused to change her mind. He needed to choose his words carefully.

He arrived at her quarters and took a deep breath as he went over what he was going to say. When he felt ready, he rang the door chime.

"Come in," he heard the captain say as the door opened. He found her sitting on the couch in her living room area. "What can I do for you, Commander?"

Frank had an entire speech laid out in his head, but it flew right out the window before he could utter a word. There were so many ways he could approach this. Should he let her know he was aware of TERRA's standing orders regarding the outpost? Should he give her the heads-up that SOLARIS was en route to take control of INFINITY?

No, he had to give her a chance. "Captain, are you sure about this?"

"Commander?"

"About destroying the outpost? Have you considered all possibilities? They may have information vital to the alliance."

The captain's reply was calm. "I've examined all options, Commander. Yes, they may have some tactical information, but it's not worth the risk of finding out. They've demonstrated their hostilities towards us. We can't risk another engagement and incurring more casualties. I'm confident whatever information they have down there will be on their homeworld."

Frank was disappointed in her justification. He waited for her to disclose more information about the transmission the outpost sent that had activated the hidden weapon on Mars, or that she had been in communication with TERRA. But she remained silent about those things, and emotionless in her response. This was someone committed to their plan.

"Is there something on your mind, Commander?"

"No, sir. It's my duty as executive officer to ensure you've considered all scenarios. It would have been negligent of me not to."

Annette nodded. "Of course. Are preparations complete?"

"We'll be ready at 1500 hours."

"Very well, Commander. Dismissed."

Frank made a hasty exit from her quarters. Well, that was that. He'd given her the opportunity to explain herself, change her mind, or at least come clean about the orders from TERRA. She'd failed in all regards. Frank's conscience was clear. As distasteful as it would be for him, he felt justified in removing her from command.

——— ——— ———

At 1345 hours, the senior staff met in the conference room. Annette laid out the plan for attacking the outpost, verifying with each senior staff member that preparations in their area were complete.

Given the tactical nature of the mission, Chief Hiroshi was in attendance. It didn't take much effort for him to convince the captain to allow him to post security officers in key areas of the ship.

When the meeting concluded, the staff headed off to finish last-minute preparations before reconvening on the command deck. Hiroshi stopped by Jeremy's quarters and informed him about what was discussed at the meeting. Kordif headed up to the command deck and programmed the Onixin navigational subroutine into the computer. Hiroshi disabled the security protocols in the computer so that it wouldn't pick up the program in a security sweep.

Finally, the moment had come. It was 1500 hours and the senior staff assembled on the command deck. Annette was in her command chair, reviewing details of the mission one last time. Hiroshi was seated next to her, a few holographic security screens displayed in front of him. Kordif was at his station, keeping one eye on Commander Rola while the other was focused on his navigation console. Onixins could move their eyes independently of each other, which allowed them to view different areas of their environment simultaneously.

Frank was at the operations table with Ingrid. He pretended to be reviewing the mission data profile, but was preoccupied with what he was going to do. There was no backing out now, and he didn't want to. Captain Nikols was about to take action against the orders of the command council and kill the last remaining population of an alien race.

"We're all set," Ingrid said to Frank. "Ready?"

"Yup." Frank was careful not to say anything more. "Captain Nikols, INFINITY is ready."

"All hands to battle stations," Annette announced as the battle klaxons blared. "Kordif, move us into a lower orbit above the target."

"Yes, Captain. Beginning descent."

Frank took a deep breath. He needed to wait until the captain took action that cemented her intent to carry out her plans.

"Are torpedoes ready?" Annette asked.

Hiroshi pulled up the weapons status screen. "Yes, Captain. Torpedoes are loaded in the launch bays."

"Program the firing sequence," Annette instructed. "Prepare to fire on my command."

That was the confirmation Frank needed. "Delay that order!" He was a bit overzealous in his announcement, and it came out as more of a shout.

Everyone stopped what they were doing and stared at him in disbelief. Annette wore a confused look. "What was that, Commander?"

Frank moved away from the operations table and toward the captain. "Captain Nikols, you're in violation of TERRA's standing orders regarding the Screen outpost."

"What orders?" Martin asked from the communications station.

Frank had to talk quickly if he had any hope of getting the crew on his side. "Captain Nikols has been in contact with the command council. They ordered her to take no action against the outpost until reinforcements arrived."

Annette stood up from her chair. "You're out of line, Commander. I don't know what you're playing at, but I won't have you spreading lies to the crew."

Frank wasn't about to relent. "We all know the outpost sent a second signal out when they attacked us. That signal activated a hidden weapon on Mars that fired on Earth. The AURORA was nearby, intercepted the attack, and were destroyed. Captain Nikols wants to retaliate against the outpost for the AURORA's destruction."

"You're relieved," Annette said. "I don't know what you're trying to do, but it's not going to work."

"The SOLARIS is en route here to take command of INFINITY," Frank said. "If you help the captain take action against the outpost, you'll all face court-martials."

"He's lying," Annette argued. "You all saw what the outpost did to us. You really think the command council would want it left alone? They're Screen. They've done nothing but kill millions in their quest for control."

"Captain Nikols, you are incapable of commanding this ship. I am relieving you of duty," Frank said, realizing she was not backing down.

"Take Commander Rola into custody," Nikols ordered the

command deck staff.

This was it. Which way would the crew go? Frank hoped logical heads would prevail. He knew the crew was loyal to Captain Nikols, but he was banking that their concerns for their careers would override their sense of obligation.

He heard the sound of a pulse gun powering up. "Commander Rola, step away from the captain and come with me," came Martin's voice.

The captain grinned.

It was time for plan B. "Computer, execute Frank One."

Suddenly, the ship veered sharply upwards and power dropped from the dampening systems, throwing everyone off their feet. At the same time, a white gas spewed from the ventilation ducts, creating a thick fog. Frank, Hiroshi, and Kordif raced to the lift in the confusion. Kordif and Hiroshi armed their pulse guns while Frank manually entered their destination to deck seven.

Frank pulled an old-style hand communicator from his pocket. The four conspirators had shut down internal communications so that the crew couldn't track them. They carried remote communicators that didn't run off the ship's comm system in order to keep in touch with each other. Hiroshi had also issued these to his security team leaders.

"Rola to Myers."

"Go ahead," came the doctor's voice.

"Taking command of the ship has failed. We're heading to meeting point A."

"I've looked outside my quarters and it appears everything has locked down."

"Acknowledged. Communicate only if absolutely necessary. Rola out."

"A good chunk of the crew should be locked in their quarters," Hiroshi said as he activated his communicator. "Hiroshi to security teams. Take into custody any crewmembers you see."

He didn't need to say more. His team knew that meant taking command of the ship had failed. They would round up any crewmembers out and about and lock them away.

Frank looked at Kordif. "Are you okay?"

"I am . . . bothered by all of this. Onixin officers have never behaved this way."

"I'm sorry you have to be a part of this, but it was the only way. The captain intends on destroying the outpost and we can't allow that."

That statement made Frank shudder. He was effectively protecting the last of humanity's mortal enemy. Trying to take control of the ship was necessary, but a part of him felt it was wrong.

He would worry about regrets later. "Once we get to the cargo bay, we'll figure out our next steps."

"I need our status," Annette demanded as her remaining officers scrambled in the thick fog to check the ship's systems. To say she was angry was an understatement. She'd never expected that Commander Rola would turn against her and try to initiate a mutiny.

Ingrid accessed environmental controls and vented the fog from the command deck. Able to see again, Annette noticed that Chief Ito and Kordif were missing. She concluded that they were part of Rola's mutiny scheme.

"The weapons systems have been put into a diagnostic routine," Ingrid reported.

"Terminate it," Annette ordered.

"I can't. The diagnostic was programmed with security protocols to cycle over and over. It'll take hours to crack through."

"Ito," Annette muttered in disgust. "Computer, halt all system diagnostics per captain voice authorization."

"Voice authorization recognized," the computer replied. "However, second voice authorization required from executive officer."

"He must have reprogrammed our authorization protocols," Martin speculated.

"What about internal communications?" Annette asked.

Martin checked his console. "They're down. Internal sensors are also out, as well as navigation control."

Commander Rola had put Annette at a disadvantage. She couldn't see what was going on throughout the rest of the ship, or even contact any of the crew to warn them what was happening.

"We need to rally the crew to help us," Annette said.

"We could do a peer-to-peer call," Ingrid suggested.

The captain was unfamiliar with that term. "What's that?"

"Except for the data crystals, computer hardware here is still the same basic design as on the capital ships. I can send a text-based message to other terminals. A bunch of us did it all the time on the AURORA when we didn't want certain communications going over the network and being logged."

"I'm familiar with that," Martin said.

"The problem is, someone will need to be viewing whatever terminals we send the message to," Ingrid said.

"Engineering," Annette said without hesitation. "We need to reassert control of the ship. Manual navigation should still be possible down there."

"What should I tell them?" Martin asked.

"That Commander Rola, Chief Ito, and Kordif attempted to take control of INFINITY. I'm sure Dr. Myers is with them as well."

"On it," Martin said as he started working on the task.

Annette thought of what Frank's next move might be. "Commander Rola may try to gain navigational control of INFINITY in engineering. We can't wait up here and hope the crew stops him. We need to get down there."

"Captain, Chief Ito placed his security forces throughout the ship," Ingrid reminded her.

"Then we'll need to send another message to all terminals alerting our people of what's happening. We need to get as much of the crew as we can out there to subdue Commander Rola and his allies."

Ingrid looked over to Martin. "Send a message to engineering, and I'll send a message to the rest of the ship."

Martin nodded and the pair began writing up the messages to be sent out. The captain motioned the backup navigational officer away from the station and checked the ship's location. As she suspected, it had moved out of orbit with the planet. Furthermore, the planet had rotated, moving the outpost away from the ship. For now, the outpost was safe from INFINITY.

Commander Rola had mentioned the SOLARIS coming to the Jemyu system. He must have contacted them and alerted Captain Diego of her plans. If they showed up before she destroyed the outpost, she faced the possibility of firing on a fellow starship. She needed to avoid that if she could. Retaking control of the ship was paramount if she had any hope of completing her mission.

"Anything yet on those messages?"

Martin shook his head. "I've displayed a message on all terminals in engineering, but no one has responded."

Ingrid had more tangible results. "Several crewmembers have responded. It looks like they're locked in their quarters or whatever locations they were working from. I've directed them to break open the doors and take any security officers into custody, along with the commander."

"Add Kordif, Chief Ito, and Dr. Myers to those to be captured," Annette directed. "If they offer resistance, I authorize lethal force to be used."

"Yes, Captain."

Annette joined Martin at his station. She looked at the displays and was disappointed no one from engineering had answered. Could Commander Anvil be involved in this mutiny as well?

"Engineering is the only way we can regain control of the ship," Annette said. "We'll have to go down there ourselves and see what's going on."

"I recommend using the maintenance shafts," Ingrid said. "It'll take time, but we'll avoid the security teams."

Annette nodded in agreement. "Lieutenant Singer, you'll remain here to monitor and respond to any communications you receive. Direct any available crewmembers to engineering. The more people we have there, the better chance we have to secure the location. Also, if any security detail tries to come up here, you're to shoot them. We can't afford losing control of the command deck."

Annette grabbed two pulse guns from underneath the communications table and handed one to Martin as Ingrid armed herself with one she nabbed from underneath the operations table. The women went to the corner of the command deck, where the maintenance shaft door was located. Annette opened the shaft, and both descended into it.

CHAPTER EIGHTEEN

Frank, Hiroshi, Jeremy, and Kordif had made their way to cargo bay one. They met with a security detail en route who provided them with a status update. So far, there had been no indication that fighting had broken out on the ship. To Frank, that meant most of the crew was unaware of what was going on. He wanted it kept that way, but knew Captain Nikols would find a way to alert them to what had happened.

Hiroshi directed the security detail to keep to their patrol. It would be easier for Commander Rola's team to reach engineering if they were a small group. If any disturbances cropped up, the group would be alerted by security.

Frank activated his DAT to show a layout of the ship. "I've charted us the most direct path to engineering. Barring that we meet any resistance, we should get there in about fifteen minutes."

Hiroshi pointed to a couple of locations on the route. "We have two security teams on our route. I recommend we take the team closest to engineering with us so they can help secure the area."

"Agreed," Frank said. "We just need to hold our ground in engineering until the SOLARIS shows up."

"It'd be nice to know when they'll get here," Jeremy said.

"Hopefully soon." Frank was banking on SOLARIS's appearance to defuse the situation. He had told Captain Nikols the ship was on its way. Maybe she'd reconsider her actions once it arrived. He looked over at Kordif. "How you doing?"

"I am fine and will continue to follow your lead."

The Onixin's lack of emotion bothered Frank. Was Kordif being truthful or having regrets about joining them? Frank wanted to press him for answers, but they didn't have time. He assumed Kordif's behavior was due to some Onixin cultural nuance.

"Let's keep moving." Frank headed out of the cargo bay with the others following behind him.

The walk on deck three was uneventful. They passed a couple of crewmembers without incident, and each acknowledged the commander as the group walked by. They reached the lift and took it down to deck twelve. No one said a word, as if breaking the silence would somehow jinx their good luck so far.

Frank's worries that they would eventually meet resistance were realized as they exited the lift and proceeded down the corridor.

"Commander." Kordif pointed down the corridor. Five officers were approaching, all holding pulse guns.

"Those aren't my people," Hiroshi said.

"Halt right there, Commander," one of the officers ordered as he and his group raised their pulse rifles.

"Mess hall," Jeremy whispered to Frank. The commander looked out of the corner of his eye and saw they were near the entrance to it.

Captain Nikols must have somehow warned the crew about the mutiny. He couldn't risk trying to talk his way past the opposing group. Frank pulled his pulse gun and fired, hitting one officer in the chest. His gun was at stun, so the impact didn't kill her. As she fell, the others opened fire as Frank's group ducked into the mess hall. Frank hoped the rifles were at stun, but suspected they weren't. If they were killed, Captain Nikols could make up any story about what had happened to protect herself.

The group raced into the mess hall and flipped several tables to hide behind as their pursuers entered, firing their weapons. Those people who were in the mess hall enjoying a meal fled from the chaos, unsure of what was going on. The bots behind the food counter recognized the presence of danger and retreated to their charging stations in the back.

It was slow going for the commander's group as they retreated backwards, hopping from table to table as they returned fire on their assailants. The four remaining security officers fanned out, making it more difficult to target and hit them. Kordif managed to hit one and take him down. Dr. Myers, who had not fired a weapon in years, couldn't even come close to striking anyone. All he could do was fire and keep them off their toes.

The commander's group reached the food counter and ducked behind it. The three remaining security officers took positions behind the turned tables and continued to lay down suppression fire.

"I will check no one is in the kitchen," Kordif said as he ducked through the door.

Jeremy noticed their pursuers weren't moving forward. "Why aren't they advancing?"

Frank pointed to the door, where eleven more officers were barreling through, firing on the group. "That's why."

"There's a maintenance shaft in the kitchen we can escape to," Hiroshi said.

"Only you need to get to engineering," Jeremy said to Frank. "I can stay and hold them off."

"One against fourteen? I don't think so." Frank wasn't about to abandon the doctor. They had to come up with something quick.

Kordif popped his head out of the kitchen door. "Watch out."

Frank, Hiroshi, and Jeremy watched as three service bots rolled out from the kitchen onto the mess hall floor. None of the officers in the mess hall fired on the bots, as they didn't see them as a threat.

"In here, quickly," Kordif motioned the group. The trio complied and hurried into the kitchen. Seconds later, they heard explosions along with screams. They looked at the Onixin in disbelief. "I overloaded their power cores."

There were no more sounds of weapons fire coming from the mess hall. Frank suspected no one had survived the explosions. His worst fear had come true. He'd wanted to avoid hurting anyone and absolutely did not want anyone killed, but he couldn't dwell on it. Kordif had given them an opportunity and they needed to take it.

"This way," Hiroshi said. They made their way to the back of the kitchen, where the storage area was located. There on the floor was a maintenance hatch. Frank opened it and crawled inside, followed by Jeremy, Kordif, and Hiroshi. Once the chief closed the hatch, he opened his communicator.

"Ito to any security team. Come in." There was no response from anyone. "Ito to any security officer, respond." Again, nothing but silence greeted him. "I think we're on our own."

Frank couldn't offer any condolences that would be appropriate. "Let's keep going," he said as he made his way down the shaft. All they could do was focus on achieving their objective.

——— ——— ———

"Exiting jump," Lieutenant Kelly Nalus announced. "Entering Jemyu system."

The SOLARIS finally reached the outer portion of the Jemyu system. The ship made its way to the inner parts of the star system at full speed.

"Locate the INFINITY," Captain Diego instructed Commander Gimron.

Standing next to Fotell at the operations table, his executive officer checked the sensor readings and located the ship. "Got 'em. She's holding position 214,000 kilometers from the planet."

Fotell, SOLARIS's Senfo operations officer, did additional scans of the INFINITY. "Captain, sensors show the INFINITY engines are powered down, as are their weapons."

"Maybe Commander Rola was successful in convincing Captain Nikols not to go through with her plan," Kelly speculated.

Captain Diego had thought about keeping his officers in the

dark about their mission, with only him, Michelle, and Jonas knowing what Captain Nikols intended to do. But Jacob didn't operate that way. The SOLARIS crew had been through so much together, they deserved the truth in any mission they conducted.

Fotell tapped Michelle on the forearm. "Commander, can you take a look at this?"

Michelle checked Fotell's scans. "Captain, I don't think Commander Rola was successful. We're picking up some weapons fire throughout the ship."

That was bad news. "Commander Rola may have needed to try taking control of the ship," Jacob said.

"Even if he wasn't successful, it looks like he at least immobilized INFINITY," Michelle said.

Jacob looked at his communications officer. "Anything, Lieutenant?"

"Negative, sir. I've been trying to raise her since our arrival."

"Keep trying." Jacob got up from his command chair and joined Michelle and Fotell at the operations table. He reviewed the scans of the INFINITY. "They're holding position. We need to get over there and see what's going on." He pointed to a section of the ship on display. "The hangar looks accessible."

Fotell checked the status of the hangar. "Confirmed, Captain. Our access codes should activate the doors."

"Since we don't know what's going on, I recommend we send a security team over there," Michelle suggested. "We shouldn't risk any senior officers going to INFINITY until we know what's going on."

Jacob concurred. "I'll send encoded orders with the team so there's no misunderstanding that we're taking command of INFINITY. Once we've secured the ship, we'll send Commander Walters over with an engineering team. They may need help getting INFINITY up and running if it was sabotaged. Jonas can then command the ship once he's got it operational."

"I'll have Chief Auguston put the security team together and brief them on the mission," Michelle said.

Jacob looked over to Kelly. "Set a course towards the INFINITY but proceed slowly. I'm assuming their sensors are still working and they know we're here, but I don't want to do anything that might provoke them. We need to be cautious."

"Understood, Captain."

"I will monitor the INFINITY and alert you of any change to their status," Fotell promised. "If they are aware of our presence, do you still believe Captain Nikols may try to carry out her plan?"

"Until we hear from someone over there, we have to assume she'll try. I'm aware that by preventing her from destroying the outpost, we're saving the Screen. I know what they did to your people and understand if you have any resentment."

"*Revib*," Fotell said in appreciation. "I could never hold resentment toward you. You have always done what is right. A part of me would like to see the Screen exterminated once and for all. But there has been too much destruction and killing on both sides. What they did to Flutori cannot be undone. I would rather focus on rebuilding our world and strengthening the alliance. Harboring hatred from the past serves no purpose."

Jacob smiled. "I hope a lot more of your people, and mine, have that sort of thinking."

Fotell had not only seen her homeworld decimated by the Screen but the loss of her entire family. If she could put aside her hatred and not succumb to revenge, Jacob was certain others could as well. He hoped he could convince Captain Nikols to put aside her own anger before she could execute her plan.

——— ——— ———

A shuttle departed from SOLARIS and headed towards INFINITY, containing Chief Auguston and his security team. The chief had elected not to fly over in a Repo, which was typically heavily armed. It might send the wrong message and inflame a potentially volatile situation. Heading over in a standard shuttle made sense.

"Auguston to SOLARIS, we're inbound to the INFINITY."

"Acknowledged," came the voice of Commander Gimron. "Be advised we're showing no reaction from INFINITY."

"We should reach the perimeter of the hangar doors in four

minutes." The chief turned and looked at his team. "Alright people. I want weapons armed and set to stun. No matter what's going on over there, they're still our people."

The team nodded in agreement. None of them wanted to get into a fight with fellow officers.

Auguston returned to piloting the shuttle. Even though SOLARIS was monitoring any changes to INFINITY's status, he kept an eye on the shuttle sensors. He would not be taken by surprise.

The shuttle reached the perimeter of the hangar. "Shuttle to SOLARIS. I'm transmitting the hangar activation code now."

A few beeps from the shuttle console, and the hangar doors parted ways. Auguston waited until the doors opened just enough for the shuttle to squeeze through. As it entered the bay, he reported what he was seeing. "Shuttle to SOLARIS. I'm seeing personnel on the hangar floor and observation tower. Everyone is armed and several appear to be trying to open the door to the corridor."

"Hangar control to shuttle. You are identified as being attached to the SOLARIS."

"SOLARIS, I'm being hailed by the tower. I'm patching them into our comm." After merging the communications, Auguston spoke. "This is Chief Auguston of the starship SOLARIS. We're here under orders from the command council, which I'm transmitting to you now."

It took a minute to get a response. "Orders authenticated, but they're contrary to Captain Nikols's mission."

"INFINITY, this is Captain Diego of the SOLARIS. Where's Captain Nikols?"

"We don't know. We received a text message that Commander Rola, Chief Ito, Dr. Myers, and Kordif tried to take over the ship. We were instructed to take them out if we encountered them, along with any security officers."

"Have you tried contacting the captain?"

"Our internal communications are down. We received instructions from the command deck by text."

"What about the other systems?"

"Internal sensors are down, and all doors have been sealed.

We've been trying to force them open."

"You listen to me and listen to me good," Jacob said in a forceful tone. "Captain Nikols has gone against the direct orders of the command council and is considered rogue. Unless you all want to join her in being court-martialed, you'll cooperate with the security team on my shuttle. Is that understood?"

"Yes, Captain Diego. We will adhere to your orders per the directive from the command council."

Auguston removed the hangar tower from the communication as the shuttle touched down on the deck. "It's just us on the line, Captain."

"Secure the hangar first and verify the ship's status. Have them send a text to display on all terminals showing the command council's orders and that all personnel are to stand down."

"Should I try to have Commander Rola and his group contact us?"

"One step at a time. We need to stop the fighting first, then try to make contact with the commander."

CHAPTER NINETEEN

It seemed to take an eternity for Frank and his group to make their way through the maintenance shafts. They had to take some detours when they heard the distant sounds of officers in the maintenance shaft network. Whether they were doing work or looking for the group, Frank didn't know. He wasn't inclined to find out, so they changed their route to avoid any encounters.

The group eventually reached their destination. Frank opened the hatch and the three climbed down into main engineering. They only saw two engineers, one of them being Commander Anvil. They hopped off the ladder and the noise alerted Ronan and his engineer to their presence.

"Frank." Ronan said nothing more as the group pointed their guns at him and his engineer.

"Where's the rest of your engineers?" Frank asked.

"We were in the middle of a shift change when everything locked down. It's just us two."

Frank motioned for the others to check the area.

"Frank, is it true you tried to remove the captain from command?"

"She's gone against orders. TERRA ordered her to take no

action against the outpost and she's ignored them."

"I can't believe that. Captain Nikols is an honorable officer."

"He's telling the truth. No one else is here," Hiroshi said as he, Jeremy, and Kordif rejoined Frank.

Frank gritted his teeth in frustration. "She lied to us and I can't let her carry out her illegal mission."

"I want to hear her side," Ronan insisted.

"We don't have time for this." Hiroshi fired his gun on both Ronan and his engineer, stunning them into unconsciousness.

"That wasn't necessary," Frank protested.

"You can worry about convincing Commander Anvil later after SOLARIS has arrived and we've secured INFINITY."

"I just found out why we're being pursued." Jeremy motioned Frank and the others over to an engineering terminal to show them the display.

Commander Frank Rola, Dr. Jeremy Myers, Chief Hiroshi Ito, and the Onixin Kordif have attempted to overthrow the captain and illegally take control of the ship. They are to be apprehended and taken into custody. If they attempt to resist, deadly force is authorized.

"I'm glad none of us took a hit from our pursuers' guns," Jeremy said. He watched as Commander Rola deleted the message and accessed the engineering system. "What now?"

"Now, we disable the program Kordif put in and move the ship away from the planet."

"Hold it right there." The group turned around and saw Captain Nikols and Lieutenant Erikson. Both were holding pulse guns. "Move away from the console."

"I can't do that," Frank replied. "I can't let you destroy the outpost."

"And I can't leave until those Screen have been eliminated," Annette said.

"Annette, please . . ." Jeremy started.

The captain interrupted him. "I don't want to hear what you have to say." She activated her holographic DAT. "I attached a piper to the main injector casing. If you try anything, I'll set it off."

A piper was a micro-explosive device, and she'd placed it on a critical area of the ship. Frank moved away from the console and motioned for his team to do the same, then took a couple steps towards the captain. "If you destroy the engines, we might get ensnarled in the planet's gravity and go down. You really want to risk the lives of the crew?"

"The crew's lives are in danger so long as those Screen exist."

Frank had to try and appeal to her pain. "I can't imagine what you must have felt when you learned the AURORA was destroyed. The crew were your friends, people you could trust with your life. They sacrificed themselves to protect Earth. We can mourn them but celebrate the sacrifice they made to save thousands."

Hearing about her lost comrades was too much for Annette. "The Screen have killed millions! I had a chance to stop them but didn't. Because of my inaction, I lost my friends. No more deaths at their hands. The Screen's reign of terror will finally end here."

"You're willing to throw away your career for revenge?" Jeremy asked.

"I'm well past saving my career, but I don't care. History will show I was willing to sacrifice it to eliminate a dangerous enemy."

"Computer, *triuped sanek alwre*," Kordif said. Suddenly, the hum of the engines grew.

"What the hell?" Annette looked around.

"It is done," Kordif said. The second part of the program he had inserted in the navigation system had now activated.

"No!" Ingrid shouted as she fired her weapon. It struck Kordif in the shoulder and the Onixin fell to the ground. Jeremy rushed to provide aid to him.

Annette pointed her weapon at Frank. "Back off!"

He raised his hands and backed away from her. She went over to the nearest engineering console and checked the readings, inputting some override commands, but nothing worked.

The captain couldn't accept coming this far and losing control. She had always accomplished any task or goal given to her. The Screen could not be allowed to exist.

"You won't win." With a quick motion of her hand, Annette activated the piper. There was a distant explosion, followed by a violent shake of the ship. Everyone was thrown to the ground.

Frank quickly recovered, got up, and rushed to the console. According to the telemetry data, the ship was on course to crash into the outpost despite the fact that they had programmed the ship to take it away from the planet, not toward it.

The ship shook again as more explosions sounded. Frank was barely able to stay on his feet while the others were thrown back onto the ground. Annette was rendered unconscious as she was slammed against a nearby ladder.

"Power core breach," the computer announced. "All personnel to emergency escape pods. Repeat, power core breach. All personnel to emergency escape pods."

Frank verified the computer's assessment. The explosion in the injectors had initiated a cascade reaction in the ship's power grid. There was nothing he could do to stop it. All he could do was try and alter the INFINITY's course.

He tried accessing the Onixin program, using the access code Kordif had given him. As he accessed the thruster controls, he looked at Jeremy. "Get everyone here to the escape pods. I'll try to maneuver the ship away from the planet."

"You can't stay here."

"Just go!" Frank shouted. "Make sure to take the captain with you."

The doctor helped Kordif to his feet. He looked at Lieutenant Erikson, who was holding onto another console. "Get the captain."

She nodded and went to get Annette, lifting the captain up and carrying her out of engineering to the nearest escape pod.

"I am mobile," Kordif said to Jeremy.

"Get to an escape pod," Jeremy told the Onixin as he grabbed Commander Anvil. At the same time, Hiroshi lifted the unconscious engineer and headed out.

"Come on, come on," Frank muttered as he wrestled with the thrusters. For some reason, they weren't properly responding to his inputs. The ship was still heading towards the planet. What was going on here?

—— —— ——

"I am reading an explosion in the engineering section of INFINITY," Fotell reported.

"She's also moving away from us," Kelly added. "She's on a trajectory towards the planet. At her rate of speed, INFINITY will impact the surface and be destroyed."

What the hell was going on over there? Jacob pulled up a display from his command chair console. The explosion was having an adverse effect on INFINITY's power core. Whoever had caused the explosion knew exactly where to strike.

"Auguston to SOLARIS. What's going on?"

"Readings show an explosion in main engineering," Jacob replied.

"The computer here is announcing all hands to abandon ship."

That was in alignment with the readings the SOLARIS command deck staff was seeing on their monitors. "There's a cascade reaction building in the power grid. Get everyone from the hangar into shuttles and over to us as soon as possible."

"Yes, Captain."

Michelle was monitoring INFINITY's trajectory. "The ship is definitely heading towards the planet. It looks like it'll strike the outpost."

"What's the likelihood of the outpost surviving if they're hit?" Jacob asked.

"None," Jonas said as he stepped onto the command deck off the lift. "If INFINITY's power core is now unregulated, it'll cause a massive explosion upon impact. No one will survive."

"What about altering her trajectory?" Jacob said.

"Without a tractor beam, we have nothing," Michelle replied.

"We have the grappling hooks," Fotell reminded her.

Kelly calculated using the grappling hooks to snarl INFINITY. "At the rate she's moving, the lines would snap under the stress."

Jacob regretted leaving the solar system without a tractor beam. He looked at Michelle. "Have the hangar deploy all shuttles to bring in any escape pods out there. I don't want any of them caught in the planet's orbit."

"We're already getting a batch of pods heading our way,"

Michelle announced.

"Lieutenant, send a message to all pods to head to SOLARIS's hangar bay," Jacob instructed.

"Yes, Captain."

"Jonas, is there any way we can alter the ship's course remotely?"

He was already working on that angle. "I've bypassed their command protocols and am in the navigational controls. But there's an Onixin program embedded in the navigation system and it's preventing me from making any changes to the ship's direction."

"Can you bypass it?"

"There's no way. Onixin programming is incredibly complex."

"Let me try," Fotell offered. "I have training in all alliance computer languages."

"You better make it quick," Michelle warned. "INFINITY doesn't have much time."

——— ——— ———

Frank was still working feverishly at the engineering console, trying to move the ship away from the planet. The thrusters were not cooperating. Although the thruster output matched his inputs, the telemetry still showed the ship was heading towards the planet. It was on a direct course to hit the outpost.

"Computer, dump n'quadrin energy tanks." If he couldn't prevent the ship from landing, he could at least prevent a massive explosion on the ground.

"Unable to comply. N'quadrin storage tanks have been locked down."

That didn't make any sense. Frank checked them; the computer showed no damage to the ejection system.

"Computer, eject the n'quadrin tanks."

"Unable to comply . . ."

"Damnit!" Frank yelled. "Computer, how many people left on INFINITY?"

"One, Commander Frank Rola."

At least the crew was safe. He thought about leaving, but wasn't willing to give up. He would not allow Captain Nikols's mission to succeed. TERRA had ordered the capture of the Screen outpost, not its destruction. He was duty-bound to prevent this catastrophe. And he didn't want to lose INFINITY. This ship deserved better than to be lost on its maiden voyage.

"Computer, reroute all emergency power to forward thrusters."

"Acknowledged."

He would stay until the end, no matter what. He focused on working the thrusters to try and alter the ship's course.

——— ——— ———

"Time to impact?" Jacob asked.

"One minute, ten seconds," Kelly reported.

"Captain, the hangar is reporting Captain Nikols is on board," Michelle reported.

"Have her and the entire senior staff confined to quarters." Jacob looked at Fotell. "Any luck?"

The Senfo shook her head. "I cannot bypass the programming. It is too complex to decipher in such a short amount of time. It would take *pasequi* to get past it."

"We don't have hours. Is everyone off the INFINITY?"

"No," Michelle replied. "Commander Rola is still there. He's the life sign we're picking up in engineering."

"Can we open a channel to him?"

"Negative, Captain," his comm officer said. "Their communications system is still offline."

Jacob was helpless to do anything. All they could do was watch the INFINITY fly towards destruction.

"INFINITY is penetrating the upper atmosphere," Kelly announced.

"Keep an eye out for any escape pods or shuttle," Jacob instructed. "He may try to escape at the last minute." He suspected Commander Rola would not leave INFINITY. He would remain there, trying to steer the ship away from the planet.

"INFINITY has entered atmosphere," Kelly reported.

"Impact . . ."

Seconds later, they saw a bright light on the holographic display over the operations table as the sensors went wild, registering the explosion. Jacob bowed his head in sorrow at the loss of a fellow officer.

"Sensors no longer detect INFINITY," Fotell reported.

Somehow, Jacob managed to speak up in the face of this tragedy. "Commander Gimron, launch probes over the crash site. We need to ascertain if there're any survivors." He was certain that Commander Rola was gone, but perhaps some of the Screen were out of the area and had survived. "Have security confine all INFINITY personnel to quarters," Jacob added. "I'm sure the command council will want us to begin interviews before we return home."

"I'll take care of it," Michelle promised.

Jacob looked around. He was not pleased with how this had played out. "It's unfortunate what we all witnessed. There'll be time to digest what's happened later. For now, focus on your duties. I'll be in my office, contacting the council to report what's occurred."

CHAPTER TWENTY

It had been two days since INFINITY's destruction. The SOLARIS had conducted extensive scans and reconnaissance at the site of the crash and across the entire planet, using shuttles and probes. Both yielded the same conclusion—there were no Screen to be found. It seemed that they were finally extinct.

Captain Diego, Commander Gimron, and Chief Auguston were busy interviewing the INFINITY's crew, trying to determine who'd known of Captain Nikols's plan. With the exception of Dr. Myers, Chief Ito, and Kordif, the INFINITY's crew were locked in quarters. Jacob didn't want to risk them trying to take over the SOLARIS, and had them bunched in large groups so he didn't have to spread out his security officers.

As he sat in his office going through the interview transcripts, he kept thinking about what Captain Nikols had done. It was still hard to accept that she'd gone against the command council's orders. Worse still, she'd directed her people to use deadly force against Commander Rola and his group to try to achieve her goal. Had the loss of the AURORA devastated her so much that it had driven her to these incomprehensible actions? TERRA officers were supposed to be better than this.

The door chime rang. "Come in," Jacob called.

His executive officer and chief engineer entered, wearing somber looks. "Here to give me bad news together?" he said.

"Bad news in pairs is always more fun," Michelle said, trying to lighten the mood.

"And we figure you could use some friends right now," Jonas added. "How are you holding up?"

"I've been better. I've been going through these interview transcripts, trying to get some understanding of why things happened the way they did. I don't think I'll ever fully understand it."

"Let the higher-ups back home figure that out," Michelle suggested.

Jacob conceded that was probably the best thing to do. "What do you have for me?"

"We've already sent our findings to your DAT," Michelle said. "A thorough reconnaissance of the crash site has confirmed no survivors. No Screen and . . ."

"No Commander Rola," Jacob muttered, finishing her sentence.

Jonas spoke up. "Our scans show none of the outpost buildings survived the explosion. There's nothing viable to recover."

"No tactical information, no Screen to interrogate," Michelle said. "Yup, this has turned out to be a real shitty day."

Jacob found her remark couldn't have been more perfect. "Where are we at with fatalities?"

"Sixty-seven dead. That includes Commander Rola," Michelle replied.

"Sixty-seven, out of five hundred thirteen crewmembers." Jacob had difficulty accepting the loss of that much life. Life lost at the hands of TERRA officers attacking one another. "You know what the sad thing is? A lot of people are going to think Commander Rola threw his life away trying to save the outpost."

"I don't," Michelle replied.

Her answer caught Jacob by surprise. "Really?"

"I have no love for the Screen, but eradicating the outpost for no good reason wasn't right. It was our responsibility to do whatever we could to either establish relations or capture them.

What Captain Nikols tried to do . . . I'll never agree with it. If people think that makes me a Screen sympathizer . . . fuck 'em."

"Michelle's right," Jonas said. "I like to think more people will believe Commander Rola died trying to do the right thing."

It was a comforting thought. Commander Rola had overcome so much in his short career. He'd been a fine officer. Jacob hoped that people would celebrate the person Frank had been rather than criticize his last act.

The door chime rang. "Enter," Jacob said. The door opened to reveal Fotell.

"Am I interrupting?"

Michelle motioned for the Senfo to come in. "Come on in and join the party."

Fotell was confused by the executive officer's words. "Party? I thought parties were always a celebratory affair."

"The commander is being sarcastic," Jonas clarified.

"Commander, you do know I have a difficult time with the human concept of sarcasm," Fotell reminded her.

"Sorry, force of habit."

"What can we do for you, Naporum?" Jacob asked.

"I have been analyzing the Onixin program in the navigation controls of INFINITY that we were unable to decode."

Jacob was aware of the program. "We spoke with Kordif about it. He designed it so the ship would move away from the planet no matter how someone tried to maneuver the ship."

"I hope I did not overstep my bounds, but I felt it necessary to verify all aspects of what happened." Fotell activated her holographic DAT and pulled up the Onixin program. "It took a significant amount of time, but I was able to decrypt the program."

Jonas looked at the code. "Good for you, because it all looks like gibberish to me."

"Onixin programming is known to be very complex. Captain, I traced its functions from start to end. It was designed to maneuver the ship toward the outpost, not away from it."

Jacob did not expect such a conclusion. "That doesn't make sense. Kordif was the one who created the program. He was helping Commander Rola try to stop Captain Nikols."

"Is there any way you could be mistaken?" Michelle asked.

"As I previously stated, Onixin programming is complex. However, I have done my due diligence and stand by my work. If you feel the need to consult with an Onixin on this, I understand."

"Shit," Michelle muttered. "If you're right . . ."

"Fotell, I have complete faith in your work," Jacob said. "But we're going to need to verify this to cover ourselves. Jonas, locate the nearest Onixin military ship and send them a copy of the program to examine."

"Are you going to question Kordif about this?" Jonas asked.

Jacob got up. "I have to. I need to hear what he has to say."

If Fotell was right, the implications were huge. Was it possible Kordif had been working against Commander Rola the entire time? If so, why? What would have been his motivation? He had only met Captain Nikols when he came on board INFINITY. There was no long-term working relationship that would make him loyal to her. There had to be a reasonable explanation for Fotell's discovery.

—— —— ——

Jacob had security locate Kordif and escort him to the captain's office. He considered the possibility that the Onixin might have had a hand in Commander Rola's death. Try as he might, he could not come up with a reason to explain what Fotell had found. He hoped Kordif could explain himself.

The door chime rang. "Come in," Jacob said, standing up.

The door opened and Kordif entered, flanked by two security officers.

"Hello, Viv'r Kordif."

"Captain Diego. You wish to speak with me?"

Jacob motioned to the security guards. "Wait outside." Once they left the office, he continued. "I need to ask you some more questions about what happened on INFINITY."

"Of course. I thought our previous conversations provided all you needed. However, I will provide any additional information."

"What did you think of Commander Rola as an officer?"

"He was a fine officer. His loss will be felt by your TERRA."

Jacob found the response to be antiseptic and lacking any sort of personal attachment. "You thought he was a good man?"

"As I said, he was a fine officer," Kordif reiterated.

Something wasn't sitting well with Jacob. Kordif was exhibiting a clear lack of admiration for Commander Rola. He was beginning to suspect what the Onixin starship would report back. "We deciphered your computer program." He said nothing more, wanting to see the Onixin's reaction. Kordif's lack of response was telling. "You have nothing to say, Viv'r?"

"Onixin programming is beyond the ability of most humans to understand," Kordif flatly stated.

"Oh, we found it wasn't that hard to decode." Jacob made his way around his desk to face the Onixin. "It was a bit of a shock to us when we discovered that it was designed to steer INFINITY toward the outpost. That's contrary to what you told me in our debriefing."

Kordif said nothing. He remained standing rigid, looking ahead.

"Viv'r Kordif, I am your commanding officer, and you will answer my questions. Why did you design the program to steer the ship toward the planet?"

The Onixin hesitated and his hands began to shake. "Captain Nikols is also my commanding officer."

"Not anymore. Answer my question."

Kordif's eyes darted in different directions. "You do not understand. Captain Nikols was my superior officer. I was duty-bound to follow her orders, no matter what my opinion was of her intentions."

"You mean your so-called helping Commander Rola was a ruse?"

"Captain Diego, in the Onixin military we are taught to obey the orders of our superior officers, regardless of what we might think of those orders. To disobey a superior officer is unheard of. It would break down the chain of command and effectiveness of our operations. A superior officer has earned the right to have their orders carried out without question."

Jacob was beginning to understand where Kordif was coming from. "In Onixin military, the chain of command is always followed, no matter what."

"If not, it would invite discord and strife. When Commander Rola told me of his plans to remove Captain Nikols from command, I was unsure of what to do."

"You could have gone to Nikols and told her of Frank's plans."

"I just told you Onixin officers must follow the chain of command. As Captain Nikols was my superior officer, so was Commander Rola."

Jacob was seeing the conflict the Onixin had grappled with. "Two superior officers giving you two different sets of orders. That's something that doesn't happen in your military."

"You do not know what that did to me. I did not know how I could appease both of them. After much thought, I concluded I must follow the orders of Captain Nikols, as she was the highest-ranking officer. But I could not outwardly betray Commander Rola. I created the navigation program that would ensure the mission would be carried out while making it appear that I was helping the commander stop her."

Jacob didn't know what to say. This wasn't a clear-cut issue of an officer betraying their superior, this was a cultural issue. He understood from working with Onixins that they put importance on following the chain of command. It wasn't just important to them, they relied on it. "But Commander Rola was acting to ensure the orders of the command council were carried out," he said. "The council has higher authority than Captain Nikols."

"We accept the word of our superior officers without question. As I never spoke with your council, I could only go by the orders of Captain Nikols."

Jacob understood now. He made his way back around his desk and sat down. "I can't begin to understand what you went through by being put in that situation. But your actions cost the life of an officer."

"That was never my intention. If I could have saved Commander Rola, I would have."

"In that, I do believe you. I'm not sure what's going to happen to you. Captain Nikols and those involved in the fighting will be court-martialed. I'm sure they'll be additional inquiries. TERRA and your military will have to figure out what will happen to you."

"I will accept whatever decision they make."

"Then there's nothing more to be said here." Jacob had gotten the answers he needed. It wasn't what he had wanted to hear, but it did support Fotell's discovery. He could only imagine how TERRA was going to deal with the Onixins on this. It could put a fracture in the alliance.

"Captain Diego, does this happen often with humans? Is it normal for your military officers to turn against one another?"

Jacob considered Kordif's question carefully before answering. "Not often, but yes. It's never easy when it does happen. Part of what we deal with is following orders while not compromising our own beliefs."

"Onixins cannot afford to be concerned with our own opinions. Orders must always be followed."

"And that's a difference between humans and Onixins," Jacob said. He activated his DAT and pressed a holographic button. The office door opened, and the security guards came back in. "Please escort Kordif to . . ." Jacob was going to say 'the brig,' but that didn't sit well with him. If nothing else, he realized that the Kordif had never wanted Commander Rola to die. "Please escort him back to his quarters. He's to remain there until he's transferred off ship."

Kordif hung his head low as he was led out. Jacob felt that, in some ways, the Onixin was a victim of circumstance, trapped in what he thought it meant to be duty-bound. The others on INFINITY had no excuse for their actions.

"Diego to Auguston."

"Go ahead."

"I want Captain Nikols and the entire INFINITY senior staff, with the exception of Dr. Myers, Chief Ito, and Viv'r Kordif, transferred to the brig."

"Chief Ito has requested Commander Anvil to be transferred

to quarters away from the others."

Hiroshi had made the request to Jacob earlier and explained why. "I'm aware of the request and approve it. Transfer Commander Anvil to his own quarters."

"I'll take care of it, sir."

——— ——— ———

Jonas Walters and Fotell arrived at the mess hall for dinner. They'd spent the last couple of hours together, with Fotell educating the chief engineer about Onixin computer programming. Given Fotell's skills at uncovering the true nature of Kordif's program, he wanted to pick her brain and learn more about how Onixins coded their computers. Jonas always thought of himself as smart, but he was doubting his abilities as he tried to comprehend this new computer language.

"Thanks for being patient with me," Jonas told her as they ordered their food from the bots. "I can't believe how complex the Onixins make their computer programs. You have to be an Einstein to figure this stuff out."

Fotell knew the term 'Einstein,' as Jonas had previously explained that expression to her. "You say you do not understand, but I could tell you were comprehending the basic concepts. Do not be dissuaded. It took me *beio-cupu* before I could grasp the basics. It will happen for you too."

Jonas didn't know what *beio-cupu* meant and wasn't about to translate that metric on his DAT. For all he knew, it took Fotell years to get a superficial understanding of this stuff.

As the pair took a seat, someone called out to Fotell. "Fotell, you must join us."

Fotell turned to see a group of Senfo at a table standing on their chairs, waving at her. She rightfully concluded they were the Senfo merchants that had been saved by INFINITY. They weren't confined to quarters, as it was established they'd played no part in Captain Nikols's mission.

Jonas thought it might be nice for Fotell to spend time with some fellow Senfo. "If you want to have dinner with them, go ahead. They might be able to catch you up on the latest happenings on Flutori."

"I have no interest in spending time with them. I will be polite and go over to exchange some brief pleasantries with them. I will be right back."

Jonas was a little surprised Fotell didn't seem interested in hanging out with them. In the last few years she had been in the exchange, she'd only come across a couple of other Senfo. Maybe this whole situation with the INFINITY had gotten her down. She had told Jonas on more than one occasion she had developed a close affection for humans, especially the SOLARIS crew. It would be understandable if she was feeling a sense of loss for those killed on INFINITY.

Fotell approached the table as the five Senfo climbed down from their seats. "Greetings, Cumondant."

"Greetings, Fotell," Deel replied as he tipped his hat to her. "We would like you to join us in celebration. It is a great day knowing the Screen have finally been eradicated."

Fotell wanted no part of their celebration. "I will not celebrate actions that resulted in the loss of humans."

Deel tipped his hat. "The human deaths are unfortunate, particularly Commander Rola. We can still celebrate that their sacrifice was not without rewards. The Screen are gone."

"I will take no part in celebrating their extinction," Fotell responded flatly.

The smiles of the other Senfo disappeared. "How can you not be happy they are gone?" one asked. "They decimated our world."

"I am aware of what they did. I suffered from what they did to Flutori, but I will not take pleasure in them being wiped out. We are better than that."

"You are *larnik*," another Senfo said in disgust.

"Maybe the near-loss of our world wasn't enough for you," remarked an equally disgusted Deel.

Fotell became enraged and threw her hat at Deel. Watching from afar, Jonas knew that a Senfo taking off their hat and throwing it was a sign they had been insulted to the highest degree.

"Do not presume to know me!" Fotell shouted. "I lost my

entire family because of the Screen. They sacrificed themselves so I could live. I do not ignore what the Screen did to our people, but I will not continue the cycle of hatred. My family would not want that for me or our people. We defeated the Screen and have rebuilt our world. That is good enough for me and should be good enough for you. If you want to celebrate their deaths, then you do it alone, but I pity you."

Fotell turned and walked away from the group. Jonas was shocked by what he had witnessed. He realized Fotell had now greatly insulted them in return. For a Senfo to walk away after throwing their hat without picking it up was also a great insult.

Fotell returned to her and Jonas's table, climbed up into her seat, and began eating her meal. "My apologies for being next to you without my hat."

"It's okay," Jonas assured her. "We don't have to stay. We can go back to one of our quarters."

"I will not abandon my meal plans because of them. I enjoy our time together."

Jonas nodded and picked up his fork. He noticed the other Senfo quickly jumping from their seats and racing out of the caf-eteria. "That was pretty impressive what you said to them."

Fotell stopped eating and put her utensils down. "These last couple of days, I had to ask myself if it is something I genuinely believe. When I think of the Screen who perished on that planet, a part of me is glad they are gone."

"There's nothing wrong with that. You've told me what they did to your world. There's nothing wrong in feeling a little satis-faction. If my world suffered in the same way, I'd probably have similar feelings."

Fotell slumped in her seat. "That is not who I am, who I want to be."

"You're not," Jonas insisted. "I've known you a long time. You're a compassionate person who's always eager to help out. You've made it your mission to try and get to know everyone on this ship. You're not a hateful person, Fotell. Don't think other-wise because you are having some unexpected feelings."

Fotell smiled and patted Jonas's arm with her three-digit

hand. "You have alleviated my concerns. *Revib.*" She decided to change the subject to something else that was on her mind. "Do you think they will end the exchange program?"

"Who? TERRA? Why?"

"Because of what Kordif did."

Jonas realized what she was getting at. "I don't think they would abandon a program that's worked so well because of what one person did. I wouldn't worry about it."

"Your words ease my concern. I would not like leaving SOLARIS. This crew has become a great comfort to me."

Jonas smiled. "Is that what you're worried about? Having to leave the ship? If you have any doubts, let me dispel them. All of us would sooner resign than see you go."

Fotell was about to tip her hat in appreciation, but realized she wasn't wearing it. She smiled at her friend. "You have restored my good mood. *Revib.*"

——— ——— ———

It was around 2045 hours on the SOLARIS. Jacob and Jeremy entered the brig to have a brief discussion with INFINITY's former captain. They headed to the far corner where Annette was being held. She said nothing as the pair approached, merely folding her arms as she stopped pacing the cell.

"We'll be leaving the system in the morning and going back to Luna Station," Jacob informed her. "Once we've docked, security will take you into custody until your court-martial can be scheduled."

"If anyone should be court-martialed, it should be him." Annette pointed at the doctor.

"It was you who disobeyed orders from the command council, not me," Jeremy reminded her.

"You were the one who convinced me to try opening a dialogue with the outpost. Because of that, they crippled my ship and destroyed the AURORA."

Jacob intervened in the conversation. "And you should have risen above your grief and hatred and continued to find a non-violent solution. You had that opportunity with the orders from the command council."

Annette waved her hand dismissively at Jacob. "What do you know? You weren't in my shoes."

"I've seen it firsthand," Jacob replied. "Years ago, when I was on the PHOENIX, we came across a planet inhabited by two races. The captain's intentions were to establish peaceful relations with each of them, even though they were hostile toward each other. When things degenerated and they threatened open warfare with each other and us, the captain didn't throw in the towel and give up. He stayed and did everything he could to find a peaceful solution to the very end.

"That's the difference between him and you, Annette. You should have pushed past your feelings and tried to find a peaceful solution for dealing with the outpost. That's what diplomacy is about. Sometimes you have to keep plugging away to make any headway, and sometimes you need to learn to walk away. You did neither. You chose to respond to them with violence. You let your feelings get in the way of your job and it cost you your career and the lives of some of your crew, including Commander Rola."

"Commander Rola's dead?" This was the first Annette was hearing this news. "How?"

"He tried to stop you from carrying out your plans. He stayed on INFINITY until the very end." Jacob noticed that the news had seemed to affect her, but he wasn't going to stick around to see if she was remorseful. "That's something else you'll need to answer for."

Jacob walked away from the cell and left the brig. Jeremy followed him, having no interest in exchanging any more words with Captain Nikols.

"It appears diplomacy is something TERRA will need to teach its future ship commanders," Jacob said to Myers as they walked down the corridor.

"This will be a difficult lesson for TERRA, but necessary."

"You know what's hard about all of this? I never saw it coming. I worked closely with her at the shipyards. I never suspected she could be capable of this."

"I don't think anyone would have suspected this from an officer with her career record," Jeremy said. "I think TERRA expected the success of the PHOENIX would naturally replicate in other ships going out to explore space. Now they're going to have to take a long, hard look at their plans. Are their officers really prepared for the challenges of space exploration?"

It was a difficult, but legitimate question. A couple of cadets had been able to form the alliance that defeated the Screen. TERRA blindly assumed that if inexperienced cadets could make such accomplishments, then their experienced officers would have no issues tackling anything they might encounter in space. What Captain Nikols had done would be a painful reality check for the command council. Jacob foresaw a lot of fallout from all of this.

"Most TERRA officers have spent their lives in the solar system," Jacob said. "TERRA will have to revamp their training program, and probably their other plans."

——— ——— ———

Ronan paced the quarters security had placed him in, frustrated by not knowing what was going on. He had been extensively questioned by Captain Diego and his senior officers, but none of the questions he'd asked about his crew had been answered. He had no idea what was going on with Captain Nikols, Commander Rola, or the other INFINITY senior officers. He wasn't even allowed access to the SOLARIS's main computer. All he knew was the INFINITY crew were in confinement and that they were slated to head back to the solar system.

The sound of the door chime was a welcome relief for the chief engineer. Maybe he could get some information from whomever was knocking. "Come in."

He was disappointed when it was Chief Ito who entered. Then again, if the chief was here, then maybe some of the other INFINITY crew were free to move about SOLARIS. "Where's Captain Nikols?"

"In the brig where she belongs," Hiroshi replied. "The only

reason you're not with her is because of me."

"What do you mean?"

"If I hadn't stunned you, would you have helped us? Or would you have helped the captain carry out her plan?"

Ronan wasn't expecting such a question. Caught off-guard, he stammered. "I, I don't know. Frank and I were friends, but I had my loyalty to the captain."

Hiroshi folded his arms. "I suspect what you would have done. You TERRA types are all the same. Follow the rules and declare unbending loyalty to each other no matter what as long as it serves your purpose. I guess that makes Commander Rola's death okay by you."

Ronan was taken aback by the news. "Frank is dead?"

"I thought they would have told you. Yes, he's dead. He stayed on INFINITY trying to steer the ship away from the planet. He gave his life trying to stop Captain Nikols. But she won. The outpost is destroyed, and the Screen are gone. You should be proud. What's the life of one commander and dozens of other officers if your precious captain got her wish?"

This was too much for Ronan. He retreated to the couch and sat down, replaying everything that had occurred from the time they were attacked, to the captain issuing her orders to destroy the outpost, to when Frank and his group confronted Ronan in engineering. "I never wanted any of this."

"No, you just wanted the captain's plan to play out with no hiccups," Hiroshi said without a hint of sympathy. "For one brief moment, I thought maybe you would have sided with us. But I was kidding myself. You would have done anything to stop us."

"No!" Ronan jumped off the couch. "I wouldn't . . ."

"Wouldn't what?" Hiroshi interrupted. "You're gonna stand there and say you would have helped us?"

Again, Ronan struggled to find the words to respond.

Hiroshi wore a look of disgust. "I thought as much. I won't feel guilty when I nail you to the wall at your court-martial." The security chief turned and left the quarters.

Ronan was in disbelief. Frank couldn't have died. "Computer, I need verification that Commander Rola is deceased."

"Per Captain Diego, all inquiries made by INFINITY personnel are restricted."

"Can I talk to Captain Diego then?"

"Direct contact with Captain Diego by INFINITY personnel is prohibited. A request can be sent to his personnel inbox."

Ronan slumped back on the couch. All of this seemed unreal. It was hard enough remembering Frank pointing a gun at him in engineering. He had hoped it was a bad dream. Even after waking up in the escape pod, Ronan couldn't reconcile what had occurred. All the intense questioning he had gone through finally made sense, and Hiroshi had no reason to lie. There was nothing he could do but see what would be waiting for him back at head-quarters.

CHAPTER
TWENTY-ONE

The following morning, three Quix, one Senfo, and three Onixin starships arrived at the Jemyu system. With the area secured, the SOLARIS departed and headed back to the solar system. It was an uneventful trip. Jacob had the ship travel at top speed. He didn't want the INFINITY crew on board any longer than necessary.

Once they arrived back at the solar system, the ship headed directly to Luna Station to dock. Under heavy security escort, the entire INFINITY crew was transferred down to headquarters.

Jacob was summoned by the command council and Commander Gimron was given command of SOLARIS until his return. She was under explicit orders to keep SOLARIS docked but to keep the crew on board. No one was permitted shore leave.

Jacob spent twelve weeks on Luna, put up in an apartment and given strict orders not to contact the SOLARIS, including his senior staff. He spent the days in countless meetings with the command council, other high-level officers, and a variety of government officials. He also testified at Captain Nikols's and the senior staff's court-martials. It was clear to Jacob that the actions of Captain Nikols had altered TERRA permanently. The next few years would be difficult for the organization.

After three long months, he was given the go-ahead to return to SOLARIS. Before he could return, he was required to meet with Admiral Vespia for new orders. Given everything discussed in all the meetings he attended, he expected SOLARIS's mission to test experimental technologies was changing.

Jacob arrived at the admiral's office and found the door open. Her bot assistant was missing. He popped his head in and saw the admiral sitting at her desk. She looked up and motioned for him to enter. "Come in and close the door behind you."

Jacob did as he was instructed. "What happened to your bot?"

"In maintenance for software upgrades." She motioned for him to sit down. "We need to go over some things before you report back to the SOLARIS. You're going to be a busy man the next few years."

That piqued his interest. "How so?"

"We can't risk another Captain Nikols incident. All current officers will be going through stringent evaluations to determine their fitness for space exploration. Those who get through the evals will undergo rigorous training. The Academy's curriculum will be revised to teach cadets deep-space scenarios. The crew of the DISCOVERY are being reassigned and the ship will remain docked with a skeleton crew. The ship will remain out of service until we can restaff it with qualified personnel."

Jacob was worried that the admiral was going to inform him that his crew would be gutted. "What about the SOLARIS?"

"You'll be the only starship conducting local space exploration for the foreseeable future. With PHOENIX out exploring deep space, SOLARIS will be tasked with exploring the unknown parts of space near us. You will be the only starship captain conducting exploration for TERRA."

The news was not a complete surprise to Jacob. In several meetings, TERRA had floated the idea of suspending space exploration. Several individuals took the idea seriously. "That seems drastic, Admiral. We have good officers out there who have what it takes to explore space. If John Roberts proved he could do it, then there are others in our ranks who can too."

"I'm sure there are, but we can't risk trusting anyone now. We need to be sure those we give command of a starship can truly handle the responsibility. What happened with the INFINITY is a direct result of TERRA's isolationist policy. We were lucky with John Roberts, but we were arrogant thinking we could send others out into space without seriously thinking of the ramifications. Luckily, you and your crew proved themselves during the jumpgate mission. Everyone is comfortable with allowing SOLARIS to continue space exploration."

Karla cleared her throat before continuing. "We'll be looking to you to consult on how officers will be trained. You'll routinely return home to provide guidance on training programs and provide hands-on training experience to officers. It's a lot we're expecting, but I know you can handle it."

It was a lot, but Jacob was up for the challenge. "I'll do whatever I can to help." When she nodded, he decided to switch subjects. "What's going to happen to Kordif? No one's talked about him."

Jacob knew that Captain Nikols, Lieutenants Erikson and Singer, and those officers who had killed fellow officers had been convicted and sentenced to life in prison. The other INFINITY officers were stripped of their commissions and expelled from TERRA. Those remaining crew members who took no action during the incident were separated and reassigned to different facilities. What he didn't know was that the command council had decided that none of them would ever serve on a starship again. They wouldn't even be allowed to go through the new evaluation process. Just serving on INFINITY had permanently tainted their careers.

"Kordif is off-limits for discussion," Karla said. "But given your involvement in the situation, I'm willing to tell you, with the understanding you never discuss him outside this office with anyone."

Once Jacob nodded, she continued. "Kordif has been sent back to his homeworld. We're still in discussions with the Onixin military leaders about what sort of punishment he should get, but in the interest of diplomacy we'll accept whatever they decide to do."

Jacob suspected she wasn't being up-front with him. "You don't think anything's going to happen to him."

"You're perceptive, Captain. No, nothing's going to happen to him. It's clear from our discussions that the Onixins don't think Kordif did anything wrong. He was put in an impossible situation and did the best he could. If he wasn't dead, the Onixins actually think Commander Rola should be punished for defying Captain Nikols. In the interest of maintaining good relations, we'll be letting the issue go."

The truth of what had happened in the Jemyu system was hidden from the public. All court-martial proceedings had been held behind closed doors, and the government had issued a cover story saying the INFINITY suffered a catastrophic failure in its power grid due to the negligence of the captain and many of her senior officers. Commander Rola had tried to stop the reaction and died as a result. This gave his family a sense of closure, with the thought that Frank died trying to save his fellow officers.

Karla continued. "With our restructuring plan, we'll be relying more on the alliance to provide us protection until our new fleet is established."

"Including the Onixins?" Jacob asked.

"We're not going to let cultural differences tank the alliance. As distasteful what Kordif did is, it opened our eyes. We need them. We need all the alliance members, but we need to be cautious moving forward. All Onixins in the military exchange will be returning home."

"But the exchange isn't being terminated," Jacob said.

"It's being put on ice. No Onixin will serve in TERRA until we get a more complete understanding of their culture. We're evaluating those Senfo and Quix currently in the exchange, but no further officers from those militaries will be accepted into our ranks."

Jacob immediately thought about Fotell. He wasn't about to lose her over the INFINITY fiasco. "If you're worried about my operations officer, I can vouch for her. She's an integral part of my crew and I will fight to keep her on board."

Karla smiled. "Good enough for me, Captain. Consider her commission on SOLARIS as safe."

That was easy. Jacob was expecting to get into a drawn-out argument to keep Fotell, even going to the command council. He didn't expect the admiral to capitulate so quickly.

The admiral could see the look of surprise on his face. "I don't think you realize your standing in TERRA. You hold a lot of weight and your words carry influence. Between your actions with the jumpgate and how you handled INFINITY, you've impressed a lot of the brass. A lot of people are looking to you to help guide us forward. You're a rising star."

Jacob was not used to that sort of adulation. "Thank you, Admiral. I'll continue to do what's in the best interest of TERRA and my crew."

Jacob was happy to be back on the SOLARIS. He met with his senior staff and went over their new orders. None could believe the drastic change of course TERRA was making. Everyone had assumed that within a year the fleet would be operating several starships in space. Now, those plans had been put on hold.

Jacob also shared the halt to the military exchange program with his senior staff. They immediately protested, assuming that it meant Fotell would be leaving. Michelle stood up and was ready to head out and confront the command council, threatening to have it out with them. After calming her and the others down, Jacob assured them Fotell's position was safe. Following the meeting, he pulled Fotell aside and personally reiterated his promise that she was welcome on SOLARIS as long as she liked.

He noticed she wasn't wearing her hat but resisted asking her about it. Whatever had happened to cause her to remove it was her business. He would leave it up to her if she wanted to talk about it.

After getting up to speed on ship status reports and reacquainting himself with some of the crew, Jacob retired to his quarters. He had an hour to himself before Michelle and Jonas showed up at his quarters. It had become a nightly ritual for them to get together to unwind. It was something they'd started after their adventure in the Triangulum Galaxy. Being able to put duty aside and be themselves was a great comfort. Tonight was different, as Dr. Myers joined them. Since he'd been reassigned to the SOLARIS, Jacob had decided to include him in their little circle.

"I can't believe TERRA is putting its plans on hold," Michelle said as she looked out of the living room window at Luna. "All our efforts these past few years have been wasted, and for what? Because one captain couldn't hold her shit together?"

Jonas looked at the positive aspect of all of this. "TERRA will be busy building new ships, outposts, and weapons platforms at a rapid pace with all the money the government has granted. From what I hear, the solar system will be well-fortified in just a few years."

"Sure, we'll have a bunch of new starships but no one to man them," Michelle said. She looked at the captain. "Jacob, does TERRA really think its people can't handle space exploration? We already got a ship out there manned by over thirty thousand, exploring the galaxy."

Jacob could only shrug. "TERRA considers PHOENIX a unique situation."

Jonas gave Michelle another reminder. "They also consider us unique, otherwise the council wouldn't be letting us explore space."

"The one perk from our little jaunt to another galaxy," Jacob joked. The crew's adventure on their former ship, the SOLARA, was classified, but Dr. Myers had been briefed on that mission due to his space exploration experience on the PHOENIX. There was no risk in talking openly about it in front of him.

Jacob continued. "Nikols's actions forced TERRA to ask some hard questions. Are we truly ready to send ships out there, manned by thousands of officers, into the unknown? How well do we really know our alliance friends?"

Neither Michelle nor Jonas could answer that with ease. They both thought about the questions. It was Michelle who spoke up first. "I hate to admit it, but you have a point. We were forced into the alliance to fight a common enemy. Even with the exchange, I can't say I'm very knowledgeable about the Quix, Onixin, or Senfo. And no one knows anything about the Aldarians. Well, except maybe you, Doctor."

"They are the one race we have extensive knowledge of," Jeremy said, referring to the fact the Aldarians had lived on PHOENIX for three years. "I was also blind to TERRA's readiness. If a cadet could take an experimental starship and form an alliance to defeat the Screen, I believed anything was possible."

"We all had high expectations," Jonas said. "We have to accept it's going to take a little longer to get the fleet ready. We should be happy that we're on the one ship that's going to be out there having all the fun."

Jacob appreciated his chief engineer's outlook. "Let's be grateful TERRA believes in us."

"I agree," Michelle added. "If I have to spend one more year at the shipyard, I'd go nuts."

CHAPTER TWENTY-TWO

The president's office notified Admiral Vespia about an upcoming meeting with President Butu. When the admiral inquired what the meeting was about, the chief of staff would only tell her that attendance was mandatory.

This concerned her. If the chief-of-staff refused to reveal the purpose of a meeting, that usually meant bad news. However, Karla Vespia had always handled any crisis sent her way and was confident she could tackle whatever issue the meeting would be addressing.

Before heading to Earth for the meeting, she first made a clandestine trip to Mars. She had some final business to attend to regarding the Screen. She was going to see what information had been extracted from the Screen leaders she ordered interrogated.

She met with her liaison at the underground facility. They immediately escorted her to the cell housing the prisoners, who had not been terminated yet. Despite being imprisoned after their people were defeated, they had remained proud and defiant. The recent extensive interrogation sessions had left them broken and battered. Both lay on their beds, barely moving, their breaths shallow.

"Report," Karla ordered as she gazed upon the prisoners. She had no sympathy for them.

The liaison handed her a paper report. "This has everything they told us. Most of it's gibberish. We don't know if they're trying to deceive us, reacting to our interrogation techniques, or giving us legitimate intel. We'll have to cross-reference their responses with the data obtained from their homeworld."

Vespia quickly flipped through the pages. "Anything regarding additional devices or weapons in the solar system?"

"None. The only weapon they admitted to was the one on Mars. They didn't acknowledge anything else that might be in our system."

Both TERRA and the alliance militaries had scanned every planet, moon, and rock in the solar system and found no additional Screen weapons or devices. Karla was satisfied they were safe. The interrogation had validated her assurance.

She closed the file and took one last look at the prisoners. "I believe the environmental system is due to malfunction in a few hours. Once they're dead, have their bodies taken to medical for dissection. Have reports created to support the autopsies, then burn the bodies."

"Yes, Admiral."

Karla turned and walked away, smiling. "*Now* the Screen are extinct."

A shuttle touched down near Lake Abaya in The Rift Valley. President Butu maintained her vacation home in this part of Ethiopia and was spending time here while Parliament was in recess.

As the shuttle's side door opened, Admiral Vespia was greeted by two of the president's security guards, who escorted her to the president's two-story lake home. Butu's chief-of-staff, Arnold, met the admiral at the front door and escorted her the rest of the way to the president's study. He said nothing during the walk, and Karla didn't try to inquire what the meeting was about. If he hadn't told her earlier, she assumed he wouldn't say anything now.

She used the time to go over every possible scenario that might be presented to her. She felt prepared for anything.

Arnold opened the door to the study and motioned the admiral inside. Karla saw President Butu seated at her desk in the center of the room, by the large sliding glass doors that looked out on the lake. When Arnold closed the door behind her, the admiral announced herself.

"Admiral Vespia reporting as requested."

President Butu looked up at the admiral but displayed no smile. To Vespia, this confirmed her instincts that she would be dealing with unpleasant news.

The president got up from behind the desk. "Thank you for coming. Can I get you anything to drink?"

"No, Madame President. Thank you, and of course I would come to see you when summoned."

"Your predecessor lacked that courtesy," Butu said, referring to Admiral Donalds. "I'm glad to see you didn't pick up his bad habits."

Karla was getting impatient. She wanted to know why she was here, not get sidetracked by idle chitchat. "Is there a reason you wanted to see me?"

"I'm sure you're aware your position as head of TERRA's command council has always been a precarious one. Since the first day of TERRA's reorganization, most people have called for your removal. It was only because of your actions after PHOENIX's return that I chose to keep you at your post. You've done well facilitating changes needed in TERRA, despite seeing most of your colleagues being replaced by ES officers."

"It was difficult for me, but I knew it was in the best interest for TERRA to survive in the new world." Karla saw no need to hide the discomfort the reorganization caused her. On any given day, she would arrive at her office not knowing if she still had a job.

Butu grabbed a paper file from her desk, opened it, and flipped through the pages. "Unfortunately, this situation with INFINITY can't be ignored. It's not enough to scale back the alien exchange program and delay the launch of ships for exploration.

We need to be sure that we weed out individuals like Annette Nikols so this atrocity never happens again. To ensure that, we can't leave long-term TERRA officers in key positions."

Karla knew exactly where this was going as the president returned to behind her desk. "We'll be issuing a joint statement announcing your retirement at the end of the month. You'll receive your full pension and the public will see this as a mutual decision on our parts. We'll make the announcement the same day we'll decommission the remaining capital ships. That will help convey to the public that TERRA is truly moving into a new era."

Karla was not about to capitulate without a fight. She'd spent too many years working hard to become the head of TERRA. "With all due respect, Madame President, I think this decision is a mistake. I've done everything that's been asked of me to bring TERRA out of its old ways. I successfully got our new shipbuilding program off the ground and know intimate details of TERRA's operations to identify areas that need improvement. I'm a valuable resource and it would be a mistake to throw such a resource away."

The president cracked a smile. "I expected you to argue with me, and I respect you for that. You haven't survived in your position as long as you have by letting people walk over you. You made some good points about why you should stay. I can go over several things to justify your exit, but there's no point in doing that. The decision's been made. I'm only telling you as a courtesy and to let you leave with your reputation intact."

"And if I refuse to go along with this?"

"You'll be arrested and court-martialed for gross negligence of duty by giving Captain Nikols command of a starship. I've already been told by our legal team that the charges are dubious and you would most likely be found innocent, but your reputation would be irreparably damaged to the point where I doubt you could find work in the private sector. You've spent too many years in TERRA to leave under such a dark cloud."

President Butu was surprised when Karla cracked a slight grin. "Now that's something I can respect. Well played, Madame

President. You covered all the bases, something I would have done."

"Then we're in agreement?"

The admiral nodded. "Have your people send me my speech I'm sure they've already drafted. May I ask who will be replacing me?"

"I can't divulge that, as we have not informed the individual."

"I take it the person will be from ES." It made sense to Karla that they would make the next head of the command council a former ES officer.

"Your instincts are correct," Butu confirmed. "I can tell you all remaining original high-level TERRA officers will be replaced with people from the ES side. A completely fresh perspective is needed if TERRA's to move forward."

"I always knew I'd leave TERRA in two ways: either dying on the job or being forced out. I'm glad to see one of my assumptions was right."

—— —— ——

After a couple more minutes of chatting with President Butu, Karla returned to her shuttle and headed back to Luna. It was strange, but she found she wasn't upset about being forced out. Oddly enough, she felt relieved, as if decades of constant pressure and looking over her shoulder were now in the past.

As she returned to her office at headquarters in Infinity City, it was already 2315 hours. None of the high-ranking officers were around, which suited her fine. Although she wasn't mad about the president's decision, she wasn't in the mood to talk to anyone.

Her DAT alerted her to an incoming message from the president's office. She suspected what it was. Sure enough, when she pulled the message up on her terminal in her office, she saw it was her retirement speech she would make to the public.

After reading the speech, she began pulling out books and other personal mementos she'd be taking with her. A knock on the open door interrupted her, and she turned to see Admiral Michael Forsent at the entrance.

CHAPTER TWENTY TWO

"A little late to be packing, isn't it?" he said.

"Why put off tomorrow what you can do today," she said as she continued to pull books off the shelves. "I know you don't care for the décor, but that's your problem when you move in."

Michael smiled. "And what makes you think I'm moving in?"

"Come on. I know they offered you my position. Don't insult me." Even though President Butu told her they hadn't offered the head of the council position to their selected candidate, Karla knew that was a lie. She wouldn't have been informed of her removal if they didn't have their candidate already lined up and ready to take over.

"Oh, they did offer me the position. It was a tempting offer, and I did fantasize about moving into this office. But I turned them down."

Karla found that hard to believe. "You've made it no secret you wanted my job from your first day on the council."

"That's true. I did want your job. You're a sneaky, under-handed person who's used anyone and anything to get to where you are. I relished the challenge of unseating you from your position of power. Now that the president has removed you, I found being head of the council no longer interests me."

"Careful, Michael. If I didn't know better, I'd say that was a compliment."

"It was." He approached Karla and put his hand over hers. "And now that we're no longer colleagues, I don't have to worry about inflating your ego and telling you how attractive I've always found you."

His admission caught her by surprise. She'd never picked up so much as a hint that he saw her in that way. "I'm twenty years older than you."

"I like older women."

"I'm very opinionated."

"I like to know where someone stands."

"I hold grudges."

"Who doesn't."

"I don't like most people."

"Same here, so we have something in common."

Michael leaned in so close, Karla could feel his warm breath on her face. She found it surprisingly exhilarating. She hadn't felt something like this . . . in so long.

Just as it seemed he was going to kiss her, he pulled back. "Call me and we'll do dinner, or don't. I leave it up to you, Karla." He winked and left her office.

Karla could hardly believe what had transpired. She dropped the book she was holding and slumped into her seat.

This had been an odd day. First, she'd been booted from TERRA but hadn't gotten upset about it. Now the man who argued with her at every turn and made no secret he wanted her job had hit on her. Had she been so consumed with her career that she had forgotten about other aspects of life?

CHAPTER TWENTY-THREE

Jacob met up with his son at the engineering bureau and offered to take him to dinner. With no firm schedule for the SOLARIS to depart the solar system, he wanted to take advantage of his time on Luna and spend as much of it with Chad as he could before the young man headed back to the Academy in a few weeks.

Father and son took a seat in a diner's corner booth. The restaurant was close to the engineering bureau and was a favorite spot for its officers.

The two enjoyed chit-chatting about inconsequential matters while they ordered their food. After the waiter bot dropped off their orders, Jacob dove into more serious matters.

"I take it you've heard about TERRA's revamped plans?" he asked his son.

"It's all everyone's been talking about. I'm not interested in exploring space, but it sucks we're not going to be out there checking out other star systems."

"Luckily, you'll have plenty of work to do if you want to continue a career in engineering design. TERRA's planning to build a plethora of new installations in the solar system. You could be a part of designing them."

Chad shrugged. "I'd rather stick with starship design."

"I'm sure there'll be a continued need for designing new ships to complement our SOLARA-class vessels." Jacob cleared his throat before continuing. "I don't know how much time we'll have together. TERRA's asking a lot of me and I'll be busy the next few years. I don't want you to think I've up and abandoned you again."

"Dad, we've been over this. I'm not mad you weren't around when I was growing up. I may only be in the Academy, but I know what a career in TERRA entails. Don't feel that you have to apologize to me for putting your work first."

"My work's important, but so are you. In a few years, you'll be an officer and I want to help guide you. I just want you to know that I won't be around as often."

"We can always talk over the comm, and it's not like you're going to be out there for months at a time. You already said they're going to keep SOLARIS close to home. Remember the first couple of years of us getting to know each other? All the stories you told me of your adventures in the fleet?"

Jacob smiled, recalling the countless tales he was able to share with Chad. "Yeah."

"I want you to continue doing that. Go out there and have more adventures to come back and share with me. I may never leave the solar system, and don't have to. I've got you to explore space for me."

Jacob was moved by his son's words. "I don't know how I got so lucky to have a son like you."

"Let's not get sappy. Just do what you need to do. I'll be fine, don't worry. In the meantime, what can you tell me about SOLARIS's maiden flight?"

Jacob wasted no time beginning the story. Of course, he had to make most of it up, as he couldn't divulge the SOLARIS being an experimental testbed and all the ugliness that had happened with INFINITY. Luckily, Jacob had enough of an imagination to come up with a believable story.

It was 0652 hours the following morning. Karla had slept very little the night before. She'd stayed at her office until she had finished packing all her personal belongings before heading home. There, she spent nearly an hour destroying files relating to her work over the years. Much of it detailed past activities she couldn't ever allow others to see. It would risk her being court-martialed and reveal secrets about other remaining high-ranking TERRA officers that were best kept buried. All the cloak-and-dagger charades didn't matter to her now. Her career was over, and she felt no need to hang onto any information she had collected over the years about the organization.

When done purging the files, she relaxed by the living room fire, sipping a glass of brandy. It was 0204 hours when she finally went to bed. She would be making her retirement statement alongside President Butu in two days, but wanted to take care of one more thing first. There was one piece of unfinished business she couldn't let go. When she retired, it would be with a clean slate.

At 0500 hours she took a shuttle to Mars. She arrived at a facility located within a secondary dome two hundred kilometers from Crimson City. The facility belonged to TERRA. Part of the facility had a section for the incarceration of prisoners most people were unaware of. For most of TERRA's existence, this part of the facility had been sporadically used. Since the INFINITY's destruction, it had its highest number of residents ever.

Karla arrived and made her way into the facility, heading directly to the incarceration area. She walked without an escort. She didn't need one. Her credentials were sufficient to permit her access to any of the restricted areas, not that anyone could ever prove she was here. At every door where she provided a biometric scan for entry, the computer immediately erased a record of the scan from its log.

The admiral arrived at the isolation section, where prisoners were kept in solitary confinement. All the former INFINITY officers who were convicted in their court-martials had been placed here per Karla's orders. It was only a temporary arrangement, as the prisoners would be relocated to facilities on Earth where most of them would spend the rest of their lives in confinement.

One prisoner would be spared the transport to Earth, as Karla had other ideas for her. She grinned as she approached the cell holding Annette Nikols, who was wearing a white jumpsuit with a serial bar code imprinted on the front. The admiral found her reading a book, one of the few luxuries afforded prisoners here. Karla was pleased to see that Annette had already finished her breakfast.

"Hello, Annette."

The disgraced former captain looked up at her visitor. "If you're expecting me to address you by title, forget it."

Karla feigned a hurt look. "I'm disappointed. I would have thought that after a lifetime of devoted service, you'd still adhere to protocol."

"A lifetime of service that got me what? Thrown to the wolves? If you're expecting me to grovel, you're wasting your time. What I did saved humanity from a lingering threat."

"Oh, I agree. Destroying that outpost was a smart move on your part. We can all be assured that the Screen are truly gone for good."

Annette looked perplexed by the admiral's response. She got up from her seat and approached the energy field separating the two. "You didn't say anything to that effect at my trial. Everything you said made me out to be this monster who should be locked away forever. That's not someone who's happy with what I did."

"I agree with what you did. My problem is how you went about it. Specifically, you went against me by disobeying my orders."

"You mean the council's orders."

"My orders," Karla stressed. "I was the council; therefore, my orders. Going against me is something I simply cannot stand for."

Annette raised her arms and looked around. "What are you going to do? I'm already in prison for the rest of my life."

"That's not good enough for me. You're an unpleasant

reminder. Anyone who's ever gone against me has paid the price. I made sure of it. You may think life imprisonment is a sufficient punishment; I don't. You defied me. A life sentence will not do."

Annette laughed. "What are you going to do? Torture me? Kill me?" She pointed to a red blinking light in the far corner behind the admiral. "I don't think they'll let you."

"Oh, you mean that camera and the others that switched to dummy feeds when I came in?" Karla enjoyed seeing the smile disappear from Annette's face. "I can assure you I'm free to do as I wish, as no one will ever be able to prove I was here. Don't forget, I was head of TERRA's security for many years. I made sure all my little tricks would work on those procedures I established."

Annette said nothing and stood in place like a statue. She watched as the admiral pulled a small device from her pocket and held it up.

"I see you enjoyed your breakfast. Bagel and lox with cream cheese and hot tea. I especially like the cream cheese. Its composition makes it easy to hide things, like the nanobots I had injected that this little device controls."

Annette took a couple of step backs as she put a hand on her stomach.

Karla chuckled. "The transmitter has a long range, so moving away isn't going to help. By now, the bots have left your stomach and are circulating throughout your body."

"You wouldn't . . ." Annette managed to sputter out.

Karla was disappointed to see the look of fear on her face. TERRA officers were supposed to be resilient in the face of death. "Kill you? Yes, I have every intention of doing so. I could have programmed these bots to kill you in any number of painful ways. But as I already said, you're a loose end I want tied up. I only care that you're dead. The manner by which you die is irrelevant. Think of it as me showing you mercy."

Karla clicked the single button on the transmitter. "I could explain how the bots will kill you, but the details aren't important. Just know that you'll be getting tired and will fall asleep, that's all."

When she was done speaking, Annette could already feel lightheaded. "No," she blurted out as she tried to walk back towards the energy field. Her legs had become difficult to move. Even her arms felt like heavy weights. She managed to get herself over to her bed and slumped down onto it, looking up at the smiling admiral. Her vision was becoming hazy.

"That's right, my dear. No need to fight it," Karla said in a soothing voice. "Just lie down and close your eyes."

Annette tried to fight the heaviness, but she had no energy. Sitting up proved to be too difficult, and she fell over onto the bed. Tears streamed down her face. She wanted to cry out for help, but her voice was lost to her. She closed her eyes, hoping that perhaps this was all a bad dream, and she would wake up in a few hours. She clung to that thought as she drifted off into nothingness.

The admiral was pleased that Annette had taken her advice. She looked so much more presentable lying peacefully on the bed, instead of on the floor in some violent pose.

The transmitter made a beeping sound, alerting Karla that Annette's life-signs had ceased. The admiral turned and left the cell block, walking casually, as if she'd just concluded a visit to an old friend.

Well, Michael did say he didn't mind someone who held grudges, she thought, and smiled.

END

NOVELS BY ROBERT STADNIK